RUNNING SCARED

Eddie Malloy is back on track. Cruising to victory on a few winners from Tunney's stables. The only cloud on the horizon is fellow jockey Bill Keating—his blackouts are getting so frequent that he's becoming a danger on the course. And there's something he wants to tell Eddie. Then Bill is found dead in a horsebox. Gassed. With traces of drugs in his body. The verdict is suicide. But as there are two horses beside him, also dead, his ex-wife is not convinced. And she has the persuasive power to lure Eddie out of the saddle and into a dangerous investigation which unnerves at least one of the suspects. Someone clearly wants to silence Malloy—for good. From the mud-spattered tracks of the English turf to balmy afternoon race-meetings in Barbados, Malloy follows a trail of fraud, bribery, sabotage and corruption to the heart of a conspiracy that threatens to devastate the racing industry.

RUNNING SCARED

Richard Pitman
&
Joe McNally

CHIVERS PRESS
BATH

First published in Great Britain 1994
by
Hodder and Stoughton
This Large Print edition published by
Chivers Press
by arrangement with
Hodder and Stoughton Limited
a division of Hodder Headline PLC
1996

ISBN 0 7451 7934 7

British Library Cataloguing in Publication Data available

Photoset, printed and bound in Great Britain by
REDWOOD BOOKS, Trowbridge, Wiltshire

For Sarah Jo, born on the 8th of July
—An artiste if ever I saw one

Joe McNally

For Mandy, Gemma and Tara who provide
an unequal home balance which seems to
work in my favour.

Richard Pitman

RUNNING SCARED

CHAPTER ONE

Bill Keating started out with a lot of friends, mostly fellow jockeys like me. But steadily he lost them. He had problems and if he'd told us what they were we might have been able to help.

But he kept quiet and when he died I wasn't the only one who felt guilty.

A few times during the opening weeks of the season I'd asked Bill if he was okay. Others were concerned about him too. Towards the end of a race he'd seemed to have trouble staying on his horse. Afterwards he'd sometimes look like all the blood and energy had been sucked out of him—white face, sunken eyes, foot-dragging exhaustion. He could hardly find the strength to shrug off our questions.

He wouldn't tell us what was wrong. We discussed it without him. Everyone offered opinions ranging from brain damage to exhaustion. Blakey had found him sitting alone after racing one day staring at the car keys in his open palm. Asked if he was all right Bill looked at Blakey and held out the keys, 'What are these for?' he asked. Blakey could tell by his vacant look that it was no wind up.

We decided that until he was ready to talk about it there was nothing for us to do except try and look after him during races. But at Worcester in early August he almost killed himself and Martin Craig.

On the way to the car park that day I'd paused by the winning post to watch the end of the last race.

They were both finishing unplaced, coming up the run-in at their own pace when Martin saw Bill, galloping a couple of lengths in front of him, grow

1

rapidly weaker. Martin urged his horse alongside Bill's as they passed the post. Bill, hands useless on the reins, bumping dead weight in the saddle, slumped to the right.

Martin leaned across trying to support him, to keep him on till they slowed but Bill lurched to his right, sliding off. Reaching out desperately in semi-consciousness Bill grabbed the bridle of Martin's mount and swung limply to the ground dragging the horse almost to its knees. Martin came down on the other side where his foot caught in the stirrup iron.

Getting hung-up is every jockey's worst nightmare; dangling by a twisted foot, dragged at the gallop behind half a ton of nervous confused metal-shod horse.

Bill Keating lay where he fell, the hooves of Martin's terrified horse just missing him as it careered off.

A soundwave of 'Ooohs' came from the grandstand behind me as Martin, rattling along on his shoulders, tried hopelessly to reach upwards and free his foot. The horse jinked flipping Martin onto his front; the hoof-printed turf thumped and battered his face as his arms and scrabbling fingers dragged uselessly behind.

The grandstand 'Oohed' again and a woman beside me shouted, 'Oh my God!'

The jocks on the first three, who'd finished close together, had turned by now at the top bend and were coming back when they saw what had happened.

Colin Blake on a big chestnut shouted to the others and they urged their sweating mounts across turning them side-on to form a broad semi-roadblock in the path of Martin's horse.

The runaway faltered perhaps thinking of going

2

for the gap to their right. Martin was unconscious now at the least, bouncing in his bright checked colours like a muddy rag doll.

I said a brief prayer. The grandstand held its breath. I could hear vague calls of 'Whoa!' from the three mounted jockeys. The runaway slowed, turned, thought about galloping back down the course but took just two more steps then stood still.

Martin lay motionless. Blakey jumped off and though every instinct would be urging him to hurry towards Martin he moved calmly wary of scaring the horse into another wild run.

Blakey was four or five paces away, his head perfectly still. He'd be holding eye contact, the first thing that would make the horse aware the situation had changed. A thousand pairs of binocular lenses were fixed on them. Breaths were held.

If the horse bolted again, if it got past Blakey it was unlikely Martin would survive.

Blakey stopped and slowly raised his fingers to gently stroke the horse's nose.

It took two steps back.

The tension in the stands was tangible.

Blakey moved slowly forward again. He'd be talking quietly, trying to calm the horse.

His fingers ever so gently to the nose again. Softly then onto its neck stroking calmly towards the reins till his fingers clasped them.

The crowd sighed and the grandstand came alive again with the buzz of conversation and some applause for Blakey.

* * *

Bill Keating recovered within an hour but it was

almost a week before Martin Craig was fit enough to attend a Stewards' Inquiry into the incident. Still protecting him, a couple of jocks told the Inquiry that Bill had simply been hit in the face by a clod of earth causing him to temporarily lose control.

The Stewards took no action. With hindsight it would have been much better if they had.

Bill asked no favours of anyone though he'd always grant them happily himself. We all liked the guy, had a special affection for him even. He'd been around longer than most of us though he'd never really got the breaks.

Enough rides to get by on but few of them any good; the plodders, the bad jumpers, the ones that made you marvel at the real genius of racehorse trainers; persuading otherwise sensible owners that their geese *would* eventually turn into swans.

Enough of the poor suckers believed it to keep jockeys like Bill Keating clinging to the wreckage of their own dreams.

Bill was thirty-nine and had a lot of metal holding his bones together; some plastic too. He'd had so many collarbone breaks they'd replaced them with synthetic ones. Recently divorced after fifteen years with a good woman in a bad marriage, he lived alone in Lambourn.

He was among six of us who regularly occupied the same corner of the weighing room; laughing, kidding, commiserating, living off each other's highs and lows, managing, most of the time, not to think of the possible death or paralysis that awaited us each time the tapes went up.

None of us had fought in a war but, emotionally, we were as close as I imagine men can get in peacetime.

4

The Worcester spill scared Bill and he dwelt on it over the following weeks, came close, I'm sure, to telling me what was wrong.

On an unusually hot Saturday in September we walked together to the car park after racing at Stratford. I quizzed Bill again about his health. He looked ill, depressed and very worried.

Leaning on his old Fiat Estate he promised to tell me everything when we next met at Uttoxeter the following Wednesday.

I watched him pull away through a lazy dust trail then got in my own car and headed home.

The Indian Summer had blessed the tiny racing village of Lambourn too and they tell me the church bells were ringing through the warm Sunday evening when Bill's teenage daughter found him dead in the horsebox.

CHAPTER TWO

'Suspicious circumstances,' said the police and kept Bill's body in a mortuary freezer for almost a month.

There was just one day in late October with no jump racing and Cathy, Bill's ex-wife, persuaded the cops to let her arrange the funeral for that day, the twenty-fourth, so that all Bill's friends could be there.

To a large extent it had been Cathy's reaction to his death that had delayed the funeral. The police had plumped for suicide almost from the outset. Come the inquest so did the coroner.

The autopsy revealed significant traces of heroin in Bill's blood and his arms showed puncture marks. But cause of death was carbon monoxide poisoning

5

from exhaust fumes.

Not the usual hose from the tailpipe; the cops said the exhaust system had been deliberately holed just below a vent in the floor of the horsebox allowing a fatal seepage of gas.

On searching Bill's flat they'd found a number of unposted letters to Cathy, some unfinished but all reflecting his total despair over the way his life had turned out. Several mentioned suicide. No 'formal' suicide note was found.

But the cops were happy that Bill had taken a heroin fix, punched a hole in the exhaust pipe, started the engine, closed the tailgate and lain down in the straw of a stall to die.

Cathy didn't believe he'd killed himself nor did his two daughters. His friends, me among them, found it hard to believe too though that was before we found out what had been wrong with him.

Still, circumstantial evidence made those who knew him question the verdict at the time. There were practical contradictions too like, where was the instrument used to pierce the exhaust? The cops said he must have disposed of it before climbing into the van.

But the main thing, the telling factor against Bill Keating running poisonous fumes into a horsebox, was that he wasn't alone in there. In the two narrow stalls next to Bill's, crumpled grotesquely in the cramped space, were two dead racehorses.

*   *   *

Autumn had given the south of England a miss this year. We seemed to go straight from warm late summer to early winter. Most of the folk at the funeral had dressed against the cold.

After the service about a hundred people filtered away along the narrow red-shale paths of the little churchyard towards a long row of vehicles ranging from a Rolls to a rusty moped with a dented helmet hanging from the seat.

It was a windless day, clear sky, coppery sun. Drivers cleared leaves from windscreen wells as more floated down from the avenue of trees.

I walked with Bill's widow, Cathy, and his teenage daughters. None of us had spoken since we left the graveside. I opened the door of the big car for them. Cathy, defiant in a sky-blue two-piece and white blouse, turned to me; dark hair, brown eyes, longish jaw, the same basic facial shape as the ex-husband she'd just buried. She asked, 'Have you got a lift?'

I nodded. She ushered the girls into the back of the darkened car and said to me, 'Come back to the house.'

'You sure?'

A short vigorous nod. 'Just half a dozen or so. Close friends. You know.'

I looked at her. She hadn't cried yet. Kate and Amy in the back hadn't either. All holding out for each other's sake.

I touched her arm. 'Thanks,' I said, 'I'll see you there.'

* * *

Cathy leased a big farm at the head of the valley. She'd been running a livery and horse transport business from there for five years and running it well. That had been one of the reasons behind the marriage breakup. Cathy had always been full of drive and

7

ambition and so had Bill.

Cathy ended up a top businesswoman. Bill ended up a journeyman jockey; he couldn't face being second best in his marriage as well as his career.

It was some three years since I'd been to Cathy's place. It had changed. Potholes and ruts in the long driveway shook the car about, weeds grew around the perimeter of the paddock and the fences were in poor repair.

I parked between two horseboxes, the road-dirt on each almost obscuring the black letters on blue background which read—CATHY KEATING EQUINE TRANSPORT.

The front of the old redbrick farmhouse looked sad and generally dilapidated too. They say you shouldn't judge a book by its cover but if I'd been a potential customer of Cathy's I wouldn't be ringing her doorbell with a lot of confidence.

Following Cathy along the hall into the drawing room I thought the inside looked pretty dog-eared too. Then I chided myself for being such an ungracious guest.

Amy, the elder daughter, dark like her mother, solemnly fixed drinks from a bar in the corner. Never speaking she simply moved inquiring eyes to the next person after filling each glass and bringing it over.

She looked like she didn't approve of these people sitting chattering in her house, drinking and trying to act normal so soon after burying her father. I knew how she felt and could never quite understand the purpose of these get-togethers, never was comfortable at one.

I moved across to the bar and spoke to Amy. 'Can I help?'

She looked up with empty eyes and shook her head

8

then remembering her manners whispered, 'No, thank you.'

I rejoined the others and listened to them reminisce for a while before Cathy invited me to join her in a walk outside. I held Cathy's long wool coat but she settled it on her shoulders leaving the sleeves empty. The light was fading and the air grew sharply cold.

Side by side we walked by the rotting flowerbeds and watched the trees steadily silhouetting against the last of the light.

Cathy talked.

About life and death, the kids, her 'worthless' career, the years of sixteen hour days, of drag-out fights with Bill, about happy times with Bill, about the divorce.

Finally she stopped walking and turned to me. 'Look at my eyes, Eddie.'

I looked.

'Take a step closer.'

Slightly uncomfortable, but I took it ... Close enough now to smell the brandy on her breath.

'Look into them.'

They were chestnut, the pupils widening in the virtual darkness.

'See any tears?' she asked.

I looked at her. 'They'll come.'

'Think so?'

I nodded.

'Uhuh. Can't cry any more. Lost the ability when Bill left.'

I didn't answer. I could see she was serious and that platitudes were pointless. There was no emotion in her face or voice. There had always been a hardness about her but I'd assumed she saw it as an essential ingredient for business success.

9

She broke eye contact and we started walking again. She said nothing more till we rounded the front of the house again, setting off the bright security light. A galaxy of frost particles drifted in its beam.

Staring into the night Cathy changed tack, 'What would I have to do to make the police investigate further?'

She'd been insistent throughout that Bill would never have risked killing those horses as well as himself. She'd protested strongly to the cops.

The uncharitable among racing folk said she just couldn't face having his death on her conscience but I knew she didn't blame herself one bit. Cathy believed everyone was totally responsible for their own lives.

She was fighting for Bill's sake, to clear his name. Same as she'd have done for me or any of her friends. Or so I thought.

'They'd want hard evidence Cathy.'

'How do we get it?'

Her use of the plural put me slightly on my guard. I had the makings of a good season in front of me and I was reluctant to be side-tracked, even for Cathy.

'You could start by finding out about the drugs; when he started taking them, who his supplier was.'

Cathy pulled the loose coat closer around her. We discussed Bill's drug taking. She reckoned he couldn't have been on it long though she emphasised that since the divorce she hadn't exactly seen him on a daily basis.

Although she had noticed his memory lapses, lack of co-ordination, blank expression at times. 'I'd thought maybe he was just getting a bit punchy but it must have been the drugs.'

We discussed Bill's problems during races and the

incident at Worcester that had really scared him. Cathy tied them up with the physical signs she'd noticed and put it all down to heroin.

I said, 'I'm not convinced heroin affects you that way. I don't think it makes you physically incapable.'

'Maybe not when you're high but what about afterwards?'

'I don't know...'

She guessed I was holding something back. 'How could we find out?'

I had to work to hold in a resigned sigh. 'Well I suppose I could ask Doc Clarke.'

She turned smartly towards me. 'When?' That business look was back in her eye.

'I'll see him on Wednesday at Cheltenham.'

'Would he know about that sort of thing?'

'If he doesn't, he'll know a man who does.'

We both smiled. A moist halo of frost lay on her fine hair. Hot breath trickled from her nostrils. She looked up at the stars. 'I've never known it so cold this early in the year.'

'Me neither.'

'Too cold for snow?'

I looked up. 'No clouds. No snow without clouds.'

She stared at the sky a while then said quietly, 'No show without Punch.'

'Mmmm.'

'D'you think he's up there watching, Eddie?'

'Somewhere.'

We were silent again for a while then she said, 'My ears are freezing.'

I smiled. 'Let's take them inside and sit them by the fire then.'

*   *   *

11

We stood in the big kitchen warming our hands on cups of tea, our backs to the dull, chipped blue Aga. Cathy, red-cheeked, said, 'If we can just prove it was an accident I'll be happy. Okay so he was taking drugs, I've got to live with that. But he must've blacked out in there after taking too much.'

She looked very stressed, stood quiet for a while staring hard into her tea cup, squeezing the fragile china with both hands, getting very intense. 'It has to be an accident, Eddie...'

The sentence came out through strangled vocal cords. The cup shattered splashing tea down her and cutting her hands. She looked at the blood on her palms then buried her face in them. Putting my cup down I stepped in close encircling her in my arms.

She was silent.

She didn't respond to me holding her, just kept her forearms tight across her chest, face in her hands.

After a minute or so I gently clasped her wrists and eased her hands away. Her brown eyes, still not crying, showed a mixture of defiance and despair. There was blood where the tear stains should have been.

Easing me away she moved to the sink and ran cold water on her hands. Tearing paper sheets from a towel roll she moved to a small pine-framed mirror and started cleaning her face.

'You got a first aid kit?' I asked.

She ignored the question, stamped the pedal-bin open, dumped the bloody tissue and tore some more which she clasped between her hands as she came towards me.

A fair measure of control was back in her face. She looked at me steadily, 'Eddie, I'm in the biggest

12

fucking mess I've ever been in in the thirty-seven years of my life. I'd have sworn I could have lived a hundred and thirty-seven and not accumulated the problems I've got.

'The business is gone, as good as finished. I'm mortgaged so high they might as well have buried me today with Bill.'

She gave a huge sigh here and began to relax in the way people do when they finally realise, win or lose, that the struggle is over. The stiffness left her limbs and she managed a smile and a slightly nervous laugh then said, 'I'm in so deep I'll need to be bailed out in ten grand increments or I'll get the bends on the way back to the surface.'

I smiled too and tried, for her sake, to prompt her into talking some more. 'What happened?'

'What didn't?' And she told me how the business had steadily spiralled downwards in the recession then plummeted as she borrowed to stay afloat. She'd cut back, laid staff off, sold equipment, now it was down to the personal stuff. She couldn't even pay the children's school fees.

Having just got myself on the right side of solvency there was nothing I could offer but sympathy. Or so I thought.

Cathy said, 'Eddie I'm certain Bill's death wasn't suicide and I need to prove it but I can't afford to push it any further ... I don't mean financially can't afford. I need someone to fight it for me. I know the police won't.'

Something else was coming. I waited.

Cathy, unblinking, looked straight at me, all defiance now, no despair. She said, 'When Bill and I started this business we took out a big life insurance policy. Somebody told me they don't pay out if it's suicide.'

'How big a policy?'

'Seven hundred and fifty thousand pounds.'

'How much do you owe the banks?'

'The guts of six hundred and fifty thousand.'

'And if it wasn't suicide?'

'An accident.'

'Even though nobody disputes that the exhaust was holed deliberately?'

She didn't reply.

I continued. 'And maybe the engine was switched on deliberately and maybe someone put Bill in that stall.'

Cathy's face showed no surprise.

I said, 'If we can prove it wasn't suicide and the police can prove it wasn't an accident then they're going to be setting up a murder inquiry.'

Neither of us had to say who we thought would be the prime suspect.

CHAPTER THREE

Next day, Tuesday, I had no rides. The only jump racing was at Newton Abbott in Devon and I was glad I didn't have to drive there. I rose at six and dressed hurriedly. It was frosty outside and I hadn't quite sussed the heating system in my flat.

I lived deep in the Shropshire countryside in part of an old barn which had been converted into luxury holiday flats. The barn was on an agricultural complex on a two hundred acre estate. The main business there for over a hundred years had been training racehorses but until recently no

14

thoroughbred had walked the paddocks for many years.

When the holiday company went bust a millionaire businessman and racing nut called Gary Rice bought the place and spent freely to set it up once more as a training establishment.

He then installed Charles Tunney, an ex-amateur jock and good friend of his (and mine) as trainer, which was brave of him as Charles had only just been granted his training licence.

It was a great adventure for Charles as was life in general. I'd never met any genuine person who didn't like him immensely. He had the knack of making everyone he spoke to feel special; he always paid total attention to what you were saying and laughed uproariously at everyone's jokes because he honestly thought them funny. Charles's sense of humour had the lowest ignition point imaginable. The really funny ones would have him wet-eyed and helpless.

Charles had persuaded Rice to pay me a small retainer to ride the stable's runners. Too small really but Charles made me feel that if I didn't ride his horses he would never train a winner. He almost had me believing I was Lester and Fred Winter rolled into one.

It wasn't too bad an arrangement, we only had nineteen horses which left me free to take many outside rides. The board and lodgings were thrown in too.

I hurried down the narrow stairs out into the chilly morning. Sunrise was still an hour away. The moon was almost full in a clear sky. Lights were on in the yard and the sounds of equine breakfasts being prepared grew louder as I approached.

I exchanged good mornings with several lads and

15

went into the house. Charles stood at the kitchen worktop under an array of pots and pans dangling from a dark wooden beam. The glare from an overhead striplight reflected from the mustard coloured walls making his face look jaundiced. In his early thirties, he was five seven with dark curly hair and unusually thick eyebrows.

The percolated coffee he was pouring looked rich and strong.

'Black for me,' I said.

He glanced up. 'Eddie! How're you doing?' As if he hadn't seen me in years.

'Morning Charles.'

'Sit down. Coffee coming right up.'

I sat at the big pine table and picked up *The Sporting Life*. Charles took a seat at the end and slid the coffee mug along to me.

'Thanks.'

'How'd the funeral go?' he asked.

'As well as funerals can.'

'How are Cathy and the kids?'

'Bearing up.'

'D'you apologise for me not being able to make it?'

'Uhuh.'

'Cathy understand about it? She wasn't upset or anything?'

'She's got more things to worry her right now, Charles.'

'Yeah, I suppose so.'

The door opened and a yellow bobble hat poked round. Underneath it was the flushed young face of Darren, one of the lads. He said, 'Padge says to tell you Kinky's got a leg, guv'nor.'

Charles sipped black coffee and nodded. 'How bad?'

16

'Fair bit of heat in his off fore. Won't make Saturday, Padge says.'

'Okay,' Charles said and Darren's head withdrew.

Kinky was a horse, King Kibbutz, Padge was the head lad and 'a leg' was bad news—lameness. The horse had been down to run at Wetherby on Saturday.

'That's three on the easy list,' Charles said.

'They'll all be fine in a week,' I said. Injuries, especially minor ones, to National Hunt horses were a regular fact of life in every yard in the land.

'Hope those bloody foreigners stay sound,' Charles said. 'If one of them goes I'll cut my throat.'

I looked up from my paper and smiled. 'Remind me never to be a trainer when I quit riding ... in fact ...' I reached for the formbook which lay open on the table. It's often known as the racing man's bible.

Standing up, I held the book in my left hand and raised my right. Charles looked at me. I said, 'I do solemnly swear never to take up the post of racehorse trainer at any point in my future life no matter how many millions of pounds, gallons of champagne, hundreds of women or any other form of enticement is offered me. I have seen enough misery for one life.'

Charles, already laughing, said, 'Mad bastard.'

The 'foreigners' Charles mentioned were two horses he'd bought from New Zealand at the start of the season. They were just about acclimatised and both showed promise, one more than the other. He was called Allesandro and he was scheduled to have his first serious gallop this morning.

We'd yet to work him with any of the other horses whose racecourse form would give us a reliable yardstick. But a jockey can tell a good horse purely

17

by the feel he gives, the way he moves under you, the power he exudes. I was convinced Allesandro was very good though I'd settled for telling Charles he might win a race or two.

At 7.45 a.m., as the sun began taking the chill out of the air, three of us jig-jogged at the bottom of the grass gallop which rose away in a long steady climb.

Allesandro grew impatient beneath me. He was a strong iron-grey gelding with a big ribcage and a rather plain head. The two bays alongside me had won five races between them. They were maybe twenty per cent fitter than my horse and Charles had told me just to sit in behind and see how long I could stay with them when they quickened up. We were to go a mile.

I could see his stocky outline waiting for us two thirds of the way up the gallop. Bryson and Whitey, both good work riders, were aboard the other two. Bryson called out, 'Ready!'

The two in front set off with huge simultaneous leaps and were galloping the moment their feet touched turf. I was still turning at this point but Allesandro quickly cottoned on and I felt him drop his bit, warning me that he was about to whip around.

He did so in an instant and launched us in pursuit.

Bryson and Whitey mastered their horses after fifty yards by which time I was sitting on their tails having my arms stretched like some old-fashioned torture.

This was an important gallop. It would tell us if Charles was going to have a class horse in only his second season training—a rare blessing. I felt a degree of tension and Allesandro sensed it making him even more eager to race his companions. Like all

18

good racehorses he loved competition and the closer he was to the others the better he worked.

But he was too keen and twice his steel shoes clipped the heels of Whitey's horse, the first time slightly losing his own balance, the second causing the leader to falter.

Whitey turned cursing angrily. I smiled at him.

Every time the pair in front collided the rebound created a temporary gap which Allesandro instinctively surged for. Fortunately for me, trying to keep him anchored, it closed each time.

Charles had wanted me just to stay as close to these two for as long as I could but I already knew Allesandro was capable of much better. As we passed Charles my arms, wrists and fingers were numb trying to hold this big horse and I caught a glance of the trainer's bemused, happy look.

Even though the pair in front quickened now, Allesandro was bursting to eat them up. His head got lower as he fought me and with two furlongs to go I simply couldn't hold him any longer and gave in.

He moved outside and passed them in two strides, snorted his turbo up to full power and quickly went away. Glancing back at a wide eyed Bryson I saw him mouth, Jesus!

Smiling as I narrowed my eyes against the wind and felt the cold slicing my cheeks I sat almost still enjoying the pulsing rhythm, the raw power that pulled us twenty lengths clear by the end.

We'd gone a third of a mile past the finish before I could pull him up and only then because I aimed him straight at a small copse where he decided discretion was the better part even of antipodean valour and slowed down quickly.

As I turned to walk him back I saw Charles

19

jumping up and down and punching the air as if he'd just scored the winning goal in the World Cup Final. He was whooping and squealing with delight and doing little jigs and I burst out laughing at the ridiculous joy of it all.

*   *   *

After riding another piece of fast work and schooling four horses I went back to my flat, made tea and a salad sandwich, sat down to read the *Racing Post* but found myself confronting the problem I'd been trying to forget all morning; Bill Keating's death.

The reason I'd been pushing it out of my thoughts was simply that I didn't know what to do about it. One of my weaknesses is an inability to say 'no' to people, especially friends. Cathy had more or less eased her worries onto my shoulders. I hadn't objected and now they sat there weighing me down, daring me to do something about them.

I should have rejected it when I'd had the chance, been as forceful with Cathy as she'd been with me. I was a professional jockey who'd once been champion and wanted to be again, an achievement that needed one hundred per cent commitment.

I hadn't the time, the inclination, nor the mental energy to get involved in any more amateur detective work. I'd had my share of it in the past two years through absolute necessity, the need to protect myself. But this was different, I had no personal stake in it. Bill and Cathy were friends but he was dead now and she was as independent as a woman could be.

Why then did I feel a complete bastard when contemplating leaving her to solve her own problems, abandoning Bill's reputation to the gossipmongers ... at least Pontius Pilate only washed his hands, I was taking a full shower.

Or trying to.

Deep down I knew I'd end up doing what I could. I was already persuading myself it was a simple case which wouldn't take up too much time or cause me any damage.

So I tried to plan the best opening move and immediately my mind moved into non-jockey gear as I reflected on how I'd handled past 'investigations'.

A couple of years back I helped track down a guy who was involved in horse-doping in a big way; a guy who, eight years ago, had falsely accused me of being involved with his racket. The Stewards had believed him and taken away my jockey's licence and with it my livelihood, half my personality and most of my self respect. Even now I hadn't got all of it back and didn't know if I ever would.

Then last season some maniac started killing jockeys for no apparent reason and I found myself on his hit list. The cops couldn't catch him so it turned into another Do-it-Yourself job which almost cost me my life.

I sat at the table this morning thinking of those two cases and how tough it had been to get started, to know how to make the first move, where to look, who to talk to ...

I sipped tea and chewed, stared blankly out of the window down at the quiet yard.

The only consolation was that I'd somehow got through those cases and I'd get through this the same. And even if I didn't it wasn't as though my life was on the line this time. Just Cathy Keating's business.

And Bill's memory.

Deciding that logic was the thing, rationally

21

applied common sense, I got up to search for pen and paper, though I knew deep down this was just another ruse to give me five minutes more before facing things.

Back at the table, yellow pad and black biro in hand, I got to work.

The problem: prove that Bill Keating's death wasn't suicide. Complications: no evidence, no witnesses and probably no co-operation from the police. Further complications: if it is suicide Cathy doesn't get the insurance money. If it was an accident she does. If she gets paid the business survives, the children's futures are secure and so is hers.

So Cathy's troubles are over.

But that would just be the start of it. Faced with a huge payout the insurance company will ask more questions than a Trivial Pursuit convention.

The police would be showing a passing interest too. It didn't help that the horsebox Bill was found in belonged to Cathy.

As a partner Bill still had an interest in keeping the business afloat as long as possible and occasionally, when he had no rides, he would do some driving. The dead horses found with him had been picked up that evening for a planned overnight trip to a new trainer in Yorkshire.

... The two dead horses that told Bill's friends it wasn't suicide ... maybe that needed some rethinking now.

If his state of mind was bad enough to write those letters threatening suicide, to behave the way he'd been doing in the final days, to be physically incapable of raceriding sometimes and, above all maybe, to refuse to tell any of us what was wrong, what would two horses have meant to him in that

22

condition?

I wrestled with it a while longer then tossed my pen down on the table and joined my hands behind my head. Something told me to leave things as they were, accept the suicide verdict and just get on with riding winners.

I rang an owner I knew, Marjorie Simmonds, who was a partner in a medium sized insurance company. We exchanged the usual pleasantries then I asked about the likelihood of Cathy's payment being withheld.

Marjorie told me that was a fairly common misconception. She said, 'The important thing is Bill's state of mind and his physical condition when the policy was actually taken out which was how long ago?'

'When they started the business I suppose. It was tied into the loan they got. Must be five years or more.'

'They'd have put him through a stringent medical for that sort of risk, Eddie, he'd have to have been as fit as the proverbial flea. If he was A1 for that I don't think Cathy will have anything to worry about.'

'Would they argue that he might have been taking heroin back then?'

'They might try but they'd have to prove it which I think would be difficult if not impossible.'

'Great. Thanks, Marjorie.'

'My pleasure. Any tips?'

'I'll give you a double: be wise and don't bet.'

'Spoilsport.'

Much relieved I called Cathy before the doubts started creeping in. She was grateful but not totally convinced. She went away to ring her lawyer.

I closed the yellow pad and put it away. Then I sat

staring out of the window. Then I made coffee. Next I played some music. After that I went for a walk. And all the time my conscience niggled. I tried to ignore it then I tried arguing with it but in the end I just couldn't shake off the belief that Bill Keating did not kill himself.

Cursing myself I got the pen and pad out again along with my diary and spent the next three hours calling jockeys and trainers, people who knew Bill, and asking questions. By midnight I had a big phone bill, a fierce headache and no answers.

It must have been after one when I finally got to sleep. Just before 2 a.m. the phone rang. I was pretty groggy when I picked it up. A voice I didn't recognise said, 'You've been asking questions about the death of Bill Keating?'

'Uh huh.'

'Well be a good boy and stop it.'

'What?'

'If you don't you'll get a chance to ask Bill personally.'

Alert now, I didn't reply. The voice-bank section in my memory was whizzing crazily through the entries to try and place the caller.

He said, 'Malloy, you there?'

'Uh huh.'

The voice, suddenly much more menacing said, 'Listen, bastard, forget it. Understand?'

I hung up.

I understood.

CHAPTER FOUR

Although late night death-threats are not as conducive to sound sleep as a good lullaby or a bad novel I awoke quite refreshed. At least the call had removed the uncertainty, eliminated days of wondering; somebody else was involved in Bill's death.

Briefly I considered telling the police about the call but decided to wait until I'd spoken to Cathy.

It was a bright, cold morning. I rode work and schooled three over fences, ate a meagre breakfast alone, soaked the racing papers with spilled coffee then went to get my kit ready for Cheltenham.

If I'd been taking my own car I'd have given it a quick inspection for foreign objects or severed brake pipes. Last night's caller sounded serious about his intentions and experience had taught me the pitfalls of complacency.

But there was no way he could know that Charles had offered me the jeep that day as my car was due a service so I climbed into the high driving seat without checking for sabotage.

I laid my mobile phone on the passenger seat and hoped to hear it ringing on the way to the races. The phone was another heavy expense for jockeys but if you wanted to survive it was as essential now as a crash helmet.

I had three rides booked at Cheltenham but there was always a chance, through either injury or indecision, that a spare ride would be available. For every horse I got safely to the start the owner had to pay me just over seventy pounds plus a percentage of

25

any prize money.

The top jocks had more than eight hundred mounts a season, most of them booked through personal agents. They could afford the luxury of refusing to ride dodgy jumpers and slowcoaches. I was among the many who scrambled for their leftovers though a steadily increasing winner flow and a thickening streak of self-preservation kept me off the complete headcases. Those were strictly for the nerveless steel-eyed youngsters whose ambition overruled pain, instinct and common sense. For now.

Unused to the high-sided jeep I went too fast on the motorway and a strong crosswind bullied me down to a speed at which I could keep going in a straight line.

I reached the course two hours before my first ride and two pounds heavier than I had to be when I got in the saddle. Some jockeys go through terrors trying to control their weight but up until this season I'd had no problems and could normally eat and drink what I liked within reason.

But coming back after the two month summer break it had taken me just that bit longer to get in shape and I'd spent more time in saunas this season than I had in my whole life. Maybe age was catching up. My thirtieth birthday was eight months away.

Clutching my phone and holding a towel round me I opened the sauna door and stepped inside the hot cabin to be greeted by three others already sweating freely, Blake, Neumman and King of the Sauna, Dave 'Puddly' Dudley, who would sweat if you aimed a hair drier at him.

Neumman didn't care much for my company. He'd ridden all Gary Rice's horses before Gary set Charles up as his trainer. I'd effectively though

26

unintentionally taken Neumman's job. I'd tried to be open with him about it when Gary first approached me, tried the no hard feelings stuff but he wasn't having it, took it personally.

In the weighing room we tolerated each other but he lost few opportunities for snide digs at me.

After updates on their sex lives and other assorted ribaldry (including Neumman slapping his long limp penis against his wet leg and asking if it sounded like excessive use of the whip), I steered the talk towards Bill Keating.

I'd spoken to Blakey last night on the phone and now I asked the other two the same question: did either of them have any inkling that Bill was taking heroin?

Were they totally surprised to learn he was?

Puddly was. Neumman said he'd stopped being surprised about anything when he'd discovered there was no Santa.

That made fourteen people I'd asked since yesterday and all I'd learned was that at least one of the previous twelve must have talked to someone else, hence my late-night call.

Puddly, elbows on knees, sweat dripping in steady rhythm from his nose said, 'Is this you off on another one of your investigations, Eddie?'

I shrugged. 'S'pose so.'

'What's in it for you?' Neumman asked.

Good question. Nothing but some peace of mind, a quiet conscience. But I didn't want to get into any holier-than-thou discussions, especially with Neumman, so I just said that Bill was my friend and I didn't think that drunk, stoned, high or sober he'd kill two horses.

Neumman wasn't satisfied. He pressed the point,

'So you're going to spend your own time ferreting around asking questions?'

Suspicious of his attitude now I looked at him. 'What difference does it make to you?'

'Come on!' He scoffed, 'You must be getting something out of it! Who's paying you?'

'Nobody.'

He stared at me. I wasn't sure if he was going to smile. He asked, 'You fucking Cathy?'

I glared at him. The others looked round sharply. Blakey said, 'You're well out of order, Neumman.'

I stood up. Neumman stayed sitting. Puddly sweated and watched. Neumman was on the high bench, fair hair clinging to his flushed forehead. His eyes smirked. I looked up at him. 'If you ever say anything like that again I'll break your jaw in enough places to shut you up for months.'

That silenced him.

A bucket of warm water stood by the door. I picked up Neumman's phone and dropped it in. A long splash sizzled onto the hot coals. I said to him, 'Add some soap. At least your phone conversations will be cleaner.'

The others laughed. I didn't even manage a smile as I went to shower.

*   *   *

I went looking for Doc Clarke to find out how much he knew about heroin addiction, see if he could guess how long Bill had been on it but the Doctor was tied up. I'd see him later in the weighing room.

With an hour to kill before my first ride I drifted around the course hoping to pick up some solid information on Bill's drug taking. Jockeys and trainers aren't the only purveyors of racing gossip and rumour nor the most reliable since a number carry personal grudges.

Others make a living at the game, among them people to whom good information can mean the difference between a diet of fillet steak and champagne and one of omelettes and tea.

They'll hear a hundred stories a week about how well a horse is doing at home, how another wasn't trying last time, how one has been trained with a certain race in mind, how a bent jockey pulled one or a crooked trainer stopped another.

A gambler's ability to sift all this then weave his findings into a clinical interpretation of the formbook will decide whether or not he survives.

Professional gamblers need at least as much nerve as professional jockeys. There are about twenty of them currently making a consistent living on Britain's racecourses and I found one of them in the Arkle Bar drinking mineral water and reading the *Racing Post*.

Allan Coe was fortyish, straggly greying hair too long for his age. Thin-faced and narrow-eyed from constantly avoiding the trail of smoke from the permanent cigarette between his lips he was, at five eight, a couple of inches shorter than me.

He'd seen me approach so didn't look up from his paper when I stopped beside him. He just said, 'Eddie.'

'Allan.'

'What do you know?'

'Not half as much as you.'

I spent the next five minutes talking to him about Bill but there was nothing he could tell me that would help.

I stood beside him trying to think up another question, reluctant to move on because I knew I had nowhere to move to. If Allan Coe hadn't heard anything it was a safe bet nobody else had.

Coe was impatient to get back to his newspaper. He said, 'If I hear anything, Eddie...'

I touched his arm. 'Sure. Thanks.' I turned to walk away.

Coe said, 'Was that what was doing him in, heroin? During a race, I mean.'

'Dunno. Could've been, I suppose. What did you think it was?'

'Somebody told me he'd just had a few too many knocks on the old napper. He had a couple of real bad falls at the back end of last season, some of us thought he'd have packed it in.'

'Couldn't afford to,' I said.

'Better than getting yourself killed.'

'For some, maybe.'

He nodded and raised his fingers slightly in farewell.

The three bookmakers I questioned could tell me nothing either though all that lack of information on Bill's private life didn't exactly add up to zero. A conclusion I could draw was that Bill could not have been using heroin for more than a few weeks. And I consoled myself with the thought that the pathologist who carried out the post mortem might be able to confirm this. With a definite timescale on the drug taking maybe I could track Bill's movements back, find out who he was seeing.

On my way to the weighing room I stopped by the parade ring to call Cathy and see if she could get access to the pathologist's report. As I dialled her number somebody tugged the sleeve of my jacket.

30

Frowning, I turned to see a little red-faced fat guy of about fifty grinning wider than a halloween pumpkin.

He pointed determinedly almost poking me in the chest. 'You're Eddie Malloy, aren't you!'

I nodded, 'That's right.'

Beaming he dug in his coat pocket for his racecard then into his inside pocket for a pen. He thrust both towards me. 'Give us your autograph!'

Bemused, I looked for somewhere to set my phone down.

He said, 'I'll hold that for you,' and grabbed the phone.

I resisted the urge to wrest it back deciding to sign and get rid of him. 'What's your name?'

'Monty.' He was pushing the buttons on my phone now.

'Please don't do that, Monty,' I said, scribbling quickly.

He did poke me this time then grinned conspiratorially as he said, 'Phoning up tips to somebody, weren't you?'

On the brink of agreeing I changed my mind in case he then started pressing me for the winner of every race. I went back to finishing the autograph but he wouldn't be put off. He poked me again. 'You were, weren't you?'

Handing him back pen and racecard and easing the phone from his grasp I said, 'Actually I was phoning my MP to register my vote for the new privacy laws.'

It baffled him long enough for me to duck under the rails and hurry away across the grass. Not wanting to risk further interruptions or being overheard in the weighing room I decided to leave the

31

call to Cathy till later.

*   *   *

I finished unplaced in the handicap hurdle, won the handicap chase by ten lengths and came cantering at the second last in the novice chase all set to make it a double when my horse completely lost concentration. A narrow brown gelding with a shortish neck he'd jumped impeccably throughout and we'd taken up the running turning into the straight. Maybe it was my fault for being over cautious—I shortened him up and asked him to pop over but he got too close, rose almost vertically and started paddling in panic, flailing the black birch with his front legs.

Just before he turned over I got the message. One of the first things a jockey learns is that the combined effects of momentum and gravity provide powerful motivation for baling out before your horse hits the ground.

Without even thinking your feet kick out of the stirrups and you start tucking up preparing to roll on impact. I was sure I had plenty of time to push clear but his hindquarters caught me in their arc and whiplashed me into the turf, pounding the wind from my lungs and rattling every bone in my body.

I lost consciousness for a few seconds but by the time the ambulancemen reached me my eyes were open though my brain reverberated in my skull. Any obvious signs of concussion when the Doc checked me over would mean an enforced suspension of up to twenty days.

You can lose a lot of rides in that time and I fought hard to keep my eyes open, to move limbs, push

32

myself up.

Back in the weighing room I sat still as the Doc placed two clammy fingers lightly behind my left ear and asked, 'How are you feeling?'

'Okay.' The jocks' pre-programmed answer to racecourse doctors. Even if your neck is twisted till your head's facing backwards you'll tell him you're fine in case he stands you down.

Moving to the front then he bent forward and held up a handful of fingers asking me to count them.

'Four,' I said with much more hope than confidence.

'How did you get to the races today?' he asked.

Even mild concussion can bring temporary amnesia.

'Drove,' I said, completely unable to remember but going for the stock answer.

I tried a smile to show my well-being but it felt like the corners of my mouth were rising in slow motion like a cartoon character.

Doc Clarke bent even lower, heavy red jowls wobbling as his bloodshot eyes stared into mine. He'd checked my limbs and general reflexes. Now he was trying to make up his mind whether I'd lied about losing consciousness out there.

He settled for the minimum period and stood me down for two days. My protests were milder than usual. The way I felt I would almost have welcomed a week to recover.

Charles had a runner in the last but he said he'd leave it to his head lad and insisted on driving me home in the jeep.

'What about your car?' I asked.

'Jamie will bring it.'

Jamie was one of his stable lads.

On the way to the car park I had to pause and rest a couple of times. Concerned, Charles looked at me as I rested against the side of a big BMW. 'You look awful.'

'Feel it.' I had a pounding headache, felt dizzy and cold in the wind.

'You're white as a sheet.'

Couldn't answer. Just stared at Cleeve Hill in the distance.

Charles said, 'Wait here. I'll bring the jeep.'

A few minutes later he pulled up beside me and helped me into the passenger seat. He leaned across and slotted my seatbelt clip home. I was aware of him looking up though I stared straight ahead.

'Still bad?' he asked.

'Be okay,' I mumbled, thinking I might never be. It had been a while since I'd suffered concussion and I was trying to remember if it was natural to feel this lousy.

Charles got in. 'Soon have you home.'

I didn't reply.

Whether I lost consciousness or simply fell asleep I don't know but when I opened my eyes again we were on the motorway. The clouds which had been hanging heavy all afternoon had burst. It was raining hard. Sheets of surface water. The trucks threw plumes of spray so big you'd have thought they were towing water-skiers.

Doing around seventy we swung out to overtake one. Visibility in the spray couldn't have been more than five yards. As we nosed ahead of him it cleared. Our tail was a few feet past his front bumper when the jeep lurched wildly and spun into the path of the truck.

We did wild pirouettes on the greasy surface.

34

'Jesus Christ Almighty!' Charles cried as he fought for control.

It seemed like slow motion. The jeep spun along in circles, listing but still maintaining momentum. Each time we came round I looked up and saw the horrified face of the truck driver as he worked down his gears trying not to stamp on his brakes.

Just before he hit us I spotted one of our wheels careering along the hard-shoulder.

CHAPTER FIVE

Soaked, bruised and dazed but otherwise unhurt we stood on the hard shoulder wondering stupidly if we could, with the help of the truck driver, roll the jeep upright again.

I could hardly keep myself upright. A terrible heavy tiredness weighed me down. Double vision made the downpour look like a biblical flood.

The jeep lay yards from us on its roof, three remaining wheels (six to my eyes) and black underside exposed to the rain and lashing spray of passing vehicles. Charles and I had undone our seatbelts and crawled through the wide space left by the shattered windscreen.

The rogue wheel which had caused our problems lay fifty feet away down a shallow embankment jammed upright in a narrow ditch almost as though it was just waiting to be set off again.

The police arrived quickly but didn't stay long. After checking that none of us was injured, they took our personal details then asked us to hang on and give full statements to a back up unit. They explained that they had to rush off to a much worse accident further along the motorway.

Before their flashing light was out of sight the truck driver was pulling away. He'd advised us to let the police come to us rather than hang around in the rain.

When the breakdown truck came we gladly accepted a lift home.

It was evening before I told Charles I thought it might have been sabotage. We sat by a blazing log fire in the living room of the big house, fed, bathed and in dry comfortable clothes. Whisky glinted in the chunky glasses we held then burned gently as I sipped. In the background classical music came at low volume from Charles's big stereo speakers. Just one lamp and the fireflames lit a comfortable and companionable semi-darkness.

From the easy chair opposite Charles smiled at me, waiting for the punchline. I didn't smile back. He said, 'Somebody tampered with the wheel?'

'I had a look at the wheel before they towed the car away. Three of the bolts holding the wheelnuts on had sheared off. They'd been sawed halfway through.'

'Who sawed them?'

'Don't know ... yet.'

He sat forward, smile fading and I told him about Cathy and the insurance and about last night's call.

He listened, long eyelashes flicking as he blinked rapidly at times, a habit he had when concentrating, sizing things up. He asked, 'Why didn't you tell the police?'

'Because I felt lousy and I didn't fancy standing around for another hour in the rain then spending the rest of the evening giving them the same statement over and over.'

He shook his head slowly which meant he thought I was stupid.

'I'll ring them in the morning, tell them I went to see the wreck at the garage and noticed the sheared bolts.'

He nodded. 'You think it was done at the racecourse?'

'Probably. Nobody could have known I would be driving the jeep there but plenty of people could have seen me arrive.'

'Maybe the car park attendants saw something. I mean you don't just quietly sit and saw away at a wheel.'

I shrugged. 'Jack it up, slip the wheel off, anybody passing just thinks you've got a puncture.'

'S'pose so.'

We discussed it for half an hour speculating on why someone would risk killing me to prevent me nosing around Bill Keating's past life. We worked our way through the list of names I'd rung last night asking about Bill.

Charles said, 'One of them has to be involved somewhere. He must've called up the guy who then rang you with the threat.'

'Maybe but it could just as easily have been a remark made by one of them that this guy then latched onto.'

'True.'

Two more drinks each brought no enlightenment and as the fire died in the grate and we downed the last of the whisky Charles became serious. 'Is it really worth your while going on with this, Eddie?'

I shrugged. It was late. I didn't want to be at the losing end of a long argument.

He moved forward in his seat. 'I know you liked

Bill and, and Cathy too but ... Well you were hardly ... you weren't *that* close. I don't think Bill would have held you to any sort of commitment.'

'Maybe not.'

Exasperation didn't sit well on his face. 'But you're going on with it?'

'Somebody tried to kill me today and they almost got you too. I'm mildly curious to find out why.'

'But if you keep trying to find out why he'll probably keep trying to kill you.'

'I'll be careful.' I got up. So did Charles.

'You can be hellish flippant sometimes,' he sighed.

Smiling I put my hand on his shoulder. 'Survival mechanism.'

'Contradiction in terms the way you use it,' he said resignedly.

'Good-night.'

'Good-night,' he mumbled and I could sense him shaking his head slowly as I walked away.

Before turning in I rang Cathy and told her what had happened. Her concern for my welfare didn't mask the obvious relief at the fact that Bill's death was beginning to look much more suspicious. She was still awaiting her solicitor's advice on proceeding with the insurance claim but was expecting a call the next morning.

I asked about the pathologist's opinion on how long Bill had been taking heroin. Cathy said he couldn't tell for certain but it would have been months rather than years, maybe even weeks.

I considered asking her to meet me at Stratford the next day but, wondering who might see us, I thought better of it and we agreed I'd go to her place for dinner tomorrow night.

Lying in the darkness, in the deep rural double-glazed silence I felt all the old doubts coming on. I didn't need the echoes of Charles's warning. I was worried about how this would end up. My luck had to run out some time.

I tried a logical analysis.

If I got killed or crippled who would suffer?

Not much counting to do—one. Me.

No wife or children, estranged from my own family since I was sixteen. Not even a dog or a cat. Charles relied on me a little for moral support and he and a number of friends would be sad if something happened to me but it wouldn't affect their lives in any practical way. Not in the least.

Death itself held no fears and hadn't done since my childhood. Being crippled scared me. Terrified me with its indignities. And yet it was a prospect I faced almost every day. A severed spine. A snapped neck.

For years I'd challenged the terror and beaten it but the day would come as it did with almost all jockeys when my nerve would go. No drawn out deterioration; the first cord works loose then frays and unwinds at speed and suddenly you know you can't ride any more. You've been spitting in the face of fear all your riding life but he wipes it off and waits and when the time comes he smiles and you both know he's won.

Now not content with danger on the racecourse I was into it in the real world ... For the third time.

But if the first two taught me anything it was to make my mind up very quickly. Don't entertain the doubts for they burrow away slowly affecting judgement and confidence and courage. Either do it or don't. In till the end or out for good. Decide now and kick the worries into touch.

Decide.

I did and the doubts as ever disappeared. My resolve hardened immediately.

And I went to sleep.

*   *   *

Next morning the only reminder of my bad fall the previous day was a mild headache. I felt okay but the doctor's suspension would stand so I still couldn't ride.

At breakfast Charles asked me if I still planned to go to Stratford.

'Might as well. Ferret around.'

'What about the police, you going to ring them about that wheel?'

I chewed toast. 'Would you mind doing it? I haven't got time to hang about waiting for them.'

'They're going to want to talk to you.'

'Tell them I'll ring them this evening. Get the name of the investigating officer.'

'They'll want to have a look at the car.'

'They can do that at the garage, can't they?'

'Suppose so.' He sighed seeing I was in no mood for arguing.

Smiling I said, 'Cheer up or I'll make you drive me back from the races.'

He only half smiled, shook his head and gave me that faraway look that says *I thought I knew you but I obviously don't*. He said quietly, 'You're a crazy bastard.'

'And don't you forget it.' I said.

I spent five minutes checking the car over. Found nothing untoward but drove warily on the first ten miles of the journey to Stratford.

A valet told me Doc Clarke was in the weighing

40

room but it irritated me to be in there when I wasn't riding, especially when I felt fit to, so I waited for him to come out.

In the same brown checked suit as yesterday he was carrying three jockeys' medical books which he shuffled absent-mindedly. He looked up as I walked towards him and raised his hand like a traffic cop when I was still five yards away.

'No!' he said.

'What?'

'Don't ask me, Eddie, you are not riding today. You're stood down till Monday. End of story.'

'I know. I'm not arguing.'

His face softened then turned quizzical. 'What are you doing here, then?'

'Looking for some info.'

'From me?'

I looked up at him. He was tall, pear-shaped and quite unhealthy looking for a doctor with his red, heavy jowls and bloodshot eyes.

'If you can help.'

'I'm pretty busy.'

'Won't take a minute. I'll walk with you.'

We set off in the direction of the secretary's office.

The doctor told me that although he was far from a specialist on drug abuse he wouldn't have thought Bill Keating a long-term habitual user. 'He just wouldn't have been able to ride at that level.'

I said nothing but wondered how many favours we'd really been doing when we'd all covered up for Bill's physical weakness during races.

Doc Clarke said the Jockey Club were looking at drug testing for jockeys within the next year or two and that it was a pity it wasn't already in place.

To catch the occasional cannabis user or the guy

41

who snorted a line of coke once a month?

God knows how many thousands it would cost to set up. They'd have been better spending it on weighing rooms some of which still didn't have adequate heating or shower facilities.

I kept these thoughts to myself, thanked the doctor and wandered towards the pre-parade ring where the runners for the first race were being walked round by their lads.

Like a stranger peeping through curtains the sun found a temporary gap in the clouds. The rain had stopped for lunch though there was plenty of evidence of its morning's work especially on the clothing and footwear of the stable-lads whose ages ranged from maybe sixteen to fifty.

A dozen of them clutching wet bridles walked smartly beside their horses who looked better fed and clothed than most of their companions, only two of whom had waterproof jackets on. The others wore cheap clothes and shoes, all they could afford no doubt.

Underpaid, overworked, badly housed ... Ambition kept the youngsters in it, the longing to be a big-time jockey. You could see it burning in their eyes, read it in the tough determined set of the chin and the confident stride.

And the old ones ... no dreams left there. But there were few bitter faces, those that felt that way would be long gone. What you saw was a calm acceptance, an inner satisfaction that their skills as stablemen had been enough to help them last. You could see a quiet peace. They were still doing something they loved.

I knew three or four of them but there was one in particular I wanted to talk to. I knew him only as Nick, a boy working for one of the smaller stables in

Lambourn. He wore an expensive waterproof and leather boots. Tall and thin he had that look about him that life in his tough home city had bred naturally into many of its natives; wary, watchful, opportunistic, it showed an almost predatory instinct for survival.

I arranged to meet him in the bar when he'd finished his after race duties.

Nick's horse finished unplaced but he told me he'd backed the winner. When he was buying his own in the Lambourn pubs he drank half pints of beer, the odd time splashing out for the full measure. When anyone else was buying his appetite stretched to a pint and a large vodka.

Nick was well known for 'sourcing' things for people. He could fill most orders or point you in the right direction as long as there was something in it for him.

The drinks I bought entitled me to ask where someone could buy heroin in Lambourn. Nick's answer was that you couldn't. Not from somebody living there anyway. A dealer from Newmarket apparently did some good business either on special trips to the village or, very occasionally, on racecourses themselves.

It cost me twenty-five pounds for the bloke's name and the same for his mobile phone number. By way of added value I asked if he knew any of the guy's customers, past or present.

Nick just smiled, opened his mouth so wide his jaw seemed disconnected then poured the remaining half of his beer straight down his throat.

By late afternoon the rain was back on its beat and my wheels splashed dirty water from the potholes in the drive approaching Cathy Keating's place.

Young Amy opened the door. I smiled at her. She looked uncertain then blushing slightly turned to call back down the hall, 'Mum, it's Mr Malloy.'

Mr indeed. Made me feel old.

'Well bring him in!' Cathy called from the kitchen.

Leaning over the sink Cathy's tight jodhpurs showed a fit shapely lower half. A loose green sweatshirt covered the rest of her slim figure. The dirty riding boots which stood in the porch had been replaced by furry pink rabbit slippers. A strand of straw stuck out at collar level of her dark shoulder-length hair.

Arms holding something under a running tap she half turned her head to welcome me. 'You're early.'

'Yeah, sorry. Couldn't be bothered going back home then setting off again.'

'Come straight from Stratford?'

'Yep.'

'How many winners today?'

'Zilch. Wasn't riding.'

She glanced round again. 'Oh that's right you got a knock. How're you feeling?'

'I'm fine. How are you bearing up?'

She turned the tap off and set a colander of vegetables on the draining board then plucked a towel from its plastic hook and dried her hands. She said, 'I'm okay.'

I glanced round to make sure Amy had gone then said, 'And the children?'

'Subdued is probably the best way to put it. Especially Kate, she's spent most of the time since the funeral in her room.'

'Hasn't she got any friends who could maybe bring her out of it a bit?'

Cathy shook her head and laid the towel across its

hook. 'Doesn't want to see them.'

I said, 'It'll take a while, I wouldn't worry too much.'

She looked at me. 'Eddie, I wish I had the time to worry about her. I wish I could allocate her a few more pounds of the one ton of worrying I do every day.'

The strain of the other night was back on her face. I didn't say anything. She threw her hands wide and I found myself glancing at the palms. Thin dark healing lines bound together the cuts inflicted by the broken cup. She said, 'God I'm sorry. You must think I moan day and night.'

'Not at all. I'm sure you take a break when you're sleeping.'

We both smiled then had coffee and sat talking while pots bubbled and lids clinked sending delicious aromas around the big kitchen.

Cathy told me her lawyer had advised her to proceed with the insurance claim and see what the insurer's reaction was. She'd set things in motion earlier today.

Though she had worries enough there are only so many things you can be blasé about and while I made light of the threatening phone call it was tough trying to put a devil-may-care sheen on the jeep sabotage.

The lines in Cathy's frown deepened. She said, 'You'd best leave it to the police now, Eddie.'

'I'm afraid that would have to be a mutual agreement along with whoever's after me and so far he ain't made any offers.'

'I thought he gave you a warning by phone?'

'Just one. He didn't bother coming back with another one after the jeep so I'm assuming that whatever deal was on offer on the phone has passed its sell-by date.'

'You think whoever it is would still try to get you even if you dropped the whole thing?'

'I think it's probable so I'm not hanging around waiting. I'll get to him first.'

She sipped cold coffee and stared at me, her long jaw dropping, pulling the liquid over her tongue. She swallowed and said, 'You're sitting there like you haven't a care in the world and I'm feeling guilty as hell.'

'What for?'

'Getting you into all this. Just for my sake.'

'For your sake and for Bill's. And Kate's and Amy's. And now mine.'

Putting her cup down she massaged her brow with both hands.

'Anyway,' I said, unfolding the piece of paper Nick had written the dealer's number on, 'it's a team effort.'

Cathy stopped rubbing and looked up. I pushed the paper across the table. 'I want you to ring that number and ask for Vince.'

Mentioning 'products' and 'wares' rather than drugs Cathy fenced around doing her best to get some commitment from Vince. His apparently genuine surprise at being asked if he could help sowed doubts in Cathy's mind and mine. Then he asked if he could ring back 'when he had more time' and try and clear things up.

She gave him my mobile number and an hour later he called saying that although he wasn't directly involved he could arrange a meeting with a certain party who may be able to 'tell Cathy a bit more'.

Would it be possible for her to come to Newmarket tomorrow?

46

Sure it would be possible.

He named a pub and a time and said the guy she wanted would be the only one there in a black suit and red waistcoat.

Cathy hung up and gave me the first warm, proper smile I'd seen from her in years. The frown ridges around her mouth and eyes curved to laughter lines. She said, 'This is quite exciting.'

I smiled at her enthusiasm not wanting to disillusion her at this point.

'What happens now?' she asked.

'The hard part. You meet Vince and find some way of getting him to tell you if he was supplying Bill with heroin.'

'On my own?'

'That's what he'll be expecting.'

The excitement faded quickly back towards worry. 'But what if he recognises me?'

'I doubt that. It's not as if your picture's in the paper every day.'

She nodded slowly, thinking. I reassured her, 'Don't worry, wherever you are I'll be no more than a few yards away.'

'What if he recognises *you*?'

'Then it'll cut things short and I'll ask him nicely to tell us what he knows.'

We spent another half an hour making plans and I left just as the ten o'clock news came on the car radio. Bumping and splashing back down the drive I listened to the usual depressing reports of international wars and violent crime and wondered what percentage of mayhem over the next few days would find its way to this little corner of England.

CHAPTER SIX

Next morning at breakfast Charles told me that the police had not yet called back. He'd reported the damaged wheel-bolts and told them where the car was. I was about to update him on the progress made at Cathy's place last night when I noticed how uneasy he was talking about it.

I sipped black coffee and asked him what was wrong.

'Nothing.'

He looked awkward, avoiding my eyes.

'Come on,' I urged.

He put down his cutlery, a piece of yolk-daubed bacon still pinioned to his fork. He said, 'I'm nervous about how Gary will take this.'

Most trainers had a number of 'employers' in that they had different owners but Gary Rice was the sole source of Charles's income. He was also his landlord.

'Take what?' I asked.

'This whole business with threats and sabotage and police and stuff. I don't think he'll see it as good for his image somehow.'

'Nah,' I said, 'he'll be fine. Something for him to dine out on.'

'You think so?'

'Yeah, I wouldn't worry.'

Charles wasn't convinced but picked up his fork again driving the impaled meat slowly round the plate on a final mopping up mission. 'I'd better tell him though.'

I nodded.

'I'll ring him after first lot.'

I could see he wasn't relishing the prospect. I asked, 'Want me to call him?'

'Would you mind?'

'Not at all.'

He grimaced, undecided. 'Think he'd rather hear it from me since I'm his trainer?'

I shrugged. 'I'm his retained jockey and the hassle's all down to me really.'

'Well, if you wouldn't mind.'

'No problem.'

His smile brought back his natural sunniness and the forked bacon, reprieve over, met its natural end.

I rode some work again on Allesandro, the big grey that had Charles whooping like a kid the other day. One of the horses he'd pulverised in that gallop had won a decent race by ten lengths at Stratford yesterday and Charles and Gary were planning a big betting coup on Allesandro's first race.

He worked exceptionally considering he was still some way short of peak fitness and as I dismounted in the yard Charles salivated over the prospect of hammering the bookmakers.

'He's in at Uttoxeter next Wednesday. If we leave that bit of belly on him we should get an even bigger price. I'll go and ring Gary now.'

Sarah, a chubby little groom, took charge of my horse and led him away to be untacked. I followed Charles and listened to him hatching plans for Allesandro with Gary Rice. Gary was at his estate in Barbados for a few days. He had another racing yard set up over there alongside his sugarcane plantation. He was always promising Charles and me a holiday on the island.

At that moment Charles looked like he needed a holiday. With considerable trepidation he asked

Gary to hold and handed me the phone.

As I took it I watched Charles trying to hurry casually away already whistling in an attempt to blot out what he thought might turn quickly into a major argument between me and his boss.

Gary took the news even better than I'd expected, calling me 'mate' all the time and offering support of whatever kind I thought I needed. He said he knew a certain Chief Constable and would be happy to have a word. I thanked him and said that may well come in handy at some point.

I hung up, adopted a deeply worried look, found Charles in the kitchen with the volume high on his radio and wound him up for a full five minutes with a dire report of Gary's reaction.

Back in the yard I watched our two runners at Warwick being loaded into the horsebox. Each had a reasonable chance of winning which was one of the reasons I wouldn't be going to watch them race.

There are few things a jockey hates more than watching horses he should be riding win races. I'd deliberately left Stratford early yesterday so that I wouldn't have to witness the stable's easy winner there. I was always glad for Charles and for the lads but the mixed feelings weighed too heavily on the black side.

When Cathy had set up the meeting last night with the mysterious Vince I hadn't realised there was racing at Newmarket today and with nothing better to do I decided to make the one hundred and forty mile drive east and remind myself how the flat jocks lived.

My car was parked by the gable end of the barn and I was checking it over methodically ticking off aloud the precautions advised in all Good-Driving

50

Manuals: 'Air, Water, Oil, Tyre-wear, Lights, Indicators, Semtex, slashed brake pipes, sawed wheel-bolts...'

I was on my knees at the front bumper when I heard an engine then wheels crunching gravel. I looked up to see a police car swing into the yard. One uniformed guy, one plain-clothes.

They followed me up to the flat where I made coffee and answered all their questions. Between them they couldn't come up with any conclusions and it struck me once again, the ambiguity of police attitude when weighed against achievement.

Still I knew it was a tough job and I tried to be courteous, tried to make sensible suggestions like liaison with Cathy's local force. I got the usual, 'Leave that to us, sir,' and the parting line that they'd be in touch and to contact them if any further threats were made.

The drive to Newmarket was as tedious as ever. I'd first travelled this road about ten years ago and the bloody roadworks on the A45 were still there. And the diversion signposts still weren't there. And, like ten years ago, I got lost and missed the first race.

I called Cathy from the course to confirm our meeting place that evening and to warn her that she might get a visit from the police.

The only real attraction flat racing holds for me is the beauty and grace of the horses which tend to be built on much cleaner lines than the jumpers. The racing itself bores me and I didn't stay long.

I wandered into town and passed a couple of hours in the National Horseracing Museum.

Five o'clock found me alone in the plush lounge of a big hotel. I sipped coffee and tried to concentrate on reading my paper but my mind kept drifting to this

51

evening's meeting and its possible consequences.

I was comfortable at the thought of being tough with Vince if needs be but there was every chance he didn't operate alone. Some said the drugs business in Newmarket was way out of control. If the big players weren't already in there they'd be sniffing around the edges.

As the racecourse emptied the lounge filled and by the time Cathy arrived she had trouble picking me out. I saw her in the doorway looking anxiously around the faces. I raised my paper. She saw me and looked relieved, tried to smile as she came over but tension kept a frown on her brow.

She wore tight black trousers and ankle boots, a beige polo neck and a short dark jacket.

I got up and kissed her lightly. She was holding her breath.

'Relax,' I said.

She tried to smile again and sat down. 'I'm nervous.'

'You'll be okay.'

She nodded. I smiled. She said, 'I've got to go to the loo.'

I stood up with her and went to get us drinks as she disappeared quickly back through the multi-paned doors.

After ninety minutes, two large gins and lots of encouragement she was still cold sober and scared. We sat in my car in the darkness. The meeting place was forty yards away, a big busy pub.

Cathy's children were staying with her mother so we were under no time restrictions. She kept going silent on me. I watched her face in the sweep of passing headlights. She looked worse than at Bill's funeral. I decided it wasn't worth the risk.

I reached for her hand. She clasped mine in hers. They were cold and clammy. I said, 'Cathy, I'm going in myself. You stay here.'

She turned to me. 'I'm sorry, Eddie.'

'It's okay.'

'Give me five minutes to get myself together then I can ... I'll probably be able to do it.'

'You won't. The longer you wait the harder it gets.'

'Maybe we can rearrange it?'

I shook my head. 'I'll go in,' I smiled to reassure her. 'I know who to look for. It won't take long to get into conversation with him.'

I pulled my hand free. Cathy slumped back in the seat. 'Jesus, I used to be a lot tougher than this.'

'You're still tough when it matters,' I said. 'Horses for courses. Will you be okay here till I get back?'

She nodded slowly.

'If I come out with him and we get in a car follow us.'

She looked at me.

'Okay? You all right to drive?'

She nodded. 'What if you're just walking?'

'Wait. I'll be back.'

I left her looking thoroughly despondent.

I heard the music as I got out of the car and the closer I got to the pub the louder it sounded.

Two bow-tied doormen guarded the entrance and if the proprietor paid them by the inch then they came considerably cheaper than your average bouncer. Both were shorter than me but plenty big enough for most of the Newmarket lads. They glanced at me and parted.

The place was big, dark, crowded, warm, smoky and loud. Music from fat speakers pounded a base beat that shook the floorboards. Excuse-mes were lost in the racket and I had to shoulder my way through tightly packed groups laughing, drinking, smoking, trying to hold conversations.

The bar was long, brightly lit, well staffed. I got a drink within two minutes and started looking around for a guy in a red waistcoat.

It was much too crowded. I envisaged myself opening bloke's jackets one by one.

After checking those at the bar as best I could I moved around. No one seemed to notice me. I criss-crossed the floor and on my third foray, as I broke through the edges of the throng, the toilet door opened and he stood framed in the light.

Tall, dark well-trimmed beard and gelled hair, black suit and a red waistcoat showing as he stood, hands on lapels, talking to someone on his way in. He was coming out.

I followed him to the bar. He moved along it speaking to everyone, well liked, it seemed. A barman pushed a drink towards him on a paper coaster. As he reached for it someone else stretched for the ice bucket and knocked his drink over.

I watched his face. He laughed and looked at the woman who'd spilled it. She was being very apologetic and trying to mop it up. It was Cathy.

An hour later on our pre-arranged signal I left the pub. Five minutes after that Cathy joined me in the car. She was flushed, smiling, much more relaxed, pleased with her 'success' which turned out to be another meeting arranged with Paul, as he'd called himself, for next Tuesday.

'I can't wait that long, Cathy.'

'It's only a few days.'

'This is Friday. I was hoping to tie something solid up over the weekend.'

54

'That soon?'

'I start back riding on Monday. I won't have much time after that.'

Her enthusiasm cooled now. The smile faded. 'Maybe you should just bale out now.'

I looked sharply at her, expecting her to take it back. She didn't. I said, 'It's not a matter of baling out. I said I'd help. I'm in it now probably deeper than you are. Somebody tried to kill me two days ago and I'd like to find out who it was before next Tuesday.'

Her petulant look was gone. She put a hand on my shoulder, 'I'm sorry, Eddie, I shouldn't have said that. It's the nerves . . . and the booze.'

'Forget it.'

While we watched for him to come out we discussed what Cathy had learned. Though he'd called himself Paul she'd heard a few people address him as Vince. 'A nickname,' he explained when she asked him about it.

She told him she wanted cocaine and cannabis and he played dumb till she hinted that she was talking biggish amounts, left him believing she wanted to deal in it to help shore up her business. She said her name was Trish. Didn't tell him where she lived.

'Nobody followed you out?'

She shook her head. 'You'd have seen them.'

'Maybe they just stood at the door, watched you get into the car.'

'Maybe. I didn't see anyone.'

We kicked it around a while longer but didn't come up with much. Doubts crept in. I wondered if I should have thought it out more, taken another approach.

The night wore on slowly. A lot of people came and

went. Vince stayed inside. Cathy fell quiet. I switched on the radio, low volume. Jazz.

It got cold. I started the engine and we got some warm air. Cathy dozed off. She snored gently. Breaths of stale gin mingled with the jazz notes...

Just after midnight I called it quits, couldn't keep my eyes open. I clipped my seat belt in and slipped the gearstick forward. As I steered out from the kerb a taxi drew up. Vince stepped from the doorway and got in.

I glanced at Cathy. She was still sleeping. The taxi pulled away. I followed it.

CHAPTER SEVEN

As we left the town the glowing tail lights in front of me grew brighter in the darkness. I was wary of him becoming suspicious and dropped back to around three hundred yards behind.

A couple of minutes later the taxi stopped. Indicating quickly I turned down a narrow track to my left, stopped and killed the engine and lights.

Cathy woke up and instinctively whispered, 'What is it?'

'He's stopped. Wait here.'

I got out leaving the door open and walked to the junction. The taxi showed no signs of moving off again. I squinted through the bushes looking for the outline of a building or another vehicle, some clue as to why they'd stopped there. Nothing.

I sensed Cathy at my shoulder. 'Is he in that car?'

'It's a taxi.'

'Why have they stopped?'

56

'I don't know.'

'Did Vince get out?'

'Don't think so.'

She heard the irritation in my voice. 'Should I shut up?'

'Just for a few minutes.'

She did and we stood craning necks, listening, willing the interior light to go on so we could check that Vince was still there.

We waited ten minutes. Cathy said, 'It's cold.'

'Why don't you sit in the car? I'll signal you if anything happens.'

'You sure?'

I nodded. Then the taxi engine revved. A minute. Revved again. Vince got out talking to the driver, 'He'll be here any minute!'

Couldn't hear the driver.

Vince said, 'I'll pay for the other hire!'

The driver must have declined the offer. Vince shouted, 'Fuck you!' and slammed the door. The taxi pulled away.

The moon appeared briefly and lit Cathy's wide-eyed face. She looked scared. I ran back to the car and started the engine while the noise of the taxi was still enough to mask the sound from Vince. Cathy got in and I told her what I wanted her to do.

She started by removing her tights.

I knew Vince was waiting for someone who could appear any time and I wanted to pick him up but we had to sit and suffer. To roll straight along just as the taxi disappeared would have looked too coincidental. I held out as long as I could. Cathy's nerve would be fraying by the second too.

There was the option of waiting to see who his contact was but that might mean missing the chance

57

to pick up Vince himself who I was sure could tell me all I wanted to know.

After maybe three minutes I touched Cathy's shoulder and said, 'Go.' Then I crouched out of sight in the back.

As we approached, Vince did what I thought he might. Assuming it was his contact he stepped out into the road. Cathy steered away from him but slowed enough for each to see the other's face.

She stopped and rolled the window down. I heard his footsteps as he walked round. 'Long time no see,' he said.

Cathy said, 'You gave me a hell of a fright. I thought it was some madman.'

Vince sniggered. 'Mad, bad and dangerous to know.'

'What are you doing out here?'

'What are *you* doing? You left the pub ages ago.'

'I had to see someone before heading back.'

'Where?'

'Home.'

'Who did you have to see?'

Cathy bristled. 'What's it got to do with you? When you buy me a drink my life story doesn't go with it!'

I saw his hand come in and rest on Cathy's shoulder. 'Cool your jets! I was only asking.'

Cathy sulked. 'Sound like a cop.'

'Last fucking thing I'd be.'

Cathy started rolling the window up. 'I've got to go.'

'Hang on. I'm meeting somebody. He'll be here in a minute.'

'Do I know him?'

'Doubt it.'

58

'Then I ain't waiting.'

He pulled his hand out as the gap narrowed and bent towards her. 'He's a very interesting man. He could help you.'

'Thought you were going to help me on Tuesday?'

'Why wait?'

'I haven't got the time.' She revved the engine.

'Look, okay! okay! I'm bloody cold, just let me sit in the car till he comes, you don't have to meet him!'

Cathy weighed it up.

He said, 'As soon as he drives up I'll get out.'

She hesitated then leant across to open the passenger door.

Vince got in saying, 'Good girl! Good girl!'

Cathy said, 'Don't call me that.'

'No offence. No offence meant ... Any taken?'

'Forget it.'

I grew increasingly uncomfortable huddled down in the back. We'd agreed that Cathy would keep him talking for a while to see what she could get out of him without my intervention. If the talking died she was to switch the radio on quite loud to kill the sound of my breathing.

Cathy probed. Vince didn't give. He probed back. She didn't expand much on the story she'd given him in the pub. After five minutes she switched the music on. Two minutes later Vince suggested something more romantic and changed the station. A few seconds after that he started asking Cathy about her sex life and within a minute was talking so dirty it made my flesh creep.

That was when I nearly closed his windpipe off with Cathy's tights whipping his head back to bounce on the headrest.

He tried to squeal but just managed a strangled

59

gasp. It startled Cathy but I nodded at her and she crunched into gear and pulled away. Vince's fingers tried to get inside the nylon. I watched his terrified eyes in the mirror and said, 'Take it easy, Vince. What is it you say, eh, cool your jets, that was it wasn't it? Thought a pervert like you would appreciate a pair of ladies tights around your neck. Or are you a stockings and suspenders man?'

He began choking. Phlegm spluttered from his gagging mouth sticking to the windscreen. Spittle ran down his chin. Cathy winced. I eased the pressure, let him have enough breath to cry, 'Jesus Christ!', then tightened it again.

Cathy cast a worried look back at me. I nodded to reassure her and she drove on. By the time we pulled in to a deserted layby I had tied the tights to Vince's headrest. They held him secure but gave him enough air to keep breathing.

Cathy switched off the engine. Vince sucked in oxygen. I stayed behind him making sure he didn't see my face. I leaned towards his ear. 'Got a pen?' I asked.

He reached for his top pocket and pulled one out. I took it. 'Hey, nice one Vince! Gold Waterman! Business must be good.'

He didn't respond. I said, 'Take pen. Insert into tourniquet. Question patient. If no response twist pen one full turn. Simple instructions, Vince, huh? Bet you're glad I remember my first aid.'

He tried to see me in the mirror. I leaned forward and angled it away. Removing all the lightness from my voice I said, 'Were you supplying Bill Keating with heroin?'

No reply. He just kept gasping. I twisted the pen. He gasped louder. I said, 'Was Bill Keating one of your customers?'

He nodded weakly.

'Is that a yes?'

He nodded. I loosened the tights two turns.

'How long for?'

'I ... he ...'

I let him catch some breath.

'Just ... a few weeks.'

'Who supplied him before that?'

'Dunno.'

I tightened again. He cried out. I said, 'Vince, don't fuck me around, I haven't the time for it. Who was supplying the stuff before you?' I eased off enough to let him answer.

'Nobody ... not with smack.'

'What, then?'

'Mo ... Morphine.'

'Morphine?' I only knew of it as a painkiller.

Vince nodded.

'Were you supplying it?'

He hesitated. I jerked it tighter forcing an involuntary whistle from his tubes. He nodded desperately.

Leaning close to his ear I said, 'Listen, I'm going to let you have enough air and comfort to ask you a minute's worth of questions. Give me the right answers and give them quickly. If you don't I'm going to cut off the oxygen supply to your brain for long enough to turn you into a cabbage. Do you understand me?'

He nodded quickly throwing sweatdrops into the darkness. I loosened the nylon and said, 'Why did he want morphine?'

'Help his headaches.' His voice was badly broken. I wondered if I'd damaged his vocal cords.

61

'You taking the piss?'

'No! No! True!'

I glanced across. Cathy was staring at me as though I were mad. I continued grilling Vince, 'How bad were the headaches?'

'Real bad. Very bad.'

'Why didn't he go to his doctor?'

'Couldn't. Was scared he'd stop him riding.'

That's when I knew he was telling the truth. I asked, 'Why didn't he stay on morphine, increase the dose?'

Vince hesitated. I grasped the nylon. His fingers came up and he shouted, 'No! He, he came for some one time and I didn't have any...'

'But you happened to have some heroin lying around which you knew would get him hooked a lot quicker than morphine?'

He tried to glance round maybe hoping that when I saw the pathetic look in his eyes I wouldn't hit him. I grabbed a handful of his hair and felt the crackling stiffness of lacquer. Forcing his head forward I said, 'Eyes front!'

I let go his hair and his head drooped feigning shame. I was certain he felt none and I became even more angry at him thinking I was stupid enough to be taken in.

I took a few breaths to calm myself. I had to analyse things coolly, ask the right questions while I had him. Eventually he told me that he had been Bill's first and only supplier. Bill had been 'referred' to him, as he put it. I forced the name of the referee out of him.

'Where can I find him?' I asked.

'Just a phone number...'

'What is it?'

62

He gave me a London number and I slipped his pen from the tourniquet and wrote it on the back of my hand. 'This better be right, Vince.' I jerked hard on the ligature. 'If I've got to call Directory Inquiries you're in deep shit.'

He gurgled. I tried to think if there was anything more I could get from him without giving away who I was. I needed him to think I was some sort of rival, another supplier maybe trying to muscle in. That's why I'd been playing the tough guy. There had to be a chance Vince was connected with the bloke or people who'd threatened me. I didn't need him running straight to them for protection.

On reflection I realised I'd been concentrating far too much on Bill Keating for Vince to be fooled but there wasn't a hell of a lot I could do now except protect my identity.

I tried to find out who it was he had been waiting for when we came along. He said it was just one of his suppliers.

I calmed my thoughts searching for further questions. Vince's breathing was still heavy, laboured. Cathy looked tense and, wondering how much more she could take, I decided to call it quits.

I eased the neck tourniquet up till it encircled Vince's head at eye level then I tightened and knotted it so he couldn't see. Then I got out, opened his door, dragged him out by the hair and kicked him into a ditch.

I resisted the strong temptation to lecture him on the number of lives he was screwing up with his filthy trade. I needed to have him think I was as bad as he was. I got back in the car and Cathy drove.

She was still only in third gear when she burst into tears.

I took over the driving. The only communication we had on the journey was when I asked occasionally if she was okay and she said yes. I think she was in mild shock. Understandable.

We sat in her kitchen till dawn broke. Half a dozen cups of hot sweet tea thawed her voicebox sufficiently to spend half an hour regretting we'd ever got into this.

'I thought you were going to kill him.'

'It had to be convincing.'

She looked tortured. 'Eddie, I honestly thought you'd taken leave of your senses. You were so cold and callous.'

I sipped tea and tried not to be angry at this woman who'd been more than happy to enlist my help when her impressions of villains were just from books and movies.

'What did you want me to do? This is the real world, you can't go in half-cocked, they'd eat you alive.'

She was gripping her cup again in that intense way, with both hands, trying to crush it. I leaned across and eased her fingers away. She lowered it to the table. 'It just seems ... well ... I don't know.'

I said, 'It's not as if I did him any real damage.'

'But what about the next time?'

I stared at her. 'Cathy, listen. I didn't take this on without knowing the dangers and I came in fully committed to handling them with whatever level of ... of resources I have to.'

'Resources meaning violence!' she accused.

'What do you want me to do?'

'Just forget it. Let's forget it.'

'You forget it. I can't. I'm in it. I have to see it through.'

64

She went quiet for a while. I poured more tea and tried playing it down telling her Vince was just a small time hood who couldn't do anything to either of us.

Cathy wanted to believe me but I could see in her dark-ringed nervous eyes that her perception of me had changed too much for things ever to be the same again. Until now her summary of me had been: someone to trust with almost anything, someone soft enough to take advantage of if needs be, someone to pull social and intellectual rank on albeit subliminally, someone who'd never be anything more than a jockey.

Now she feared me.

I was sorry for that. But a bit of me was satisfied. In her mind Cathy had long since bundled me up and slotted me into a category, confident that I was the sum of all my parts and that she knew exactly what they were. Now she'd discovered one more and, even worse, didn't know which others were hidden.

Looking through the heavy condensation on the window above the sink I saw a watery sun struggle up and suddenly felt very weary. My headache was back. I needed sleep and a few hours of my own company.

I finished the cold tea and got up. 'I've got to go.'

Cathy rubbed her face and drew her hair back. 'What time is it?' she asked.

'Gone half seven.'

'Jesus, those horses need feeding.'

'And I've got some that need riding.'

She nodded glumly. I reached for her shoulders and kissed her goodbye. She didn't smile. She said, 'What next?'

'I'm not sure but we'll soon crack it.'

'How?'

I looked at her. 'Somehow . . . Don't worry about it, you've done your bit, there's nothing else you have to be involved with.'

'Are you going to see this other guy, the one Bill saw before Vince?'

'Maybe. I'll see what I can find out about him first.'

She looked at me like I was a lost cause but managed to tell me to take care. I told her I'd stay in touch.

In the car I rang Charles and apologised for missing first lot and told him I'd try and make the second.

He didn't ask where I'd been.

The yard was quiet when I got back and the second lot were back in their boxes. One van had already left with two runners for Wetherby and one was preparing to take another pair to Warwick. Charles had gone to Wetherby in his car.

In the kitchen I made toast and coffee and listened to Radio 5 though I didn't take much in. This was the last day of my suspension and I was determined to make the best of it by tracking down the guy Vince had fingered. I wanted everything over with as soon as possible so I could concentrate on my riding again.

Back in my flat I rigged my mini tape recorder to the earpiece of the phone and dialled the number. It rang out a dozen times and I was just about to hang up when a woman answered, said good-morning, announced her name and thanked me for calling The Allied Bank. Knowing that Vince had put me away I was tempted to hang up but thought I might as well ask. The woman, still speaking like an automaton, said she was sorry but no one of that name worked there.

I banged the phone down and the cable swayed

and I wished it was round Vince's throat and that I was still holding the ends.

I made a pot of coffee and sat down once again with pen and pad hoping that my plodding logical approach would at least help me fill part of this empty day.

What had I learnt? That Bill Keating was baited, lured onto heroin by an unscrupulous dealer. That Bill had been suffering severe headaches (which could have explained his virtual blacking out during races). That Bill wanted so badly to keep riding that he risked his life on the course and risked drug addiction off it. Would a man so driven then kill himself?

No way.

Yet the police were convinced it wasn't an accident.

So somebody must have murdered him.

Before I could find out who I had to find out why. There was a high chance the drugs connection was in there somewhere. If so there was an equal chance Vince was involved and that he'd now reported his encounter with a guy whose only interest was Bill Keating.

For whoever made the threatening phone call and sabotaged the jeep, putting two and two together was not going to be difficult.

I managed an ironic smile as I threw the pen down and poured that whisky. Cathy had taken cold feet—it looked like she'd get her insurance money anyway, no one else seemed to give a toss about Bill, I stood to gain nothing personally from finding his killers yet I couldn't quit now even if I wanted to.

Sitting target.

CHAPTER EIGHT

I was sure Bill had been murdered but at the moment it seemed I was the only one who cared. It was time other people did.

The racecourse medic for the midlands, Doc Clarke, had known Bill better than any of his colleagues. The least he could do was tell me if Bill's medical records pointed to any severe head injury. I rang Warwick races to confirm he was on duty then drove there at speed.

He was filling in forms in the ambulance room, his arm surrounding them like a kid protecting exam papers. He didn't look too surprised to see me. He said, 'Back on Monday, Eddie?'

'Yeah.'

'Looking forward to it?'

'Can't wait.'

Slowly he took off his reading glasses and stared up at me. 'You look . . .' he searched for the word, 'impatient.'

'Good on the spot diagnosis, Doc. Add frustrated and thoroughly pissed off and you've got the full picture.'

Putting the glasses down he shifted in his chair. 'And something tells me it cannot all be laid at the door of your enforced two day rest.'

'Correct.'

'And something further, some uncomfortable premonition, leads me to the conclusion that it is I whom you think may be able to help relieve this unfortunate condition.'

I'd never had occasion for serious conversation

with this man but I hoped his grammar didn't become more convoluted the longer he talked.

I dragged an old three-legged stool across the room and sat down opposite him. Instinctively he lifted the papers he'd been working on and turned them over. Big fleshy earlobes framing heavy jowls he watched me apprehensively. I said, 'Bill Keating was murdered.'

He stared at me. 'Says who?'

'Says me.'

'Why and by whom?'

'I don't know.'

I told him about the drugs and Vince and the headaches and Bill's obvious determination to keep right on living. I withheld the threats to me and the busted car—he'd have washed his hands of it and sent me straight to the cops.

'And that is all you are basing your assumptions on?'

'It's all I've got.'

Picking up his glasses again he said, 'I fear it is not sufficient.'

I knew it wasn't but I persevered, trying to get him on my side, reminding him of what Bill was like as a man, as a professional.

He said, 'So professional it now seems that he risked his life and that of his colleagues through riding while obviously unfit.'

'Come on, Doc, that wasn't Bill! It must have been the illness, the headaches playing on him.'

He raised his eyebrows. 'They must have been some headaches, Eddie. Headaches of brain tumour proportions.'

That made me think. Suddenly suicide lurched back into the frame. If Bill had been suffering from

69

something like that he wouldn't have waited to die in agony … But he'd have told someone, surely. And he'd never have killed those horses.

But he wouldn't be thinking straight, maybe he forgot the horses were even in there.

We talked some more and the Doc agreed that for Bill to know about a tumour it would have to have been diagnosed by an expert so somebody somewhere would have records. I told him I'd get Cathy to check with Bill's GP and with the coroner.

The Doc agreed to keep an open mind and see if he could pick up any clues 'without badgering people'. Slightly deflated but less frustrated I got up to leave knowing that the threats and attempt on my life still punched big holes in any suicide theory.

As I reached the door he called me back. Tidying his papers, he said, 'A thought occurs to me…' He waited for my prompt.

'Uhuh?'

'I could go back and examine Bill Keating's brain scan result. It was no more than a few months ago and any abnormality, especially invasive tissue, would show quite clearly.'

He was right. These days every jockey had to have a pre-season scan to make sure a build up of falls hadn't caused permanent damage.

I smiled. 'Great idea!' Then the obvious occurred to me. 'But wouldn't it have been examined and spotted at the time?'

'Should have been but one never knows. I think it is worth checking.'

Annoyed at myself for discouraging a potential ally I said, 'Of course it is. When can you do it?'

'I'm free Monday and Tuesday, I'll try and arrange something then.'

70

I scribbled my mobile number and handed it to him. He promised to let me know immediately he had something and as we shook hands I saw that trace of a gleam in his eye, the one Cathy had shown, the spark that said, this is a break from humdrum life, this is exciting. Then I remembered how the reality had affected Cathy and I vowed to try and shield this nice old doctor from it for as long as possible.

On a roll now I rang Cathy and told her about the scan. She showed little enthusiasm. I said, 'I want to talk to the girls.'

'Why?'

'They might know something. Bill may have confided in them.'

'He wasn't the type.'

'Maybe not but I have to find out.'

Her long sigh came down the line. I said, 'Cathy I'm sorry but I need to know why Bill was killed.'

'Eddie...' she sounded tired, 'can't we just drop it?'

'Cathy, we went through all this last night.' Reluctant as I was to remind her of who got me involved in the first place I was ready, if necessary, to make her feel very guilty about it.

I explained that Bill may just have confided in someone. He had no girlfriends I was aware of and he hadn't spoken to any of the lads. If Cathy knew nothing then it was just possible that his daughters might.

Cathy offered to question them but I doubted her commitment and persuaded her to let me drive over right away. I agreed it might upset them and promised to handle it as sensitively as I could.

All four of us sat at the kitchen table with tea and cakes and I encouraged Kate and Amy to reminisce

71

about their father, especially the good times. I moved things round gradually to the time they'd spent with him in his final months but if they knew anything, which I doubted, they weren't telling.

It was dark when I got back to the yard. I parked and walked towards the block of yellow light coming from the kitchen window of the big house. Drawing closer I heard laughter and cursing and glasses clinking.

To my right horses snickered contentedly in their boxes. Somewhere in the corner a shod hoof scraped at the concrete under its straw bedding. The familiar smell of hot fresh droppings reached my nostrils. Two of Charles's dogs ran from behind the barn and came barking towards me for a pat. I bent to stroke them and welcomed myself back to the real world— for a while anyway.

Under a pall of tobacco smoke in the kitchen a raucous card game was in progress at the big table. Charles had on his Yankee card-sharp gear, metal bracelets on shirtsleeves, plastic cap-peak low over his eyes and loud-checked waistcoat. A couple of the lads saw me and shouted. Charles, without stopping dealing said in his Bronx accent, 'Pull up a chair, Ed and draw some chips.'

I declined politely and settled for a large whisky, news of our runners today (two winners and a second) and the relaxed atmosphere. I laughed at their antics, watched everyone get pleasantly drunk and enjoyed seeing Charles in tearful paroxysms of laughter at some of the jokes. For a couple of hours Bill Keating didn't enter my mind, nor did Vince or Cathy or brain scans or syringes, tumours or overturned cars.

They saved themselves till I was asleep and formed

72

a horrific nightmarish amalgam which woke me in a mucksweat around 4 a.m.

*   *   *

Next morning on the gallops Charles was bright-eyed and bullish. Yesterday's winners had taken his strike rate for the season to thirty-eight per cent.

He and Gary Rice liked a bet and he saved his high octane enthusiasm for the rare well organised betting coup. Plans had been redrawn for Allesandro, the big grey New Zealand horse. Instead of going for a small race at Uttoxeter Charles had pencilled in a hottish contest at Chepstow on Saturday next.

The reasoning was that among better opposition the price would be bigger and the prize money greater. The more work the horse did the more obvious it became that he was very good indeed.

We were easing off on his exercise now. Charles reckoned he could win at Chepstow around ninety per cent fit. The lack of top condition would be obvious to racecourse experts and his price in the betting market would swell accordingly.

As I pulled him up this morning after a nice half-speed gallop I felt mildly frustrated. This was one time I'd have loved to have gone all out on him. I hadn't raced at full tilt for four days, hadn't ridden at all yesterday and I could have done with that burst of exhilaration to blow clear the thoughts and worries cramming my mind and the sticky residue of that recent nightmare.

Still it would be all the better tomorrow when I was back in the saddle up at Newcastle. Charles had no runners but I'd been booked by two different trainers for three rides.

Over breakfast I updated Charles on what had been happening. He grimaced when I told him about Vince and I got the impression he'd much rather not know about any of it.

After spending an hour with the Sunday papers I did some cleaning around the flat, washed shirts and underwear, idly polished a couple of race trophies I'd collected and tried consciously to ease some of the tension that was building as I waited for 'their' reaction to my grilling of Vince.

At the very least I'd expected the phone to ring by now, expected to hear that cold voice telling me the consequences of my actions. Thoughts of a personal visit from them (I don't know why I was convinced that more than one was involved) had crossed my mind and I'd been carrying and sleeping very close to a metre of fairly heavy stainless steel chain I'd found in the barn.

The next positive move would come from Doc Clarke when he looked again at Bill's brain scan and until he came back to me there was nothing else I could do.

Papers read, silverware polished, flat clean, clothes flapping on the line I could find nothing else to occupy myself. The temptations of eating and drinking presented themselves but were quickly banished by visions of two hours' dehydration in the sauna.

I changed into my running gear and headed downstairs. Stopping halfway I returned for my shining chain. As I wrapped it round my fist the tension cranked up another notch. The longer they waited before coming for me the bigger the whack someone was going to get.

Out in the fields I ran myself to a gasping sweating

74

mud spattered standstill then stood luxuriating in a hot shower.

Draped with a towel, my hair still dripping, I thought I heard my name being called from the yard. I went to the window. Charles, obviously agitated, was beckoning me. I opened the window. Charles said, 'You'd better come down.'

He looked serious. I asked, 'What's wrong?'

'Kenny Hawkins has been in a bad accident.'

My blue mood which had at least been working itself towards a paler shade plunged back towards navy. I got dressed and went to the big house.

Kenny Hawkins was a friend, a jockey who, like Bill, had been riding for a long time. He also lived in Lambourn where, last night on a dark road a couple of miles from the village his car had plunged forty feet down an embankment. Latest reports from Newbury General said he might never walk again let alone ride.

There's a camaraderie among jockeys that is tough for outsiders to understand. Watch them finish after a big race. The fiercest rivalry between starting gate and winning line becomes effusive and genuine delight for the successful jockey. You'll see some almost fall off in their eagerness to congratulate their victorious colleague.

Every day of our lives we take risks. It is a very rare day's National Hunt racing where no one falls, a rare week that nobody breaks a bone, a rare year when no jockey retires for good through injury. And every so often one of us dies on the racecourse.

We live with this all the time—seldom talk about it—never let it get us down but it's there and it binds us, all rivals, more tightly than any team spirit. Sure there are fights and fall-outs and bad guys but that bond is there till the day you're no longer a jockey

75

and it's one of the things that makes retirement so tough.

We were always prepared for bad news on the racecourse. When someone suffered off it it seemed grossly unfair. Fate taking us when our guard was down. I felt sick for Kenny and for his wife and children.

I rang the hospital to find out about visiting arrangements. They said he wouldn't be fit to see anyone for a couple of days. I felt like telling them not to underestimate the recovery powers of jump jockeys but I decided not to tempt fate.

That night I lay awake wondering if there was any connection between Bill's 'accident' and Kenny's. They lived within a mile of each other, had been riding for about the same length of time and at a similar level of success. Each even had two daughters though Kenny was not divorced.

That was one difference. The other was that Kenny was still alive.

*   *   *

Next morning the early racing bulletin said there was an inspection at Newcastle at eight—snow on the course. November was still eighteen hours away, what kind of winter was in store?

It was cold in Shropshire but the grass was green and frost-free. I schooled a couple over Charles's line of four portable fences and after breakfast we rang Newbury Hospital again—no change.

At 8.21 a.m. it was announced that racing at Newcastle would go ahead. Snow still lay on the course but a thaw was expected. Even though the track management didn't have the best weather-

76

forecasting record in the world, I had no choice but to set off north in the hope that racing would be on.

It was, though all I could manage from three rides was a second and a fourth. A gloomy atmosphere hung in the weighing room as we talked of Kenny's accident. The northern-based jocks didn't see that much of him but he was one of their own just the same.

In mid-afternoon a few of us got talking and Jeff Dunning suggested doing something for Kenny if the prognosis turned out as bad as we feared.

'Like what?' Bobby Cranley asked.

'Sort a race out for him,' Dunning said. 'Make sure he comes out with a few quid.'

'Like a few of us fix it up between us?' somebody asked.

Dunning said, 'Yeah, why not?'

From the back a mocking voice said, 'You fucking daft? You'll all end up warned-off.'

I recognised Neumman's tones—the guy who'd bad-mouthed Cathy in the sauna at Cheltenham, the guy who'd lost his job to me. Dunning strained to see who was objecting and Neumman worked his way through the huddle. Neumman had a habit of sneering when he spoke making his big nose twitch as his lips moved. His eyes were a cold greyish blue. He said, 'Give yourself a break, Dunning, you'll end up screwing up the system for everybody.'

'It'd just be a one-off,' Dunning said, 'for Kenny.'

Neumman scoffed, 'Fuck Kenny. Let his little brother look after him. He's got more than enough. Got a private jet, two Rollers and more houses than a fucking Monopoly set. Kenny can go to him for charity.'

Everybody looked at Dunning. He said, 'He

77

shouldn't have to rely on hand-outs.'

Neumman said, 'What do you think yours will be seen as?'

Dunning looked away knowing Neumman had a quicker mind and a sharper tongue. Neumman smiled slyly.

Fixing races wasn't something that appealed to me but at least Dunning had proposed it in good faith. I was suspicious of Neumman's hard stand against it. What difference did it make to him?

I said, 'What's your beef, Neumman?'

He became aware of me for the first time. His smile disappeared. The others watched him. He said, 'Just like I said, why get dropped in the shit for Kenny Hawkins?'

'Who's going to drop us in it?'

He flushed then tried to bluff. 'Didn't know you were into bent races, Malloy.'

'I'm not but I've got the choice. I can say yes or no to Dunning's idea same as the others can, same as you can so why the big song and dance? If you're not interested just say so.'

'I'm not, I—'

'Well stay out of it then. You're a non-runner. Nobody else wants your advice. If you're not in the team you don't get a say in the tactics.'

He grew redder. 'So you're in, Malloy, is that what you're saying?'

'Maybe, maybe not but why's it getting you so het up? You running some little scam of your own? Scared of somebody queering your pitch?'

Everybody watched him. He started blinking rapidly. He said, 'You're out of order, Malloy.'

'Says who? You the only one that can voice an opinion?'

78

'You just better not repeat that to anybody.'

He didn't sound convincing. I said, 'Tell you what, you keep your opinions to yourself in future and I will too. Deal?'

Aggressively pushing away his fringe of fair hair Neumman, unable to forgive or forget the fact I'd got his job said, 'Isn't Rice paying you enough?'

'Everything between me and you comes back to that, Neumman, doesn't it? If that chip on your shoulder gets any bigger you'll have to start declaring overweight on every ride.'

The others laughed. Neumman's pale face reddened. 'I hope you all get fucking caught!' He turned away. Jeff Dunning called after him, 'If we do we'll know who shopped us!'

He didn't look back.

After my final ride I showered, dressed hurriedly and rang Doc Clarke from my car. He had said he'd be at Portman Square in London, Jockey Club HQ, checking Bill's scan. The receptionist told me he was in a meeting. I left a message and headed south. An hour later he hadn't returned my call. I rang again and was told he was still unavailable.

At 5.25 p.m., fearing they'd close up for the night without passing the Doc my message I phoned again. The receptionist was still there but the Doc had gone. I asked if she'd passed my message on. She was evasive at first but said she had.

Back home I sat by the phone and kept my mobile switched on too. At 8.20 p.m. it rang. I answered. A familiar voice said, 'Eddie?'

It was Peter McCarthy, an old friend of mine who worked for the Jockey Club Security Department. 'Mac! How're you doing?'

'Under pressure, Eddie.'

79

I mouthed it as he said it—his stock reply to the question.

'Social call or business?' I asked.

'Business.'

'Uhuh?'

'You've been calling Doc Clarke today?'

'That's right.'

'Do me a favour ...?'

'What?'

'Don't call him again.'

That familiar little thrill zinged through me—the one that said the next jigsaw piece was about to slot neatly into place.

'Why, Mac?'

'I can't say just now.'

He knew me better than that. 'You'll have to say just now or I put this phone down and call Doc Clarke and keep calling him till I hear what I want to hear.'

'Which is what?'

'Which is what did he find in Bill Keating's brain scan that suddenly means I'm *persona non grata*?'

'Nothing.'

'Mac, come on, it's Eddie you're talking to.'

'He found nothing.'

'Mac! Why lie to me? You know I won't give up.'

I heard the long familiar sigh of submission. 'Eddie, I'm not lying. The Doctor found nothing because Bill Keating's brain scan was not there.'

'Not where?'

'In the files. It's missing. Disappeared.'

80

CHAPTER NINE

Just after ten next morning I met Mac at a service station on the M5. His dark curly hair had picked up a few more strands of grey since I'd last seen him and his cheeks were chubbier, as was the rest of him. We sat by the window, traffic whizzing past fifty feet away. Mac was halfway through a big fried breakfast, forkfuls stoking his sixteen stone bulk with more fatty calories.

I said, 'You're getting to the age where you ought to be watching your heart.'

He chewed, swallowed and said, 'My grandad ate this every day and lived till he was ninety-seven.'

'Yeah but I'll bet he didn't sit around all the time or let himself get stressed out like you.'

Spearing half a sausage he said, 'You're the only one who ever sees me stressed, Eddie. You're the only one who causes me so much grief.'

I smiled, 'If it wasn't for me you'd be a nobody.'

Chewing he said, 'If it wasn't for you, I'd be Head of Security.'

Mac had been involved in both of the serious cases I'd got tangled up with. We'd bailed one another out an equal number of times and owed each other nothing but respect and a rather guarded friendship.

When he finished eating we sipped coffee and sort of mentally circled one another in the ring looking for an advantageous opening.

Eventually Mac said, 'Doc Clarke told me what you talked about on Saturday, do you want to give me a full update?'

I did, withholding nothing. At no point of the story

did he look surprised. 'Have the police been back to you about the jeep?' he asked.

'Not yet.'

He brandished his pen. 'Who's handling it?'

'Can't remember. I've got his name at home.'

'No matter.'

I said, 'Have you called the police in yet?'

He shook his head.

'When do you plan to?'

'We don't.'

'Come on, Mac, you've got more than enough to give them with what I've just told you never mind the stolen file.'

'Stolen file?'

'Bill's scan.'

'Who said it had been stolen?'

Irritation rose. 'You're not going to say it's just been lost.'

'Misplaced. Temporarily.'

'Mac—'

'Eddie, there are hundreds of scans stored in that room.'

'Mac, don't try and tell me it's been misfiled or something. You said last night it had disappeared, come on!'

'We'll have to wait till everything's been searched at least once more. Even then, how can we call in the police for a missing file? We'd be a laughing stock.'

'It is the missing file of a man who died in suspicious circumstances. A man whose headaches were so severe he risked drug addiction to relieve them. The headaches may have come from a damaged or diseased brain. Now who is hiding something here?'

Mac spread his hands, open, innocent. 'Nobody's

82

hiding anything, we—'

'Trying to protect some stupid bastard who made a wrong diagnosis? Didn't spot the problem when he should have?'

'Eddie, supposing somebody did make a mistake, it wouldn't be the first time. Why would we indulge in all this subterfuge you're accusing us of?'

'To protect your interests!'

'Whose interests?'

'The Jockey Club's. The medical guys. The ones who could probably be sued for millions for letting a brain-damaged jockey ride in jump races.'

He shook his head slowly, that irritating half-smile and downward glance telling me I was being silly. He said, 'Look, every one of those scans is examined scrupulously. The doctor who checked Bill's is absolutely certain it was one hundred per cent healthy.'

'What's his name?'

'It doesn't matter.'

'Of course it does! Who is he?'

Four women eating together stopped chattering and, as one, looked curiously in our direction. Mac smiled and nodded to them without effect. Their necks remained craned, their eyes and ears primed for a scene.

Mac, bending low, said quietly, 'I can't tell you. Don't get annoyed.'

I gritted my teeth. 'There must be a copy of the scan somewhere.'

He sipped coffee, shaking his head.

I continued, 'The people who take them, the lab or whatever it is, must keep a copy.'

'They don't.'

'Okay, well maybe they can remember something

about Bill's scan.'

'They take hundreds, maybe thousands a year. They don't just do work for us, you know.'

'Surely it's worth speaking to them, to the guy who did Bill's?'

'How is he going to remember?'

'Have you tried?'

'We've got other cases going as well.'

'Mac! . . . Oh, this is a waste of time. Why did you agree to meet me? I've got better things to do.'

'Eddie, like before, when I know something I'll tell you. If I can help I will.'

We spent another ten minutes arguing, going nowhere. I tried to persuade him to have the police pick Vince up or put him under surveillance. He agreed to see what he could do but he was probably just trying to shut me up. I mentioned the similarities in general circumstances between Bill and Kenny Hawkins who was reported slightly improved this morning. Mac dismissed any connection.

No further forward on my part I left Mac ordering another coffee and Danish pastry, 'to heat me up for Exeter'.

He was on his way to the races there. I wasn't riding today and I decided I was on my way to London, to the clinic I'd visited in June for a brain scan.

I had to park ten minutes' walk away. It was early afternoon and the sun was out in a clear sky. Tall buildings shielded the bright streets from the wind. It was much warmer than Shropshire had been this morning. Some people were in shirtsleeves. Crossing between long lines of parked cars I took a few wrong turns and had to ask directions.

When I found the place I stood across the street

84

looking up at the window, wondering what to do next, how to approach this. I needed to speak to the bloke who'd done Bill's scan. I had a vague recollection of the one who'd done mine—well I thought I'd recognise him if I saw him again—but what would I say? I couldn't just walk into reception and ask to speak to the little fat guy which was as much as I could remember about him. Could hardly say, I'd like to book a brain scan. Maybe they'd already been approached by Mac's people, told to keep quiet.

Turning at the bottom I walked back. Checked my watch; a few minutes after one. Maybe he'd come out for lunch.

Maybe he'd had lunch.

Maybe he didn't eat lunch.

Oh, he ate lunch all right if my recollection of his girth was reliable. I decided to hang around for half an hour in the hope that he'd appear. It didn't take me long to start wishing I had the car to sit in. The fresh air was perfectly pleasant but I soon started wondering who was watching from the windows, seeing this loiterer, this street wanderer, this furtive glancer.

After almost forty minutes a black cab stopped by one of the buildings and a beautiful woman in a tight skirt and high heels got out. She paid the driver and click-clacked away along the pavement, her hips stirring my testosterone with every swing. As the cab driver sorted his change I had an idea. I crossed the road and got into his cab. 'Where to, mate?'

'The shop where they turn out dolls like that.'

He smiled in the mirror as his eyes joined the path of mine in watching the redhead move sexily away from us.

'Plenty in Soho,' he said.

'Nah, soiled goods.'

'Where's it to be, then?'

'Can we just sit here a while?'

His reflection looked at me.

'I'll pay twice the meter.'

'You waiting for someone?'

'Sort of.'

'Well, I can't sit for too long. Blocking the road.'

'Bear with me. If it gets awkward you can move on.'

He opened his window and produced a tin of rolling tobacco. The redhead had stopped at the end of the street. Then the man I was waiting for waddled out of the clinic door and down the steps about twenty yards in front of me. I sat forward waiting to see if he'd get in a car. He walked to the end of the street and touched the redhead's elbow. She bent and kissed him.

The driver glanced back at me. We both watched them. They turned right and walked out of sight.

'Drive to the end of the street.' I said. He did. The couple were still walking, didn't look like hailing a cab.

I gave the driver five pounds and got out. 'Keep the change.'

I walked about fifty paces behind them, the view of the redhead's rear a lot more fetching than her companion's. Several questions were in my mind not least how in hell did he get her? Another was when would they either reach their destination or stop a cab. The little guy didn't look like he cared for exercise and the lady's stilettoes weren't the most comfortable footwear for a long hike.

After five minutes I twigged it. The guy was

86

showing her off, strutting as well as his build would allow enjoying the admiring looks of male passers-by and blokes in parked cars. A few minutes later they crossed a busy road and walked up the steps of the Ritz Hotel. One of the commissionaires smiled and opened the door taking a while to close it after the redhead had gone in.

I stopped and considered my dress standard. Leather jacket, sweatshirt, jeans and trainers. I'd have to bluff it. I sprinted across the road and up the steps. The commissionaire who'd let them in stopped me. 'Can I help, sir?'

Looking anxious I said, 'I have rather an urgent message for the gentleman who has just gone in.'

'Mr Conway?'

'Yeah. We tried to catch him leaving the office. His secretary said he'd be here.'

'I can give it to him.'

'It's personal.'

He looked at me then at his friend. I said, 'Look if I'm not back out in two minutes you can come and get me.'

He hesitated then nodded, pushing the door a foot open behind him. I went in trying not to look too out of place, trying to keep from drowning in the opulence. I asked a bellboy where the restaurant was and got there in time to see Mr Conway and his ladyfriend being warmly welcomed and led to their table by the *maitre d'*.

I left. No lunch for me but plenty of food for thought. I went walking in Green Park and chewed on it.

Conway was a salaried worker in a clinic. Even the kindest eye would have seen him as short, fat and unattractive. Yet here he was parading a gorgeous

87

woman before fawning staff at the Ritz. Now either he was a top-notch hypnotist or he had a lot of money. The latter was favourite.

Where did he get it?

If he earned it legally it sure wasn't from scanning brains. Would such an obvious bon viveur relish loading jockeys and the like into a big machine all day and taking pictures of what was under their thick skulls?

Mr Conway was up to something.

I got back to my car and found two big white teardrops of birdshit on the windscreen. They took some shifting before I got myself through the traffic and onto the M4 towards Newbury. I planned to visit Kenny Hawkins in hospital.

On the drive I tried to figure Conway's angle. If he was making his money gambling or pimping or something then he was doing a lot better at it than his day job which I reckoned couldn't be paying more than twenty grand a year. So why didn't he quit and take up the lucrative employment full time, make even more?

I kicked his little bubble figure around in my head for an hour and could only come up with one conclusion—whatever he was making he was doing it through his main job at the clinic. Now unless he did something else there except operate that scanning machine, how was he earning the money? Moonlighting? Offering an 'informal' service while his boss wasn't around? But how much would he get from that? And would there be any real call for it? Perhaps Mac would know.

By the time I pulled into the car park at Newbury General no credible theory had presented itself. I parked and got out looking warily around, conscious

88

of being back in the world of serious accident victims.

They wouldn't let me see Kenny but Carol, his wife, left his bedside to come and spend five minutes with me. Mid-thirties, small, blonde, very round blue eyes, thin lips, she was as impeccably made-up and dressed as ever though the strain was obvious from halfway along the corridor. I kissed her lightly. She gripped my hand very hard.

We sat in a corner of the waiting room and I brought coffee and hot chocolate from a machine. She sipped it and tried to smile.

'How is he?' I asked.

'Better. Sleeping just now.'

'What are the doctors saying?'

'Wait and see. That's what they say. But there's not an ounce of optimism in their eyes or their faces when they say it to me.'

'It's early days.'

She nodded and looked down at the chocolate suds in her cup. 'Long days.' She said quietly, then, 'You expect it to happen on the racecourse if it's going to happen at all. Every day he went out there I didn't know if I'd ever see him again or if they'd bring him back on a stretcher. For what?'

She looked at me, one of his gang, one of the kamikaze band who encouraged each other. I didn't answer.

She went on, 'For broken bones and depression. Sixty thousand miles a year. Kow-towing to fat owners and so-called trainers who don't even teach their horses to jump...'

She was getting upset but needed to get it out. She turned towards me. 'He's too old, Eddie. I told him. It was his birthday two weeks ago, I told him then. Thirty-nine...'

89

She was talking like he *was* injured on the track. I tried to bring her mind back to it. 'What happened? How did the car come off the road?'

'They don't know. He just went through the crash barrier on the bend going into the bridge.'

'Were the brakes faulty or something?'

'They don't know. Still checking.'

A woman's voice behind me called out, 'Carol!'

Carol looked past my shoulder and had to battle not to swivel her eyes upwards in despair. Quietly she said, 'Excuse me a minute, Eddie.' And forcing a tight smile she got up and went to meet the woman.

I turned and watched them. The woman was about sixty, short and heavy, her camel coat well past her knees, expensive shoes and hair-do, auburn, no grey showing. She stood waiting for the dutiful kiss and I assumed it was either Carol's or Kenny's mother.

Carol didn't kiss the man who was with her. He nodded and looked coldly down at her. Carol's back was to me now so I couldn't see her reaction.

The man looked like Kenny, maybe a couple of years younger, kind of chubby faced, broad across the bridge of his nose, well cut dark hair, ears which stuck out quite noticeably. At around five eight he'd be a couple of inches taller than Kenny but I was fairly sure it was his brother.

Carol spent a couple of minutes with them then nodded towards me. The man left them and approached me holding out his hand and smiling showing some good dental work. I got up to shake hands.

'Joe Hawkins,' he said, 'Kenny's brother.'

'Thought I saw a resemblance. Eddie Malloy.'

'I know.' There was coldness behind the smile now.

'I was sorry to hear about Kenny, we all were. He's

well liked.'

'Yeah, he works hard at it.'

Resentment there.

He said, 'Listen, I'm going in to see him now. I'll be telling him not to worry, especially about money...'

He waited for some reaction from me. I stayed quiet.

'My brother doesn't need charity, Malloy.'

Somebody had been talking. I played dumb. 'What does that mean?'

'You know what it means. Run all the bent races you want but keep your charity for the Salvation Army.' A slight raising of eyebrows and widening of eyes asked me silently if I understood.

'Nice meeting you,' I said and sat back down.

Joe turned back towards his mother, passing Carol with barely a glance as she returned to where I sat.

Watching them go through the doors leading to Kenny's room she said, 'What did he want?'

'Just introducing himself.' Even before he'd spoken to me I'd had no intention of telling Carol or Kenny we were planning the coup on their behalf.

'Creep,' she said. 'And Mummy thinks the sun shines out of his arse.'

'And you don't?' I said, smiling.

'If I never saw him again in my life it would be too soon. I don't like him, don't trust him. I try to make a point of being out when he calls to see Kenny.'

'What does he do?'

'Describes himself as an international businessman. International rip-off artist would be more like it.'

'Dodgy businesses?'

'Lucrative ones as far as I can make out but he won't tell anyone exactly what he does, not even

Kenny or his mum. Just throws his money around trying to impress people, mostly Kenny and his mother. He always envied Kenny, always tried to make an impact on him, make Kenny envy him with his cars and boats and stuff.'

'And did he?'

'Nah, Kenny's never been like that. A reasonable car, a decent house … as long as he's riding he's happy.' Her eyes clouded then as she realised that the main ingredient in his happiness had just run out.

I reached for her hand. 'Carol, you don't know how things will turn out. It wouldn't be the first time the doctors have been wrong.'

Slowly she shook her head and wiped the tears with a fresh Kleenex. She squeezed my hand, 'Thanks for coming.'

I walked her to the door of the ward. 'How are the children?'

'Okay. Pretty much okay.'

'You got my number?'

'I think so.'

I lifted a card from the desk and scribbled it anyway. 'Ring me if there's anything I can do, day or night.'

'Thanks, Eddie.'

'Tell Kenny I called by.'

'I will.'

She nodded and I watched her slim sad figure walk back for a rendezvous with one man she loved and another she almost hated. Who would have guessed they were brothers?

Still unsettled I checked my car over before leaving then headed for Lambourn about twenty minutes away.

As I pulled into Cathy's place the glow from the

setting sun seemed to warm the redbrick house and surrounding buildings disguising the tattiness and steadily creeping decay.

The ramp was down on one of the big horseboxes by the wall and as I parked Cathy appeared at the top in too-big wellies holding the dribbling spout of a hosepipe. 'You should have phoned—I'd have put my party frock on.'

'You look as if a good party's just what you need.'

'Don't I know it.'

I walked up the ramp. 'Can I help?'

'No thanks. Just one more stall to clean and that's it. Well, apart from two horses to muck out which I was hoping to get done before dark.'

We talked as she worked and I told her what had happened in the last forty-eight hours. She seemed a bit more receptive than last time. We moved from the van to the stables and Cathy chivvied each horse gently around its box as she deftly forked droppings and soiled straw into a big barrow by the door.

She'd just finished the last box, scattering clean straw and banking it neatly against the walls when some sixth sense made her turn round to see the big gelding raise his tail. 'Oh no you don't,' she said, stepping swiftly across to stand behind him, 'bedding's too dear to have you mess it up right away.' She cupped gloved hands below the arched tail and caught the steaming droppings as they popped out settling into a neat pile on her hands and wrists. Carrying them past me to the barrow she smiled and said, 'Come into the house now and I'll butter you some nice scones.'

I declined the scones but sipped coffee as Cathy ate. I asked if Bill had ever mentioned his brain scan around the time he went for it.

'Not that I can remember.'

'Did you get his personal effects?'

Her look hardened. 'You make it sound like there was an auction for them.'

'I'm sorry. I was wondering where Bill's medical book was.'

'I've got it along with his other things.'

She went to the study and brought back a fat cardboard file.

In his medical book the date of Bill's scan was clearly marked, okayed and initialled although I couldn't make out the scrawl.

Something came to me. 'You got Bill's bank statements?'

She got them from the folder.

I worked back through. Cathy said, 'What are you looking for?'

Still studying them I said slowly, 'I'm ... looking ... for ... this.' My finger rested on the date a five grand loan he'd taken out had registered on his bank statement—four days after his scan had been done. Three days after that he'd withdrawn the full five in cash.

In my mind another piece fell into place. I wondered how much of Bill's money that fat little bastard Conway had spent on the redhead.

My first inclination was to drive south again in the morning and punch it out of him. Then, looking at Cathy, I had a better idea.

A much better idea.

CHAPTER TEN

The temperature rose a couple of degrees and it rained steadily through the night. As I drove across country the strong winds forecast for the afternoon began rehearsals, increasing gradually, changing the angle of the rain.

Eight races today, lots of runners, by the end of racing the Uttoxeter track would be like the Somme. I parked and ran, head down, for the weighing room.

Before setting out I'd spent an hour or so on the phone trying to trace an ex-jockey called Alan Tuttle. Tutty had retired three years ago after one fall too many. There were no compulsory brain scans at that time but Tutty's doctor suggested he take one. He did and it showed that the next time the lights went out they might not come back on. Last I'd heard of him he was driving around farms and stables selling animal feed but nobody I spoke to had seen him for over a year.

The weighing room was busy and I asked every jock about Tutty but no one could help. My first ride was in the third, an eighteen runner hurdle. The jockeys in the first couple of races had come back soaked and mud-caked and valets cursed and worked furiously cleaning and drying.

My instructions from the trainer were to stay in the first six which for my own comfort I interpreted as get to the front and hold on as long as you can. That way I had half a chance of staying relatively clean.

I jumped the chestnut off and the rain and wind decided to make me pay for trying to avoid the mud. Down the back straight raindrops came at me horizontally as though a regiment were firing them. The poor horse ducked his head and slopped through the heavy ground dreaming, no doubt, of his warm stable and a full haynet.

Three from home as tired muscles cried enough my horse lost interest and reduced speed so dramatically I thought he'd strained a tendon and started pulling him up.

The remaining bunch engulfed us in seconds, their hooves firing back an unrelenting battery of squelchy sods.

The first assault hit hard changing my colour and texture in seconds. Some of the lumps could be weighed in pounds and they hurt. Others closed airholes. One with a stone in it struck my helmet like a bullet.

As the field pulled away the clods followed a higher arc and rained on us like muddy mortar bombs.

Back in the weighing room I caught a glance of my face in the mirror: a panda stared back at me. Big white eyes which had been covered by my goggles looked out from an otherwise mud-blackened face. I smiled bringing another white contrast to the picture.

It was while I was cleaning myself up that I got talking to Denis, one of the valets. I mentioned Tutty and he said he'd seen him only last week in Somerset standing beside a tractor he'd just managed to overturn. They'd spoken briefly. Tutty was working on a nearby farm. Denis gave me directions.

My second ride finished unplaced in the last and I carried another half stone of Staffordshire mud back in on my boots and colours. Showered and dressed I ate a smoked salmon sandwich with half a cup of black tea then set off for cider country.

I called at three farms before finding Tutty. It was

96

after seven, dark. His sullen employer told me he was in 'the big barn at the back fixing the milker'.

He was in the big barn at the back resting dreamily in a giant's armchair of strawbales and smoking surreptitiously. He didn't hear me walk in and, by his own confession, nearly shat himself when I called his name.

He'd changed little; lots of red hair, very hairy hands and arms too, acne-pitted face, green eyes. He got over his shock and I told him why I'd come. He said he'd be happy to help. We sat a while reminiscing in the gloomy barn. One dull dirty striplight glowed weakly among the metal beams high above us and the acrid smell of animal urine drifted around in invisible waves of varying strength.

Bats swooped among the flaking rust of the beams.

Tutty rolled another cigarette and poked it into the flame of his Zippo lighter.

'You'll burn this place down.' I said.

He looked around at all the dry bales. 'Best thing for it.'

'Bit of a bastard, your Guv'nor?'

'Mmmm.' He drew on the cigarette.

'Looked it,' I said.

'Not just him,' Tutty said wearily, 'the lot of them. The wife's the worst. Looks at me like I was shit on her shoe.'

He glanced towards the door before continuing. 'Cow ... We've got two hundred and fifty cows here and she's the biggest one. And the three kids, horrible little sods ... not a saving grace among them. Make the Manson family look like the Waltons.'

I smiled. 'Never mind, if this works out you should end up with a few quid.'

'That'd be a first. When do we start?'

'Tomorrow.'

'Days off are kind of hard to come by, Eddie, what do I tell him?'

'Tell him you quit.'

'Just like that.'

'Shitty job anyway. You've got to be able to get better than this.'

'Will you feed me till I do?'

'Sure.' It wasn't a big risk. Tutty always hated being idle. 'Can't promise steak and caviar,' I said, 'but you won't starve.'

Clamping the thin cigarette between his lips he held out a dirty broken-nailed hand. 'Deal.'

We shook on it and I counted out a hundred pounds to cover expenses. I also gave him my mini tape recorder.

*   *   *

Back at Uttoxeter next day I rode a winner for Charles though the horse came home very tired. The rain had stopped but the going had become exhaustingly sticky as the ground dried. It was like struggling through suet pudding.

That evening I drove to Shrewsbury railway station to meet the six forty from London Euston. Tutty came striding towards the car, a wide smile splitting his pitted face. He got in, still smiling.

'Your face'll stay like that,' I teased.

His eyes sparkled. 'It went great. Brilliant.'

I smiled too. 'Good.'

Back in my flat Tutty sat opposite me by the fire a half-full glass of whisky in his fist. I sipped mine and waited while he stood the recorder upright under the lamp on the mantelpiece. He switched it on and I watched the tape start spooling in the yellow light.

Sounds of doors closing, Tutty coughing to clear his throat. A woman's voice. Couldn't make it out.

Tutty leant forward and turned up the volume.

His voice now, loud and clear.

—Yes, I'd like to speak to Mr Conway if it's possible.

—I'm afraid he's busy. Can I help?

—Not really, thanks. When will Mr Conway be free?

—He could well be tied up all day.

—Would you be kind enough to contact him just now and give him a message?

—What's the name?

—My name is Mr Tuttle. Would you tell him Bill Keating sent me?

A long pause. Doors opening and closing. A phone ringing somewhere. Then her voice again.

—Would you like to follow me?

—Sure. Thanks.

More door sounds then after the final click no more extraneous noise, no echo. I pictured a small room with soft furnishings.

—Sit down. What do you want?

Cold voice, accent slightly Americanised.

—Are you Mr Conway?

—What do you want?

—You *are* Mr Conway?

—Yes, I'm Mr Conway now tell me what you want.

—Well, it's kind of difficult. I used to be a jockey. Retired three years. Well, invalided out really. Thing is, I want to give it another go. I reckon I've another couple of years in me. Anyway, problem is I got bombed out after a dodgy brain scan and I need to

99

pass another one before they'll give me back my licence. Is this making sense to you?

—Keep talking.

—Well, look I hope I haven't got this wrong but Bill Keating, God rest him, Bill told me a while back that you were the man to see.

—For what?

—For help?

—What exactly did he say?

—Just said you were the man. Said he had similar problems and you helped him get his licence.

—And you didn't ask him how?

—Oh, we chatted for a while.

I smiled across at Tutty.

—What would you do if you didn't get your licence back?

—Well, that would cause me problems. I've been promised a few nice horses to ride, you see.

There was a long pause. I visualised Conway trying to weigh things up, trying to figure out exactly how much Tutty knew. Tutty's voice came on again.

—Do you think you'd be able to help?

—Depends. Could you come back this afternoon and let me have a preliminary look?

—Sure, what time?

—Two fifteen?

—Fine. See you then.

Door sounds again, feet in corridors then street traffic then nothing.

On the way from the station Tutty had filled in the gap. When he'd returned in the afternoon Conway had asked him to change into a hospital gown so the next half hour or so wasn't on tape. Conway did the scan then asked Tutty to get dressed and wait for him in his office.

Having verified the most significant part of Tutty's story, that he could not produce a clear scan, and probably checked too that he *had* been a jockey Conway was a good deal more forthcoming in the second part of the tape.

—Well Mr Tuttle, if the Jockey Club send you along for an official scan I shouldn't think there would be too much trouble in us ensuring you get your licence back.

—Brilliant. I appreciate that.

—No problem though it is, of course, a rather costly procedure.

—Oh. What would be the total charge?

—Five grand.

—Is that inclusive of VAT?

I chuckled. Tutty smiled across at me.

—That's the bottom line. No more to pay.

—Would it have to be upfront?

—'Fraid so.

—That does cause me a minor problem, just temporary, you understand.

—That's a shame.

—How would you feel about payment in kind?

—It doesn't excite me. Cash has a certain solidity about it, makes me feel more secure.

—Well it would be cash, the end result, I mean.

—Fine, come back when you've got it.

—Depending on your own, eh, resources Mr Conway you could have a hell of a lot more than five grand come Saturday night, if you listen to what I'm saying.

—Cash makes me listen, Mr Tuttle, sharpens my hearing to concert pitch. Other forms of payment render me the equivalent of tone deaf.

—(Long sigh) Bill gave me the distinct impression

101

I'd find you an easy man to deal with.

Tutty said it just coldly enough to set Conway wondering again exactly how much he knew. Enough for blackmail?

—Let me hear your proposal, Mr Tuttle.

—Tomorrow afternoon I'll ring you with the name of a horse which runs on Saturday. The horse will win easily at a good price if bets are placed, eh, discreetly.

—You expect me to do five grand's worth of work in exchange for a tip?

—It's not a tip. It is the name of a horse which will definitely win. It is the biggest investment opportunity you have ever had in your life and it's the first of five I'll give you this season if you agree to discretion in placing your money.

Long pause before Conway answered.

—And if that's not acceptable to me?

—Then we'll just have to negotiate on some other basis.

That slightly cold tone again. Tutty had been superb. He sat looking pretty chuffed.

—Here. Ring me with the horse tomorrow. If it wins come and see me again on Monday.

—Mr Conway, listen. When I give you the horse the first part of the deal is done. When he wins the second part is done. If you don't bet on him that's too bad, we don't move back to square one.

—Ring me Friday. Goodbye.

—See you next Monday.

Door noises. Footsteps. Traffic. Quietish whooping noise as Tutty celebrated. Then silence.

Tutty reached up and switched it off. I congratulated him, 'Brilliant, absolutely brilliant. You should be on the stage.'

He just sat smiling widely and raised his glass. A

couple of drunken hours later he fell asleep on the sofa. I left the fire burning and threw a blanket over him before wandering off to bed my head full of plans, plans which had been sharp and defined before the first whisky but were now fuzzy edged, blurred by alcohol.

*   *   *

I'd told Charles about Tutty and he was more than happy to have him around for a while. Gary Rice was talking about buying some more horses and Charles said there might be a job going in a few weeks. They knew each other well from their riding days and, next morning, both stood watching me canter past on Allesandro, our big hope for tomorrow at Chepstow.

After breakfast we returned to my flat and I called Jeff Dunning, the jockey who'd suggested fixing a race to benefit Kenny Hawkins and his family. The news on Kenny was no better. He'd regained full consciousness but it looked almost certain he'd be paralysed from the waist down. I told Jeff I'd been doing a bit of thinking and asked if we could get together this evening for a chat.

He was riding at Hexham, I was at Market Rasen more than a hundred miles further south and it would be a week or more before we were both riding at the same track again. We agreed to meet in a pub near Thirsk giving both of us a roughly equal trip.

I then rang Cathy to find out how her insurance claim was progressing. She'd heard nothing. I persuaded her to ask her solicitor to ring the insurance company for an update and told her I'd call back later.

I gave Tutty some more money and asked him to

spend the next three days in Newmarket. His job was to find Vince and track him discreetly if possible, see if he recognised any of the people Vince did business with. I gave Tutty a description (and told him he might be wearing a polo neck to hide bruises) and the name of the pub he hung out in.

I said, 'Leave messages on my answerphone, I can dial into it remotely from my mobile.'

'Okay.'

'Don't take risks.'

He smiled.

'I mean it, Tutty, I just want to find out who he's seeing and how regularly and where they might fit in. They're mostly flat folk so you may not recognise too many of them but there's half a chance we'll get something out of it. And it's better than sitting around here.'

'Or shovelling pigshit.'

'Exactly.'

Before leaving I fixed the recorder to the phone and Tutty rang Conway and told him that Allesandro would win the first race at Chepstow tomorrow. All Conway said was, 'Okay.'

At Market Rasen I had a mount in each of the first four races. I picked up a spare in the fifth. Neumman was supposed to ride it but he took a heavy fall in the novice chase and the doctor made him give it up which made it doubly pleasing for me when it won.

That gave me an extra boost. I was already on a high with things taking shape around Bill Keating's death and I was buzzing as I headed for the car park in the dusk. I was in and away before I realised I hadn't checked the car for booby traps. There could have been a wheel missing never mind loose.

I'd had no more threatening calls and it had been

over a week since the jeep capsized. I was getting complacent. Then again it now looked like Conway, ultimately, had been behind the threat and the sabotage. The quick reaction to my calls around a few jockeys that first night pointed to Conway having a close contact in the weighing room, maybe someone else he had a hold over, another jockey with a false scan tucked away somewhere.

Since that night I'd pretty much stopped questioning jockeys about Bill and certainly had never mentioned Conway's name to any of them. Apart from Jockey Club officials Tutty was the only one who knew and I trusted him completely.

Maybe Conway simply thought I'd taken the hint and given up.

Whatever, things seemed to be coming right. At first my inclination had been that drug dealers were involved with Bill's death. But Conway's little scheme threw new light on it.

Bill had failed his pre-season scan. Conway had offered to fix it for him for five grand and pass a clear scan back to the Jockey Club—God knows whose. But Bill quickly found out why he'd failed the scan, discovered the results of riding with a degree of brain damage. Under pressure towards the end of races it had become too much, caused blackouts.

Reflecting on that perhaps Bill didn't think he'd had much value for his five grand. Maybe he threatened Conway with exposure and Conway set up the fake suicide.

There had to be a chance too that Conway was tied in with Vince or some other dealer on a commission basis. Who better than Conway to know the potential agony of continuing to ride while in Bill's condition? How easy for him to say, 'Incidentally, if the headaches become too much I'd recommend this guy. He'll sort you out with a real good painkiller.'

So it could be a joint operation. That meant I couldn't leave Tutty in among it for much longer. He'd be useful to Conway for as long as he was giving winning tips. That fact alone should keep him safe for a while. Until they discovered his source they'd have to see he came to no harm.

That was the theory.

Speeding north on the A19 I flipped open my mobile and the number buttons glowed warmly in the winter dark. I punched in Cathy's number. Amy answered and called her mother and Cathy told me what I was hoping to hear, that the insurance company were in the throes of finalising payment. I congratulated her. She asked me to dinner on Saturday night. I accepted.

Another piece neatly in place. One more worry wiped from my mental slate. I reckoned I was within days of finding Bill's killer. Just Kenny Hawkins to be sorted out now and I had that planned all the way to the jackpot.

Things were going well. Too well.

I was due a setback.

Overdue.

CHAPTER ELEVEN

When I reached the pub Jeff Dunning was there and before the first drink was finished I discovered he'd been doing almost as much thinking as I had.

Rather than just arrange bets on genuine tips Jeff already had a pool of volunteers actually ready to fix a race. All they needed was the right opportunity. They wanted a small field, which would help them 'arrange' things more easily regarding the way the race was to be run. Five or six runners would be ideal.

They also wanted a quiet midweek meeting on a small course. Two reasons here: it would be easier to manipulate the betting market and get a good price for their winner and it would, theoretically at least, minimise the damage to ordinary punters who tend to bet most on big handicap races on busy days.

Jeff's brown eyes shone with enthusiasm, his dark curls bobbing as he threw back half his beer.

Never in my life have I been involved in race-fixing, no good can come of it in the long term for racing and anyone who takes part leaves himself open to blackmail for the rest of his days.

The most I'd expected from Jeff was his co-operation in getting the best possible information about genuine horses which were expected to win. Without naming Conway I told Jeff I knew a guy who'd stung a number of good people and that this would provide a nice chance for revenge and help stake the coup for Kenny.

If between us we could give Conway four straight winners then I was confident we could sting him with the fifth tip and make enough to set Kenny Hawkins up for life.

'How?'

'Let this guy back the first four tips himself then tell him the fifth is the last one and the biggest of all and that we insist on handling the stake money.'

'Then what?'

'We keep his winnings and give them to Kenny.'

'And this guy of yours will just say ho-hum and sit back?'

'Maybe not but there'll be nothing he can do.'

'How come?'

'It's a long story.' I didn't want to tell him about the tapes or Bill Keating, not until we'd cleaned Conway out then passed the evidence to the cops.

Jeff said, 'Wouldn't it be better to have an even bigger certainty with our idea. You're not just relying on a hopeful tip then, you *know* you're on a certainty.'

'Bar a fall,' I reminded him.

'Bar a fall but we'll pick a nice easy hurdle somewhere.'

'I'm not into fixed races, Jeff, but if you're determined to go ahead I won't say I wouldn't like to take advantage of it.'

He beamed, 'Good!' and told me the plans were solid and would go ahead. He confessed that a few of the lads were tempted to make some serious money for themselves as well as helping Kenny.

When I was convinced he couldn't be dissuaded I threw in an idea someone had put to me a few years back, one which would increase the jackpot.

'If we play it right we can rip this guy off without him even knowing, that would cut down any chance of reprisals.'

Jeff sipped some beer. 'How?'

'You know how quite a lot of betting shops operate first past the post payouts?'

'Sorry, Eddie, I'm not really a betting man myself.'

'Nor am I but I heard this one years ago. These first past the post shops are exactly what they say, they pay out on the first horse to pass the post no matter what happens in the Stewards Room. You could break every rule in the book during the race making disqualification a certainty but these shops still pay.'

'So?'

'So what you want to do is fix not just who's going to finish first but the second horse too. Using first past the post and official result shops we then place half the stake money on each and get whoever is on the winner to sling some weight away before the race or even during it. He weighs in light and gets disqualified but we still collect on first past the post. Then when the second gets promoted we collect on him too on official result.'

Jeff smiled in admiration. 'Brilliant.'

'Isn't it?'

'But how does it increase the take? Surely we'd be just as well putting the lot on the winner.'

'Why risk it? Spreading a lot of money for the same horse will raise suspicions somewhere twice as quick as it will if two are being bet. It'll help us get a reasonable price about both rather than a short price about one. Also it gives us a chance of saving something if one of them falls.'

He was nodding, thinking. 'I like it. I think I like it.'

'And, *and*, if it's only a five horse race we can set aside some of this guy's stake money to bet the three planned losers on course which will push out the prices of the two we'll collect on.'

'For someone who didn't want into anything illegal you're getting pretty hot on this one, Eddie.'

He was right, I was buzzing. I tried to excuse it. 'Well, if you guys are determined anyway all I'm doing is acting on the information. It's not as if I'll be riding in the race or anything. And it's not as if I want anything out of it personally.'

Jeff smiled. 'Whose conscience are you trying to ease, yours or mine?'

'Mine mostly, I suppose.'

109

'You're too straight, Eddie.'

'As far as I'm concerned you can never be too straight in this game, not if you want to stay in it for any length of time.'

'Then retire honourably with no money and plenty of arthritis?'

'Maybe.'

I could have argued that that was the price of honesty but morality ain't the in thing these days, in too many people's eyes it spells naivety. And anyway with plans to take advantage of a fixed race still bubbling in my head I hardly felt saintly myself.

Jeff knew a number of people spread around the country who could get the money on discreetly. I warned him to keep it strictly between us until the last possible minute. It might be months before the right race came up and if anybody got wind of the plans before then the sting would be ruined. Even the jockeys riding in the race didn't have to be briefed until the day itself.

Joe Hawkins suddenly came to mind and what he'd said to me at the hospital. Someone who'd been in the weighing room when this plan was first hatched had either mentioned it directly to him or Joe had picked it up from general gossip. I didn't tell Jeff about my run in with Joe but I re-emphasised how important it was to keep this strictly between the guys who'd be directly involved.

Jeff agreed and also said he'd speak to everyone about getting some bait in the way of winners. The first one—Allesandro at Chepstow tomorrow—depended on me. If he lost we lost Conway and the whole thing was down the tubes taking Kenny Hawkins's future with it.

The long drive back from Yorkshire passed

110

quickly. The last few days had introduced a number of factors into the Bill Keating equation and I spent most of the trip turning them over time and again, looking for a balance.

Midnight slipped past dropping me quietly into Guy Fawkes Day. Mentally I ticked off another twenty-four hours clear of threats but the more I thought of Conway the more I wondered if I was underestimating him because of his size, his ridiculous posing? He didn't look capable of scaring anyone let alone killing but he undoubtedly had the money to pay someone else to.

It also made me wonder if I'd done the right thing sending Tutty on the spying mission to Newmarket.

But if Conway was ruthless he was greedy too. If he suspected Tutty knew everything it depended which vice was the stronger. Conway seemed to be doing very nicely and if he decided to go without Tutty's tips for the certainty of removing him from the Keating picture then I'd made a serious blunder. There was no way I could let Tutty meet him again, not without some protection.

Still over an hour from home I worried myself into calling my answerphone to see if Tutty had left a message. I dialled. Away to my right a silver crescent moon seemed to move with me. I pictured it shining through the window of my empty flat as the phone rang out in the darkness.

The machine clicked on and I punched in the code to access my calls: just two, one from a trainer, one from Cathy. Nothing from Tutty. Nothing from the villains.

Cathy sounded happy, excited even. Maybe the insurance payout had been confirmed. I hoped so, it would leave the major share of the cash from the

111

planned coup for Kenny and his family. Then I'd hand Tutty's tape of Conway to the cops, leave it to them to get the evidence to jail him for Bill's murder and get on with riding winners.

All ends tied up neatly and me home free.

The moon still tracked me. I glanced up and made a pact with it: when this was over I was finished with investigating, done with other people's problems. The shining armour would come off for the last time. It could lie in a corner somewhere. And rust.

CHAPTER TWELVE

Nerves seldom troubled me these days. Even for the Grand National they sometimes surface only in the final ten minutes or so before the race. At the off they slip back to wherever they live and put their feet up for another year.

However, as I sat in the weighing room at Chepstow they were out in force. It was only a novice hurdle but a hell of a lot depended on the outcome. Apart from the more sinister aspects this horse looked like being Charles's first real good one. He'd had a number of winners but mostly in run of the mill races. One top notch horse could make a trainer and if Charles had a few new owners it would help make him secure if Gary Rice ever moved on.

Gary was there in the parade ring impeccably dressed as ever. He had a lot of money invested in the way he looked: designer clothes, perfect teeth, deep tan, luxuriantly thick dark shining hair. In his early thirties, nobody seemed to know exactly what he did for a living. Charles thought he dealt on the money

112

markets mostly in the Far East but Gary didn't discuss it and nobody pressed him.

My nerves were disappearing now as race time drew near but I could tell from Charles's frequent blinking that he wasn't the calmest person on the course. Many trainers give you riding orders, some are very specific. Charles just kept hopping from foot to foot and saying to me, 'Ride your own race, Eddie. You know what to do. Use your judgement. You know the score. Come back safe. Look after him.'

He wouldn't or couldn't shut up. Even Gary started looking at him strangely. He kept chattering till he legged me up into the saddle. I looked down. 'How much have you got on, Charles?'

He glanced at Gary. Gary smiled. Charles swallowed. He said, 'I'm scared to tell you.'

I was sorry I'd asked. More pressure was not what I needed.

Charles clutched my ankle as we walked round the parade ring unaware of his tightening grip. As we left to go down the horsewalk I said quietly, 'Charles, you're cutting off the circulation to my foot.'

He glanced up, apologised and loosened it a bit. I smiled, 'Charles, let go or you'll get dragged to the start at the gallop.' Still looking very absent-minded and worried he released his grip and stood watching us go through the gate like a mother with her only child on his first day at school.

I had eleven opponents. Cutty Sark, a big slashing bay horse was the hot favourite and there were three others better fancied than us. Allesandro was eight to one.

We cantered to the start and Allesandro didn't move too well in the heavy ground, couldn't properly use his smooth well balanced action. I could tell it felt strange to him as he made the extra effort to pick his feet up. His ears twitched in confusion.

We circled at the start. The starter's assistant checked our girths. The starter climbed his rostrum cursing halfway up as his muddy boots slipped on a step. We pulled our goggles down. Horses pricked ears, tensed muscles. Reins tightened. Line formed.

'Ready jockeys!? Come on!'

The tape flew up. Boots clamped. Knees locked. Bottoms rose from saddles and we headed for the first.

I kept him towards the outside, gave him a clear look at the hurdle which came up alarmingly quickly.

Approaching it he wasn't concentrating, fired up to race he seemed more intent on fighting me than on looking at the first jump. I wanted to get him into an even stride but the ground sucked at his feet every time he put them down.

I was reluctant to discipline him so early but he'd never have found the right stride on his own so I slapped him down the shoulder with my whip. The response was immediate and thrilling as Allesandro launched himself well out over the hurdle passing three others in the air.

Not wanting to be in front too soon I settled him back to an easy rhythm for the next mile letting him pop away at his jumps without firing him up again.

Chepstow in soft ground taxes the strongest of stayers. When it's heavy only the fittest finish faster than a trot. Content to watch the leaders tire themselves in pulling further away I concentrated on educating my inexperienced horse, confident his class would tell in the end.

But maybe I went too easy on him. We lost more ground on the pack and by the time we entered the

114

half mile long home straight mild doubt had become nagging worry. We were fifteen lengths adrift of the leaders.

The others, battle weary in the mud, began dropping back quickly.

Anxious to avoid being caught in the tide of tiring horses I edged Allesandro hard over to the inside rail until I felt the constant, mildly painful rap-tap-tap of my paper-thin boot against the white plastic.

The noise, like a tyre riding the ridged line of a motorway hard shoulder, warned me it was dangerous to move any further in. But things were getting critical now.

We couldn't afford to lose this race. If I could just push the pliable rail out it would offer Allesandro a strip of fresh turf for the run to the finish.

The noise of my boot on the plastic upset him a bit and quickly pulling my whip through to my left hand I tapped his shoulder to keep him running on the better ground.

That galvanised him and he found his stride and quickened. But approaching the third last we were still twelve lengths behind and as we came off the rail to meet the jump he felt all wrong and landed sideways so badly I could see his hindquarters.

I felt then that I might as well have kissed his ass and mine goodbye along with all the stake money.

The leader went fifteen lengths clear. We were in fourth. I pictured Conway watching the race on TV and Tutty in some pub in Newmarket smoking furiously. Carol Hawkins's pinched desperate face loomed, Kenny slumped in a wheelchair. Gary Rice, sweat beading his tanned forehead. Charles, long eyelashes flicking as he blinked uncontrollably and fought that dreadful pit of the gut sensation that only

115

comes from knowing you've risked far more than you can afford on a horse that's going nowhere as the winning post gets nearer. Like watching yourself go spread-legged towards a circular saw...

There was nothing else for it but to ask the horse for everything though it was against all my instincts. Giving a young horse a very tough race on its debut can sour it for life. Apologising aloud to Allesandro in advance I let him find his feet again after the mistake, gathered him up and started kicking and pushing and shouting at him.

He responded, increasing speed, trying to get that rhythm again. He quickly found it but just as quickly I drove him beyond it. This time he adjusted almost immediately, accelerating well now past two horses. I kept driving, determined not to use my whip till he stopped responding. He jumped the second last well though still ten lengths adrift of the leader, five behind the second.

But he was getting the hang of it now, taking hold of the bit the way he did at home as if to say, let me at them. He continued to quicken and found that huge ground-devouring stride I knew he had. We flew past the second horse and went in pursuit of the leader as he jumped the last where I asked Allesandro for a big one. He gave me it and relief flooded through me.

The leader was still two lengths clear but his rider swung frantically back and forth as though trying to slide up a banister. His elbows pumped, the right one breaking tempo to whack his whip down on the bay's rump.

I glanced across and smiled as we passed him but he wouldn't return my stare, unwilling to give me the satisfaction of seeing the frustration in his eyes.

Allesandro went clear without feeling the whip and

116

was galloping more strongly when he passed the post eight lengths clear than he had been at any other stage of the race.

Eventually I managed to pull him up and as we came back in off the racecourse I saw Charles, halfway down the grassy slope, being helped to his feet by Allesandro's lad and Gary Rice. In his anxiety to greet us he'd slipped in the mud. No one was laughing more loudly than he was though I guessed much of it was fuelled by the release of nervous tension.

He never admitted to me how much he'd had on Allesandro that day but he did say he would never again bet such a large amount. The way it had made him feel, putting his sanity on a razor edge for so long, just wasn't worth it.

I wondered if our fat little friend Conway had backed it and if so for how much. He was primed now, ready for the next stage. Thoughts of him stayed with me. Later, standing under the hot shower soaping myself, I envied him his gorgeous redheaded woman.

Fresh smelling and smooth faced I turned up at Cathy's for dinner. Kissing her lightly I said, 'There aren't many women I shave twice a day for.'

She smiled. 'More's the pity for you.'

She wore a tight black dress, her hair in a different style and some serious jewellery decorated her neck and ears.

'You look very glamorous,' I said.

'Thank you.'

'You suit your hair up like that. Classy looking.'

'I'm a classy dame.'

A brief image of her catching horseshit leapt to mind but I suppressed it.

'A classy dame who's not cooking tonight?'

'Thought I'd take you out.'

She hadn't mentioned this when I returned last night's call, just confirmed that the insurance payout had been cleared. She looked at me and said, 'Is that okay? Doesn't damage your male ego or anything, having a woman buy you dinner.'

'So long as you don't mind me being underdressed.' I was in a casual jacket and cotton trousers, denim shirt, no tie.

'You're fine. Everybody will think you're my toyboy. Come on, we'll have a drink before we go.'

Her manner had changed and I didn't care much for it. The flippancy didn't quite hide the fact that she was trying somehow to reassert herself with me. Not that she needed to as far as I was concerned but she was doing it for herself, to get back to happier days when she had money and success and I was just a jockey.

I wasn't sure she even knew she was doing it but it was almost tangible—let's forget all that murder nonsense, everything that happened that night at Newmarket, Cathy's got money again, another chance of success, a new opportunity to pitch herself up there with that social class she's always aspired to, pined for, even.

That was the way she was and it didn't matter that much to me, wasn't worth a big argument and if she'd kept it at such a petty level she wouldn't have got one.

But from the moment we entered the restaurant she steadily started applying the pressure, suggesting, cajoling and in the end even attempting to browbeat me into quietly dropping my interest in Bill's death so 'everyone could get on with their lives'.

It was as if she was scared I would turn up

118

something sooner or later and that the insurance company would ask for their money back. Maybe a combination of that and her ambition to get back on the fast track to success.

Those were thoughts better kept to myself but under increasing pressure from Cathy I voiced them.

Not a good decision.

CHAPTER THIRTEEN

She got very angry, denied there was any personal motive in wanting me to leave off Bill's case. She claimed that all she was interested in was letting her daughters get back to some sort of normal life. I wasn't sure right then that I believed her but I gave her the benefit of the doubt.

We left it at that and ate dinner but throughout the meal her temper bubbled and her eyes burned with indignation. Only the fact that she was well known in the restaurant kept her from blowing up completely.

When she thought we were being observed, which was most of the time, she acted quite convivially but alert as a sniper she grasped any opportunity to fire harsh whispers at me.

The night ended in cold goodbyes at her door.

For the second day in succession I arrived home in the early hours of the morning though this time considerably more down than yesterday. I pressed playback on the answerphone: nothing from Tutty. He'd been gone more than forty-eight hours.

Wearily I undressed and slid between cold sheets. I was very tired but Tutty's safety played on my mind. So did Cathy's barbs. Between them they kept me awake for a long time.

When I drifted to sleep I went deep and though my subconscious must have heard the hammering on the door it took a long time to drag me to the surface and force my eyelids open. Even then grogginess tried to tell me I was dreaming.

It was two CID officers. My first thought was that Tutty had been found dead in a ditch somewhere but they were just following up my 'complaint' about the sabotaged jeep and the threatening call.

They explained they'd come up with nothing despite interviewing all the car park attendants at Cheltenham and asked if the wheelnuts could have been cut through elsewhere. Had I stopped at services? Could it have been done at the yard? Had I had any more calls?

Everything they asked confirmed they were at a loss for leads. I couldn't tell them about Conway, not until after the sting. It would probably be two or three months before I had to involve the police, time enough for these early days to be conveniently glossed over.

An hour later they left the yard none the wiser and I had lunch with Charles. He was still on a high after Allesandro's victory and he and Gary had sat up late, discussing plans for him, vintage champagne helping them plot a course for the Cheltenham Festival.

One of the added benefits of the horse's success was that Gary had decided to bring forward his new purchases so there was a job for Tutty as soon as he liked. I looked forward to giving him the news—if he ever got back in touch.

By dusk I'd still heard nothing from him and I was seriously worried. He knew he was due to see Conway again tomorrow to set up the next stage. He knew we had to have another meeting before he saw him. Even if he'd been unable to track Vince down he still should have phoned me.

What if Vince had twigged he was being trailed? What if Vince was Conway's accomplice, partner, whatever you want to call it and they'd trapped Tutty?

Come five fifteen I couldn't wait any longer. I set the answerphone and headed for Newmarket.

The first place to try was the pub I'd seen Vince in though this time he was the last person I wanted to meet.

Just one bouncer on the door tonight. Still dark and smoky inside though not so crowded. I bought a drink and drifted around as the music boomed out, wondering what would happen if Vince suddenly appeared. I was confident he hadn't seen my face last time but if someone since had marked his card the confrontation would be interesting.

At the far end of the room tables and chairs were laid out and right along the back wall half a dozen tables fronted a padded bench-type seat.

A few dark figures, couples, groups, sat close together. Trying to look casual I worked my way among them. Then I saw him. Looked like he was slumped against the wall in the corner. I went over and sat down beside him. His eyes were closed. He was breathing heavily. On the table stood an empty beer glass and two empty whisky glasses. A corner of the long velvet curtain lay half across him like a cloak. I nudged him. 'Tutty!'

He moaned and moved away from me. I gripped his arm. 'Tutty!', shaking him gently. Slowly he came awake, eyes unfocused, drunken. 'Eddie,' he said quietly staring at me like a dumb animal. His eyes

121

drooped closed again. I looked around to see if we were being watched. Nobody bothering.

I shook him again. 'Tutty! You okay?'

His green eyes opened again, unusually dull. He said, 'Sorry, Eddie ... Sorry.'

'Don't worry about it. Come on, let's get you home.'

I helped him up and we weaved across the floor. I didn't want it to look like I was rescuing him, it would make too many people wonder, remember it. So I played drunk too, arm around his shoulder, laughing, spouting garbled banter and slapping him playfully.

I eased him into the car and fixed his seatbelt. By the time I got in he was asleep again. Pointless and probably unkind to wake him now. I started up and headed for home.

It took a while to rouse him and I almost had to carry him upstairs. I laid him on my bed and drew the quilt across. He moaned quietly. I switched the lamp on and sat by the bed for half an hour, unsure if he was sleeping off a drinking session or trying to recover from something more sinister.

Finally, with a third late night playing on me and my eyes heavy, I eased him onto his side fearful of him vomiting and choking. I returned to the living room and leaving the central column of the gas fire burning against the dark and the cold I lay on the couch and drifted into sleep.

Next morning, dazed but unhurt, Tutty was a sorry sight. Over coffee and toast he explained that he hadn't been able to track Vince down, a task he'd seen as an almost do or die mission. He'd kept holding off from phoning me in the hope Vince would appear. The longer he went without finding

122

him the more of a failure he felt.

Leaning towards me across the table, squinting against the morning light and grabbing earnestly at my sleeve he said, 'Eddie, I'm sorry. I'm sorry. I didn't want to let you down. That's what made me do it. You don't know what it's been like the last three years...' He looked desperate. I said, 'Forget it, Tutty, I know what you're talking about.'

He went on as though he hadn't heard me. 'I was good, Eddie. They talked to me on the telly, wanted me all the time for interviews when I rode winners...'

He rambled pathetically on for a long time frequently using one of the saddest expressions in the English language—if only.

When he finally ran out of words and self pity his green eyes were wet and I think I felt sorrier for him than he did for himself.

Pouring more coffee I reassured him as best I could that I was only glad he was alive and unhurt. I told him about the job that was waiting for him and moved him as calmly as possible towards tomorrow's meeting with Conway.

Making him aware of the dangers I told him it was imperative that the meeting take place in public: Conway mustn't have the chance to harm him.

He tried to shrug that off, determined to take risks, happy to take them. He saw it as a way of redeeming himself and it took me a while to talk him out of that frame of mind. It wasn't easy, he was still half drunk.

When half a dozen cups of coffee failed to get him back to his old self I suggested another couple of hours' sleep before he called Conway.

It was early evening when he finally woke and after a shower and a light meal he seemed much more level headed. Time to call Conway. I fixed up the recorder,

123

dialled and handed Tutty the receiver. The number rang out. No answer.

We kept trying without success. Tutty was getting frustrated. I said, 'Forget it, call him at the clinic in the morning and arrange it for the afternoon.'

Tutty was concerned, 'I still think he'll get suspicious if I insist on meeting him in the park. Why don't you drive me and I'll go in and tell him my friend's waiting outside in the car.'

'He'll get even more nervous then, wondering how many people know about his little scam.'

'No, no. I'll just tell him it's someone who's given me a lift, say all he knows is that I'm trying to arrange a brain scan, all official like.'

I thought about it. 'What if he walks out with you and sees me?'

'Park fifty yards up the road.'

It was worth considering. Conway may well be suspicious of Tutty's motive for insisting he saw him in a public place. I said, 'Let's sleep on it.'

'Okay. Fair enough.'

We did and decided Tutty's idea was best. We had breakfast with Charles who got Tutty really enthusiastic about working for him. 'When can you start?' he asked.

Tutty looked at me. I said to Charles, 'We've a little bit of business to tie up in London today, after that Tutty's pretty much his own man. I might have to beg him off you for the odd afternoon here and there but not for much longer.'

Tutty looked mildly disappointed at this news. Charles didn't find it hard to resist asking what our business was. After the car incident he'd wisely taken a conscious step away from what he called my 'outside interests'.

124

Just before nine we set off for London. There was only one jumps meeting today up at Carlisle and for the first time this season I'd refused the offer of a ride. Just one, in the novice chase, which looked to have little chance. I hated turning anything down though I was as diplomatic as possible with the horse's trainer.

Once again London had escaped the worst of the weather. We'd travelled through heavy rain which only died out as we approached the city boundaries. The streets around Piccadilly were dry and still full of cars. I dropped Tutty outside the clinic and moved fifty yards up where I double-parked, engine running.

Fifteen minutes later he was back out, smiling. Watching him approach in the mirror I scanned the doorway of the clinic to see if anyone followed him out. Nobody.

He got in pulling the door closed with four times the force needed, something I'd noticed when we left this morning.

I said, 'Short 'n' sweet.'

He beamed. 'The way I like it.'

'It went well?'

'Brilliant.'

'Did he back Allesandro?'

'Not for much but he backed it and *he* is keen for more,' he chuckled, 'he is *begging* for more!'

'What did he say about doing your scan?'

'Prefer to delay it a bit, was what he said. Would rather wait until all the information had been given, till every horse had won.'

'What did you say?'

'Argued a bit to make it look good then agreed to give him four more. Couldn't stop his fat little tongue coming out to lick his lips. I'd love to play

125

poker with him.'

I laughed, as happy for Tutty as I was for my own plans. All we needed were three more good winners before the big one.

The sun broke through as we snaked along in convoys of city traffic. I said, 'Want to go down and see Kenny, see how he's doing?'

Tutty said, 'Sure. Great idea.'

And we headed west.

*　　　*　　　*

Over the next six weeks or so we had no need to visit Conway again. Working together with Jeff Dunning and the northern boys we managed to give him three more winners before priming him for the big one in early January.

Tutty settled into his new job at the yard though he was excused riding duties because of potential head injuries. Cathy Keating drew her insurance money and got the business back on an even keel.

It looked like Kenny Hawkins would never get beyond sitting in a wheelchair but he got some money from the Jockeys' Insurance Scheme and the Injured Jockeys' Fund were looking after him. He and Carol still had plenty of worries but the way things were going they were soon going to have the financial ones eased considerably.

I had no more tough-guy phone calls, no sabotaged cars. The police came back once more just after Christmas then seemed to let it drop completely. Everything now pointed to Conway as being responsible for the murder of Bill Keating.

On New Year's day Jeff Dunning told me everything was in place for the coup at Sedgefield

126

four days later. Conway was ninety-six hours away from losing an awful lot of money. After that I'd hand the tapes to the cops.

Tutty set up the final meeting.

CHAPTER FOURTEEN

'Serious money,' Tutty said, waving the mini tape in the air as he came in. He took the stairs up to my flat two at a time. I followed listening to him enthuse over how much Conway was going to lose.

Slotting the tape into the small machine he set it running and stood it on the mantelpiece. He'd met Conway in a park so there was little background noise. Conway complained about the cold and commented on Tutty not wearing a coat.

Tutty looked at me here and said, 'Thought he was about to rumble me with the tape recorder.'

The machine had been in the inside pocket of Tutty's suit jacket hence the reason for him leaving his coat at home. On the tape he told Conway he didn't feel the cold much. After a longish pause, a trundling sound (a girl with a pram, Tutty said) Conway spoke.

—Well what have you got?

—I gotta horse as the saying goes.

—When?

—Thursday, Sedgefield.

—How good is it?

—It's the biggest certainty that ever looked through a bridle. It's the one we've all been waiting for for years and it's the last one we're doing.

—What's its name?

127

—I can't tell you now.

—Come on, Tuttle, you gave me the others in plenty of time.

—This one's different. A hell of a lot of planning's gone into it and we can't afford a cock up. I'll ring you with the horse's name five minutes before the off.

—Don't be so fucking silly! What do you take me for?

—That's the deal.

—How do I get my money on?

—You give it to me.

—Now you *are* taking the piss.

—Look, we can't have people putting bundles on this without any thought for the SP. You run around on the morning of the race trying to get five or ten grand on you'll ruin the price for everybody including yourself.

—So what's the difference between me putting it on and you?

—I told you, a lot of planning went into this. We've got agents prepared up and down the country. They're all going to move into different betting shops at exactly the same moment so that even if suspicion is raised by the bets it'll be too late for the shops to feed the money back to the course and bring the price down.

—Yeah, then they're all going to move back out of the shops with my fucking winnings in their hippers! Don't take me for a mug, Tuttle.

—You'll get your cash, don't worry, just the same as the rest of the syndicate will.

—And who makes up the rest of the syndicate?

—I can't tell you.

—No, because the syndicate's probably you and a couple of your bent mates trying to stitch me up. Give me four winners to hook me and then come up with the bet of the century to rip me off for my stake money. You must think my head zips up the back.

—Hey, listen! No sweat as far as I'm concerned if you don't want in on this one. You know my interest in this and you know what our deal was so I'll ring you on Thursday with the horse, you do what you like but when he wins you do the brain scan as agreed.

Tutty looked at me and said, 'I stood up here to leave and he started getting panicky.'

—Wait, listen, what would you do in my position? Wouldn't you be suspicious?

—I suppose I would but those are the terms and that's it. I'm not controlling the coup, I'm just passing you privileged information and telling you the rules of the game.

—Well I ain't playing it.

—Fine. Nice doing business with you. I'll ring you Thursday.

Soft footfalls as Tutty walked away then a faint call. Tutty stopped walking.

He smiled, 'Stood and made him come to me.'

Conway's voice again.

—Are you going to be at Sedgefield for the race?

—Sure am.

—What if I come with you?

—You're welcome to.

—When would you want the money?

—Tomorrow afternoon at the latest.

A long pause then Conway again.

—Look, you're not just dealing with me here. I want you and your friends to know that the stake money will be coming from some very powerful people.

—Fine. How much are we talking about?

129

—Fifty grand.

Tutty watched for my reaction, a silent ooohh! He laughed, 'That's what I nearly did.'

He spoke on the tape.

—That's a bit more than I'd expected.

—I told you, you're not dealing with mugs.

—Can you get the cash for tonight? We'll need a couple of extra days to distribute that to the agents.

I smiled at Tutty, 'Nice one.'

Conway spoke.

—I can have it for noon tomorrow.

—Okay. Where do you want to meet?

—Come to my house.

—Where do you live?

—Near Kingston, take this card.

—Okay, Mr Conway, see you tomorrow.

—Listen . . .

—Uhuh?

—If this fucks up in any way whatsoever it won't be a brain scan you'll need it'll be a life support machine.

—Cheers.

Tutty got up and switched the machine off. 'Nice turn of phrase Mr Conway has, eh?'

I nodded. 'Do you think there are some others in this with him?'

Tutty said, 'If he's serious about the fifty grand I suppose there must be.'

'Scared?'

He shrugged slightly. 'No reason to be if everything goes to plan, is there? The horse I give him wins. Hardly my fault if it then gets disqualified, I've kept my end of the bargain.'

'D'you think Conway will see it that way?'

'Eddie, are you trying to put me off? If you are

130

it's working.'

'I'm serious, Tutty, I just want you to be aware of what you're getting into.'

Helping himself to a large whisky he said, 'I'm into it now anyway, aren't I? A bit late to back out!'

He was right.

*   *   *

It was smart of Tutty to ask for an early pickup of the money but in one way I regretted it. If it had been in the evening I could have gone with him but at noon on the Tuesday I was well on my way to Leicester where I had three rides.

But Conway and his fifty grand filled my mind. It was way above what I'd been expecting and if we could get it all on at the expected prices and everything worked out there would be more than enough money for Kenny Hawkins and his family. Half of it would keep him comfortable for life.

But Conway's threat that some big players were involved with him troubled me. They wouldn't hand it over to Tutty and stand on the doorstep waving goodbye. Someone would probably tail him. All we could think of to combat that was to rent a car and leave it in one of the two car parks of a motorway service station.

Tutty would drive straight there with the cash and park on the northbound side, leave the car to go and have a cup of coffee then head across the bridge to jump in the rental car and travel south again.

We'd have to hope whoever was tailing him stayed in their car in the northbound park.

Just in case they were tailing him south again he was to go to a certain hotel and call my mobile

131

number then we'd make further plans.

The first race was twelve thirty. I was riding in it and was so anxious to hear from Tutty I was tempted to tuck my mobile phone in my breeches. How the Stewards would have viewed me taking a call while jumping the open ditch is another matter.

But Tutty didn't phone at half twelve. He didn't phone at all and the winner I rode that afternoon gave me no satisfaction whatever. My mind was so full of doubts and fears for Tutty I don't even remember riding the race.

I tried ringing the hotel at various points throughout the day but nobody fitting Tutty's description had been in. By the time I left the course, just after three, a heavy dread weighed me down. The money didn't seem to matter too much any more, the coup could go to hell. I just prayed that they hadn't harmed Tutty.

It took me two hours to reach the hotel. I cruised the car park, headlights searching the dark for Tutty's rental car: nothing.

I sat a while wondering if they'd beaten the plans out of him and were sitting inside waiting for me. In the end I had to go in and see.

But Tutty wasn't there. Nobody approached me.

I clutched at the straw offering the idea that maybe Tutty had forgotten my mobile number. I dialled my answerphone: nothing. The lump in my stomach grew heavier. I dug out Conway's address and set off for it with zero optimism and high apprehension.

The place was in darkness. Biggish place standing in a large garden, one of a dozen posh houses in a tree-lined avenue.

No lights and no sounds as I prowled around keeping close to the walls. There was a huge garage at the back solidly locked. No cars parked in the drive. Conway had to come back sometime and I thought of staking the place out, sitting all night in my car. I wasn't riding next day.

But a hard frost was setting in already and if Conway had abducted Tutty he might not return till after the race had been run. Till after he'd persuaded Tutty to give him the name of the planned winner.

My heart grew heavier at the thought. Tutty didn't know the name of the winner yet. Nobody would know that till the morning of the race till we saw exactly how many horses would start and which would monopolise the betting.

We'd assumed that fact alone would keep Tutty safe from abduction, the simple common sense that couldn't be argued with: all we had at the moment were the original race entries and the knowledge that all six were planned to take part. But if a couple went unsound or were withdrawn for different reasons then things would have to be put on hold. Conway should have understood that, should have known Tutty would have no name to give till raceday morning.

God knows how they were trying to get out of him something he couldn't give.

I shivered in the dark and headed out to check the last thing I could think of: if the rental car was still at the motorway services.

It was. Exactly where we'd left it. I'd have to call the rental company in the morning and ask them to collect it. Deep in gloom I drove back to the flat to wait by the phone.

CHAPTER FIFTEEN

I stayed at home all day Wednesday waiting for some word. None came. At noon Jeff Dunning rang asking where the stake money was, saying he'd set up all the links needed to get the bets on. I told him we'd had one or two problems and that I'd call him back by two o'clock.

The dilemma I faced was: did I tell him about Tutty's abduction?

I had little doubt now that I'd soon get a call from Conway or one of his people. He'd want to exchange Tutty's safety for the name of the horse.

If I told Jeff what had happened he'd know the main reason for fixing the race had gone. There would be some chance he'd want to cancel the coup completely, run the race straight. On the other hand he'd said some of the lads intended to make a few quid themselves from it so they'd be keen to go ahead anyway.

The only real loser in their eyes would be Kenny Hawkins. My main aim was to protect Tutty so I would have to give Conway the name of the winner and the only way to do that was to pretend to Jeff that everything was okay.

The problem there would be what to tell Conway, the name of the winner who would then be disqualified or the runner up who'd be promoted after the Stewards' Inquiry. Or did I tell him about the whole scam and let him decide what to do? If I did that he'd know we'd been planning to rip him off and might kill Tutty anyway.

Also, if I gave him just one horse he'd splash his

fifty grand around any old way and ruin the SP for everybody. I thought long and hard then called Jeff back.

'Jeff, this guy's having problems coming up with the stake money. He says it's going to be tomorrow morning.'

'Eddie, come on! That's too late!'

'For your people, I know it is but I've just made a few calls and I've managed to set up some contacts who can collect in the morning and split themselves over a big enough area.'

'You sure?'

'Certain.'

There was a long pause and I knew Jeff was probably wondering if I was setting him up too.

I said, 'Jeff, I'm being straight with you, honest.' The lie flowed easily. 'If he doesn't come up with the money in the morning I'll let you know. You can cancel everything if you want to.'

'Ring me before ten one way or another.'

'I will.'

Another pause, keeping me waiting, tempting me to ask. I held out. Jeff said, 'Thimbelina will be first past and Sun Tonic will get the race in the Stewards' Room.'

'Okay. I'll ring tomorrow.'

Putting the phone down I let out a long breath then jotted down the names though they were already branded on my memory.

Then I sat listening to the clock tick, watching the hands. At twelve minutes to eight it started snowing outside, light flurries. Gradually it thickened till the yard lights cast big floating shadows from the snowdrops onto my blind.

I started wondering if Sedgefield might be snowed

135

off and couldn't make up my mind if that would be a good thing.

The clock ticked on. The snow kept falling. My frustration and fear deepened. At ten twenty-three he finally called.

It wasn't Conway's voice, didn't recognise it from the tapes.

'Your pal Tuttle said you've got something to tell me.'

'Where is he?'

'Right beside me. His ear's a bit swollen from me punching it but would you like a word in it anyway?'

'Put him on.'

'Eddie!' Panic there, terror.

'You okay?'

'You've got to tell them, Eddie!'

'I will, don't worry, Alan.' Didn't know why I used his first name. 'They'll let you go then?'

'Tomorrow, after it wins. They promised.' His breath was coming fast.

'Okay, tough it out. I'll see you tomorrow. Put your man back on.'

'Very co-operative bloke, your friend.' London accent, not cockney.

'When will you let him go?'

'After the horse you're going to give me wins.'

We both knew I was in no position to bargain or ask for promises.

'The horse's name is Thimbelina. She runs in the second at Sedgefield but you must back her first past the post.'

'What?'

'She can be a bit unruly, hangs a lot in a finish and sometimes interferes with others. She's been disqualified before after winning so you must place

136

your bets in a shop which takes first past the post.'

'And where do we find these shops.'

'Most of the independent bookies in London will give first past if you ask for it.'

'You better not be ripping us off here, Malloy.'

'I'm not but listen, spread the money as thinly as you can or the price won't be worth having.'

'We've got it sorted. You just make sure it wins.'

'It will.'

'It had better, hadn't it Tuttle?'

He hung up.

Grotesque caricatures of a battered half dead Alan Tuttle filled my dreams that night.

*   *   *

By morning the temperature was up and my tyres squirted dirty slush aside as I left to drive north. For the first time in my life I was glad I had no rides booked. Concentration on the job would have been impossible. I wasn't even tempted to pack my kit in case I was offered a spare.

I'd already called Jeff Dunning and told him the cash was safely in hand. I wasn't looking forward to explaining the deception after the race but Tutty's life was more important than Kenny's long term financial security.

If Thimbelina didn't pass the post first at around one thirty-five this afternoon Tutty could end up as Conway's second victim. Even if she did win his safety couldn't be guaranteed.

I reached the course just after twelve thirty and went straight to the weighing room. Jeff and the others were there. The tension was tangible. All the more so because all of us were fighting it,

137

trying to act normal.

Jeff was riding in the race along with Bobby Cranley, Jake Brassey, Bernie Collins and Craig Macafferty. We acknowledged each other with brief nods and grunts all anxious to form a huddle and reassure each other but knowing we couldn't. We were the only ones in the weighing room who knew what was happening. Or we should have been.

I wandered back outside. Two minutes later Jeff joined me.

He said, 'Everything going smoothly?'

'As far as I know.' I looked at my watch. 'They should have started placing the bets about five minutes ago.'

'How many bodies?'

'Enough.'

'I hope so.'

'I see Bobby and Jake are riding in the first. Hope they come back safe.'

'Jesus, don't even think it.' Jeff lit a cigarette and the smoke rose tunnelling through his dark curls.

'How's the ground?' I asked.

'Soft.'

'Much snow here last night?'

'Jesus, Eddie, I'd rather talk about nothing than talk about the fucking weather.' He sucked in nicotine looking nervously around. Two stewards walked past. Jeff flinched.

'You'll have to cool it,' I said. 'You won't be worth a toss come race time.'

His head moved in bumpy little nods and the cigarette went back to his mouth.

I watched the first race, a selling hurdle, on the TV in the weighing room. It didn't matter who won this as long as Bobby Cranley and Jake Brassey didn't

138

have a fall which put them out of the next race.

The tapes went up and I wasn't even concentrating on it when Bobby's horse came down at the first.

I turned to one of the valets to double check. 'Was that Bobby's?'

He nodded staring in concern at the screen. Bobby was still lying motionless when he went out of camera shot. Dear Jesus don't let him be hurt. I grabbed a pair of binoculars and hurried outside.

If Bobby couldn't ride in the next the trainer would replace him with somebody else, somebody who couldn't be pulled into the plan at this late stage, somebody who might completely, if unwittingly, bugger things up.

Halfway up the stand steps I raised the binoculars and aimed them in the opposite direction from all those around me. Bobby was on his feet.

Let him walk now ... Please.

He walked, ducked under the rails, looked fine.

Thank you, God. Thank you.

I turned the glasses towards the action and kept praying that nothing would happen to Jake Brassey. Nothing did. He finished second.

I couldn't bear to go back to the weighing room and spent the next fifteen minutes sitting in my car not wanting to talk to anyone. To Tutty maybe, to tell him to hang in there.

Five minutes before the off I was back in the stand watching the field canter to the start.

Five Go Mad At Sedgefield.

I'd walked through the betting ring, almost more bookmakers than punters. Clerks blowing on cold hands, rubbing pens rapidly between palms for friction heat.

Glossop was evens favourite. Thimbelina was five

to one, Sun Tonic nine to two, both lower prices than we'd expected. Some of the money being placed in the shops must be finding its way back to the course. Hoping the prices didn't keep shortening I made my way towards the stand.

Mist was gradually thickening on the far side. That should help, I thought, give the lads more confidence if the Stewards can't see them properly.

The nearer the off time came the more nervous I got and when the tapes finally went up I couldn't even bring myself to watch it. I walked back down the steps and went behind the stand, leant on a wall and listened to the commentary booming from a speaker above me.

I had no idea what the tactics would be. I just knew that as they came over the last Thimbelina and Sun Tonic would have to be first and second.

The toughest bits to listen to came as each hurdle loomed, the parts where the commentator called ... 'and as they approach this one' or, '... as they come to the next'. If Thimbelina came down Tutty would crumple just as quickly only he would probably never get back up.

As they moved down the far side for the last time all five were still standing. I concentrated on the commentator as he steadily increased volume and tension in his voice. '... Visibility's getting poorer out there but Glossop still leads from Sir Abu and ... it looks like Thimbelina in third then comes Sun Tonic and Robespierre still last.

'Beginning to bunch now coming to the next, getting difficult to see them as they rise at it ... and one's gone! There's a faller!'

Please God not Thimbelina.

'... can't quite pick it out, looks to be ... Sir

Abu...'

Breathe again.

'... no it's not!'

Jesus!

'... it's Robespierre!'

Let him be right this time. My heart pounded.

He confirmed it. '... Robespierre's gone at the third from home badly hampering Sir Abu who has a stiff task now and it's Glossop still leading but only by a length now from Thimbelina, two to jump, getting easier to see them as they start to come back towards us and Glossop's still galloping strongly in front as they approach the second last, the other two having to be pushed along to stay with him, Sir Abu out of it, approaching the penultimate flight Glossop goes two lengths clear...'

What the fuck was Cranley doing on Glossop? He was making it almost impossible for himself to stop the horse now so close to so many watching eyes. And Glossop was favourite.

'... but Glossop barely rises at it! He mis-timed that completely! Hit it hard and his jockey did well to stay in the saddle! Thimbelina takes it up now from Sun Tonic...'

Go on baby.

'... Glossop's rider doesn't look happy and he's pulling him up after that mistake.'

Well done Bobby.

'... Thimbelina's three clear of Sun Tonic now who's struggling and it looks like she only has to jump the last...'

My eyes were tight shut but the picture in my mind had never been clearer as I visualised the bay mare galloping towards the final hurdle. No mistakes now, please, it's the last thing I'll ever beg for...

'... the mare's four clear as she comes to it and she's up ... and over! Lovely jump and she's coming away now from Sun Tonic...'

Thank God.

The tension drained from me as though someone had physically pulled a plug out. My only thought now, cowardly as it seemed, was to get away quickly so I didn't have to tell the lads that Kenny Hawkins wouldn't be getting any big payout.

But running away was pointless. I'd have to explain what had happened and soon. Jeff and the others would be bursting to visit Kenny and give him the good news.

I wandered reluctantly back to the weighing room knowing I'd have to sit through the hubbub which would start as soon as Jake Brassey sat on the scales. I hoped he could act. I hoped they all could.

The five who'd ridden in the race would be excited, ecstatic at pulling it off. But all the natural jubilation would have to be curbed or people would get suspicious. It wasn't the Gold Cup Jake had won it was a crappy little handicap hurdle at a small course, no real call for celebration.

The others would have an even tougher time curbing their instincts. Bobby would have to appear downhearted at having to have pulled up the favourite so close to home. Glossop had looked perfectly sound as he walked back and the Stewards would probably have Bobby in for questioning.

I stood by the door of the weighing room, said a quiet well done to Jake as he walked past clutching saddle and weightcloth against mud-spattered red and yellow colours. He smiled and made for the scales.

I kept staring out into the grey afternoon waiting

142

for the inevitable query from the Clerk of the Scales. A few seconds later it came.

The gruff voice said, 'You're five pounds light, Brassey.'

'What!'

'Five pounds light.'

'I can't be, sir!'

I heard the scales chair squeak as Jake turned to look at the needle. I turned too, it would have been unnatural to keep staring away from the drama. It was a thing that happened very rarely, maybe once every six or seven years.

A Stewards' Secretary had joined the Clerk and was double checking Jake's weight against the racecard. The secretary hurried away.

The grey haired Clerk looked up at Jake, 'You know I'll have to object.'

Jake slumped forward in despair, the saddle and weightcloth slipping from his hands to the floor.

Rather overdoing it, I thought, hoping he wouldn't top it off by actually fainting.

Slowly as though all the lead had slipped from the weightcloth into his boots Jake gathered up his gear and, head down, shambled into the sanctuary of the changing room.

The PA system blared, 'Objection! There is an objection by the Clerk of the Scales to the winner of the second race. Customers are advised to retain all betting tickets until the result of the objection is announced.'

The result was a foregone conclusion. Jockeys were allowed a small weight loss during a race to account for the effects of exertion but anyone weighing in five pounds light was destined for disqualification. The lodging of the objection was

143

simply a formality.

I earnestly hoped that Conway's man had remembered to tell him the bets had to be first past the post.

The race was quickly awarded to Sun Tonic. Jeff wasn't riding in the next and I waited outside for him. Padded jacket over his muddy breeches he came beaming towards where I stood against the paddock rail. Reluctant, ashamed to shake his hand if he offered it, I turned away before he got the chance, motioning him to follow me.

In the car I told him what had happened. He took it bad. His look changed quickly to one of deep suspicion and mistrust and I knew that whatever I said it wouldn't change his opinion. He was certain the whole thing had been elaborately engineered by me for my own ends.

The fact that the first past the post idea had come from me didn't help things.

Up till now I'd told no one in the weighing room about Conway. Tutty knew but he'd been sworn to silence and McCarthy, the Jockey Club Security man knew but he wouldn't have let it out. I had two reasons for keeping quiet. The main one was that if Bill Keating had obtained a false scan there was a big chance one or two others had too and they'd have a major interest in saving Conway from exposure.

Conway himself had just learned from Tutty that I was involved. It would be tough enough fighting him without some of my own colleagues working on me from the inside.

The other reason was that I'd been concerned at how quickly Kenny's brother, Joe, had got to learn about the initial suggestion for the fixed race. When he'd mentioned it to me the day I met him at the hospital I'd wondered who'd told him. My conclusion was that it was Neumman, the guy who'd slagged Jeff off for suggesting it. But I couldn't be sure.

So I told Jeff as much as I dared and it was pretty much the truth with just the names and the motives left out. But, understandably, he wouldn't buy it. His final words to me were that it was 'a load of fucking bullshit'. He slammed the car door then and strode away steam-driven back into the course.

I watched him go hoping that once his anger cooled he'd realise I'd never have ripped Kenny off. Jeff and I weren't bosom buddies but he should have known me well enough not to have said all the things he'd just said.

Sighing sadly I started the car and headed for home, my thoughts shared between Tutty and the five guys back in the Sedgefield weighing room who'd probably never trust me again. That fact alone stoked a rising anger, a grim determination to nail this fat little bastard, Conway.

CHAPTER SIXTEEN

The next three days were among the most miserable in my life. I got calls on Thursday evening from Bobby Cranley and Jake Brassey both asking how I could possibly do that to Kenny. Neither would listen to reason and swore they'd never talk to me again.

Jake called after Bobby and, frustrated and guilt ridden, I came within an ace of telling him the whole damn story.

145

Friday and Saturday were spent at Market Rasen and Towcester miserably waiting for word from Tutty. Saturday evening right through till Sunday's frozen dawn found me hunched in my car outside Conway's dark and silent house.

I couldn't go to the police for fear of dropping the race conspirators in it, not to mention myself. Couldn't even turn to McCarthy of Jockey Club Security for the same reason. I had told Charles back at the yard, but only because Tutty worked for him. He listened in resigned silence then shook his head slowly, throwing me one of those, you've really done it now, looks.

In desperation I even drove to London on Sunday lunchtime to stake out the Ritz on the chance Conway would be there with his redhead celebrating the big win. Nothing.

It was dusk when I got back to the flat, tired and dishevelled. I looked in the bathroom mirror through bloodshot eyes at almost forty-eight hours of beard growth and I sighed and ran a hot bath.

Towelling myself dry under the harsh light I began to resign myself to the prospect of Tutty turning up dead somewhere. My doorbell rang while I was still naked, someone leaning constantly on the button.

Pulling on a blue striped dressing gown I hurried downstairs. 'Who is it?' I shouted but couldn't make myself heard above the shrill bell.

I opened the door. Tutty took his finger off the button and walked in slamming the door behind him and turning the key. He leaned against it staring at me through bruised swollen flesh. Dried blood cracked on his chin. His two front teeth were missing.

Dirt and blood soiled his red hair, dull now. It usually shone with health. Though his green eyes

146

were little more than slits I could see the mixture of fear and relief in them. His head was back, leaning on the door. He swallowed twice, Adam's apple bobbing, as though preparing to talk. But nothing came out.

I reached for his arm, put mine round his shoulder and helped him upstairs. With warm water and a soft cloth I cleaned him up as best I could, wincing with him at the tenderness of each injury. He still hadn't spoken. A torrent of questions was building up in me but I held my tongue.

I helped him from the stiff-backed chair to the big easy chair under the lamp by the fire. Quietly I said, 'I think Charles has got some good painkillers. I'll get them.'

'Just a drink, Eddie.' His voice was croaky, weary.

'You sure?'

He nodded.

'Whisky?'

'Big one.'

I poured for both of us and couldn't help flinching as Tutty tipped the burning liquid into his battered mouth. He made a sour face but soon took another slug then laid his head back staring at the ceiling. He was quiet for a minute.

I sat in the easy chair opposite him and remembered the last time we'd sat here, remembered his bubbly enthusiasm, his vitality as we'd listened to the Conway tape.

Now he slumped like a broken soldier. He was wearing a dark polo neck and light cords and for the first time I noticed, as he sat spread legged, the long looping stain on the trousers from the groin down both thighs where he'd obviously urinated in either fear or desperation. The anger rose in me again and I

147

silently promised Conway the hammering of his life when I caught up with him.

Tutty must have read my mind. Still looking at the ceiling he said quietly, 'Get out of this, Eddie.'

I waited in silence.

'They'll kill you,' he said, then his head tilted forward and he looked at me and drank some more.

It took almost half an hour for him to tell me the story. When he'd arrived at the house Conway had asked him to follow him to the basement where he said he had the cash in a bag. Tutty had gone with him down a flight of stairs into a brightly lit room where about fifteen stone of solid thuggery was waiting to beat the information about the horse out of him.

He couldn't give what he didn't have and suffered a lot of pain to convince them he was being truthful. He gave them my name and number and told them to call.

'Sorry, Eddie, I had to.'

'Of course you did, don't apologise.'

The rest was down to waiting. The big guy stayed with him. Conway disappeared for a couple of days, returned the day after the race very pleased with himself then started planning with the big guy how he was going to get me, how he could use Tutty to set me up for the same treatment.

'Where were you all this time?' I asked.

'In the basement, never left it.'

'Jesus, I spent half the weekend sitting outside the place.'

'Don't go back, Eddie, listen to me.'

'How did you get away?'

'That's what I'm going to tell you, that's why I'm warning you.'

148

He took a mouthful of whisky and swallowed it before it burned his wounded mouth too much. Then he told me what had happened that afternoon.

The big guy was with him in the basement watching sport on TV when the door burst open and two guys in suits dragged Conway in. Conway's man jumped to his feet but one of the suits immediately raised a gun. Tutty said he looked completely cool, utterly professional. Conway's man stayed where he was till the guy told him to get out of the room and wait outside with his partner.

Then he came and sat at the big table across from Tutty. He motioned towards Tutty's injuries and asked if Conway and his man had inflicted them. Tutty said yes and the man told him he'd make a deal.

He would make sure they suffered ten times what they'd handed out. In return Tutty promised he'd come back and tell me that I was to forget all about Conway. Forget about everything except riding horses.

When I tried to pooh pooh the message Tutty got angry for the first time. 'You don't know what you're into here, Eddie. You're playing at it! I knew as soon as these guys walked in they were the real thing. The guy was quiet spoken, no mouthy threats, but I'd bet my last fucking penny he would kill you as quick as look at you.'

'So what did they want with Conway?'

'I don't know and I don't care.'

'What did these guys look like?'

'Killers.'

'Physical descriptions.'

'Forget it, Eddie. I've done what I promised. I'll sleep here tonight. I'm leaving in the morning.'

'Where are you going?'

'I don't know but I'm too fucking scared to stay here.'

I spent the next ten minutes trying to convince him he'd get his confidence back as the injuries healed, that if he ran now he'd always be running but he was absolutely determined to leave.

He was afraid to sleep in his own flat so I let him have my bed and I slept on the sofa. Or lay awake on the sofa summarising everything in my mind, the total losses: the friendship and trust of five colleagues, Tutty's well-being, his confidence, companionship, maybe even his long term health. Not to mention an estimated quarter of a million pounds worth of winnings which would have gone to help Kenny Hawkins and possibly one or two others.

Perhaps that had been the motive for Conway's abduction, the money. Or his apparent abduction. I'd tried to convince Tutty that the whole thing was probably set up by Conway to dissuade us from trying to find him.

Tutty said that if that was the case it had worked. He was certain the hard men had been genuine and I'd resigned myself to his leaving in the morning.

But the longer I lay awake into the night, the more I thought about it, the stronger my conviction grew that Conway had engineered the whole thing. I was sure that if I could find him soon I could recover most of the money and redeem myself with Jeff and the lads. Also, it would make Tutty feel safe again.

Tomorrow I'd get right back on the fat little bastard's trail.

*　　　*　　　*

But the trail really consisted of nothing more than

150

anger and optimism on my part and as those feelings faded with the passing fruitless weeks I steadily grew resigned to the fact that Conway had completely disappeared.

He never returned to his job at the clinic. I visited his house at least three times a week, even tracked down his redheaded girlfriend who turned out to be a high class call girl who could barely remember Conway's name. She said she hadn't seen him since Christmas but she wasn't short of replacements.

All this trekking around while still trying to ride winners for Charles and Gary Rice. It gradually started to wear me down.

I was still *persona non grata* with Jeff Dunning and the northern lads and one or two others were beginning to shun me as well. Neumman's sly digs in the weighing room increased in frequency and intensity and by late January I'd had just about enough of everything.

Then I got what appeared to be a break. On the evening of the twenty-sixth I got a call from a man saying that if I was still looking for Conway he was in a position to offer some advice. I asked how much it would cost. He said just half an hour of my time.

We arranged to meet after racing next day in the car park at Huntingdon races.

I sat in my car as the crowds filtered home in the gathering gloom and lights popped on in the convoy of vehicles snaking towards the exits.

I'd told the guy what I drove and my registration but as the car park emptied and dusk deepened I wondered if he was going to turn up. Then I began wondering about the wisdom of meeting a stranger here.

He'd sounded soft voiced and pleasant, quite old

151

really but I recalled his words: he'd offer advice about my search for Conway not information on where he was.

I reached into the narrow compartment on the door beside me and felt the heavy links of the chain I carried for protection.

Suddenly there was a face at the window, smiling, sixtyish, friendly with gold-rimmed glasses and a neat white moustache. He opened the door, 'Mr Malloy?'

'That's right.'

He slipped a black glove off and stretched into the car offering his hand. 'Ernest Goodwin.'

Alias if ever I heard one.

'May I, er, come in?'

'Of course.'

He took off his hat, a black homburg, smoothed back his thick white hair and got in. He wore a dark suit and an immaculate gleaming stiff collared white shirt and dark tie.

He must have been an exceptionally handsome young man, still good looking, fine featured, just some loose flesh betraying him now.

He smiled, friendly and winning and I wished for a moment he was my grandfather. He said, 'Gets very cold when the sun goes down.'

'It does. Did you come in a car?'

'Oh yes. Parked back there. Thought it would be much easier finding you if I prowled around on foot.'

I nodded unable to resist returning his affable smile.

'And so it proved,' he said, 'so it proved.'

And the delay courtesy light went out leaving both our faces in shadow.

'Mr Malloy, as I said on the telephone I have some advice to offer you in relation to Mr Conway.'

152

'Do you know him personally?'

'I know of him.'

'Do you know where he is?'

'Indeed I do.'

'Will you tell me?'

'I will tell you something which will prove even more valuable to you than Mr Conway's present whereabouts. I will tell you that if you persevere in your search for the man you will be endangering your health.'

'In what way?'

'In the way that some gentlemen prefer to practise persuasion, gentlemen who, let me say, feature slightly farther down the food chain than you and I. Thoroughly unpleasant people.'

'You're here to threaten me.'

He sounded shocked, turned to face me square on. 'Absolutely not! I came to warn you and to try and save you an awful lot of suffering and heartache.'

'Very charitable of you.'

'Indeed.'

'Do you work for Conway?'

'I work for a man who is much more important, much more powerful than Mr Conway. And he is desperately anxious to avoid hurting you. Please heed what I say and give up this pointless pursuit which I can tell you will prove totally fruitless anyway.'

'If that's the case then why is your boss so worried?'

'Worry is not a thing the gentleman in question has ever experienced. I can see you're a determined young man and I do not particularly want to spend a long time arguing with you. I have delivered the message as instructed as I believe Mr Tuttle also did and I would urge you most strongly to act on my advice.'

So he knew what had happened to Tutty.

I said, 'I'll think about it, Mr Goodwin. Thanks for taking the time to come and see me.'

'My pleasure Mr Malloy.'

He got out. The courtesy light illuminated his white hair till he straightened and fitted his hat on. Bending forward he leant in again smiling, 'Goodnight to you. Drive safely home.'

I smiled back. 'Won't you give me just the tiniest clue to Conway's whereabouts?'

He blew air from his cheeks. 'You're very persistent.' He considered things for a few moments then said, 'A couple of weeks ago Mr Conway left on a sea voyage. Take it from me that he will not be returning.' The smile faded and he walked away into the dark.

I waited half an hour watching for his car lights but nothing appeared.

Driving home I began to doubt my theory that Conway had set up his own abduction. Why go to these lengths just to keep a curious if determined jockey off his tail? Why not have me beaten up like Tutty or even killed like Bill?

But if it wasn't Conway then who had abducted him and why were they so anxious that I give up my search? And again why not simply have me severely beaten? What was behind the softly softly tactics?

Before this meeting I'd been almost on the verge of giving up anyway but I don't like being threatened and I didn't want whoever was behind Goodwin's visit to think they'd been successful in cowing me.

So I stuck at it for another fortnight though I knew I was going nowhere. The visits to Conway's house, the calls to the clinic to see if he'd turned up yet yielded nothing but frustration and a steady grinding down of my spirits. By 7th February I'd decided I was a fool to take all this on my own shoulders.

Other people had responsibilities here, if not to Kenny Hawkins then at least to Bill Keating's memory. The Jockey Club for one. It was time their security team started sharing the legwork.

I called McCarthy. He couldn't see me till the 10th. We agreed to meet for lunch in Wantage.

With that arranged I thought I may as well take action on the other thing that was bothering me, the way Kenny had lost out on his big payday. I didn't know if word had already filtered back to Kenny. My guess was it had so I felt I had to show my face, give him my version.

I decided to visit him and explain the whole thing. Maybe then Jeff Dunning and the others would see I'd never been anything but straight.

After that I'd hand the tapes over to McCarthy, let him help me find Conway. If he was still alive.

CHAPTER SEVENTEEN

I rang Carol Hawkins and arranged to visit Kenny at home on 9th February. She said she hoped I'd cheer him up and invited me to stay for dinner.

I'd ridden a winner and a third from three rides at a very cold Ludlow and by dusk frost was already settling on the soft Shropshire landscape as I headed south for Lambourn and Kenny's house.

He'd been out of hospital since before Christmas and though it looked like he'd be stuck in a

155

wheelchair for the rest of his life there seemed a strong likelihood he'd now get a very fat insurance settlement.

The weighing room gossip was that his rich brother Joe had hired a bigshot lawyer who was arguing that the local council had been negligent in the maintenance of the crash barrier guarding the bridge where Kenny had gone over. There was talk of a million pound plus settlement and that made me feel much better about the coup falling apart.

For most of the day I'd found myself feeling nervy about the prospect of meeting Kenny but the closer I came to his house that evening the more I felt a burden was about to be lifted. And God did I need the break.

By this time tomorrow the Conway thing would be out in the open with the security people so everyone would soon get to hear about it. Then Jeff Dunning and the others would maybe understand the pressure I'd been under, they'd see I hadn't ripped off Kenny or anyone else.

People would also realise that Bill Keating's death may not have been suicide after all.

And I'd have cleared the air with Kenny. I'd be free to concentrate on riding, on the Cheltenham Festival which was only a month away. I already had eight booked rides and the more time I had to study the formbook, to concentrate on the weaknesses of my opponents, the better chance I'd have of riding winners.

I smiled at the prospect. Allesandro, Charles's grey who'd done us proud at Chepstow, already looked a banker in the opening race at Cheltenham, the biggest meeting of the year.

A rectangle of pale light from the kitchen window

lit the short driveway beside Kenny's cottage. I parked and lifted out the two bottles of wine I'd bought: one red, one white.

It must have been more than two minutes before Carol answered my knock. She looked harassed and upset as she welcomed me with a kiss on the cheek.

'You okay?'

She nodded, closing the door but her round blue eyes had been crying. She wore a light blue blouse which had a large water stain just over her left breast. Thick strands of blonde hair had worked their way out of the carefully tied back bun and one of her gold earrings was missing.

I was concerned but she'd said she was all right and I didn't want to press it. She led me into the neat living room. One tall lamp and the flames of logs burning in the inglenook gave a cosy light casting shadows on racing pictures and a handful of trophies placed carefully around the room.

The curtains were drawn, the house silent but for the crackling logs. Carol offered me the easy chair by the fire and while pouring drinks tried to lighten the atmosphere with small talk about the weather and today's racing. She handed me an inch of whisky in a cut glass tumbler then sat down opposite me sipping orange juice.

'Teetotal?' I asked.

She sighed deeply. 'Eddie, I've seen enough alcohol recently to, to ... well I wouldn't care if I never saw another drink.'

Kenny still hadn't appeared and I was beginning to put things together. 'Is Kenny okay?'

She straightened in her chair though it seemed to take some mental effort, a determination to press on. She looked at me resignedly. 'If pissed out of your

157

brain is okay then Kenny's okay. If you don't mind not having dinner with my husband as arranged then we're okay too.'

'Don't worry about me.' I was mildly disappointed though slightly relieved that I wouldn't have to face him. But my main feelings were for Carol who, hard as she was trying to hide it, was obviously depressed. I thought it might help if she talked about it. 'Has he been drinking a lot?'

'Fits and starts. He can go weeks without touching it then something seems to set him off and he binges for days.'

'Maybe he just gets depressed, misses the riding.'

'He does, I know he does but he's handling that, Eddie, he'll talk about it. That bastard of a brother seems to wind him up, it was him that started Kenny on his last drinking bout after another argument.'

'Is this Joe, the guy I met at the hospital?'

'That's him, the helpful supportive little brother,' she said scornfully. 'They've been at each other's throats for a month over this insurance claim, the accident, you know.'

'I'd heard Joe was putting a big lawyer on it.'

'He's trying to but Kenny doesn't want his big lawyers or his money, says he'll handle things himself.'

'And Joe won't let him?'

'I don't know, Eddie, Kenny won't talk about it.'

'Wouldn't Joe tell you?'

She sneered, her thin lips cutting a dark line in her small face. 'I don't even stay in the house when he comes here. The kids and I have spent more time at my mum's this year so far than we did the whole of last year.' She sipped juice and wiped at the stain on her blouse. 'The way things are going we'll be moving

158

out for good.' She said that quietly, addressing the fireflames more than me.

'Maybe it's just Kenny's way of handling things, Carol. He's got to adjust to never walking again never mind not riding.'

'It's easy for you to defend him, Eddie, it's not you that has to clean up after him or wrestle him out of that chair when he's unconscious. You're not wiping vomit off your shirt or trying to explain to the children why daddy's behaving like this.'

She had a point. 'I'm sorry, you're right.'

'Don't apologise,' she said quietly, 'You came for dinner and some pleasant chat, I shouldn't be taking things out on you.'

'You're not, don't worry. I'm happy to listen.'

More earnest now she said, 'I thought he'd have been okay, Eddie, honestly or I'd have put you off coming. He seemed to really be looking forward to seeing you when I told him you'd called.'

'Forget it, we can do it another time.'

'Mmmm.' She was staring into the fire again, its light emphasising her pale skin. We sat quietly for quite a while, only the crackling logs broke the silence then a long low moan came from the back of the house. Carol looked at me. 'I'd better see if he's all right.'

A few minutes later she returned leaving the door slightly ajar behind her and almost tiptoeing back across to her chair.

'Is he okay?'

She nodded.

'Are the children at your mum's?'

'I took them there about two thirds of the way through his first bottle of vodka.'

Carol brooded silently for five minutes more then

suddenly started pulling herself together, apologising needlessly for everything and insisting I have another drink while she finished preparing dinner.

We ate rack of lamb together at the big pine table in the kitchen. Carol apologised for the setting saying the dining room was being decorated.

She talked about how life had changed since the accident. When it got back to Kenny's drinking something she said pushed me into telling her what I'd intended to tell Kenny.

It seemed Kenny had been pulling himself steadily together again after drying out from a three day bender around Christmas time. On New Year's day he promised Carol he'd quit drinking but on the 8th January he'd gone on another three day bout.

That was three days after the coup that was supposed to bring him the payoff and it made me wonder if Kenny had heard about it and about my failure to come up with the stake money. Maybe that was what set him off boozing again.

If that was the case then maybe Kenny thought I was as big a bastard as several others did. I couldn't have left his house that night with that on my mind so I explained the whole thing to Carol though I left out Conway's name and what his scam had been, pending Mac's reaction to the tapes tomorrow.

Carol confessed that she had known about the planned coup, Kenny had too and they were both very grateful for the thought behind it. They'd also heard about my part in it going wrong but both had refused to hear a bad word against me, insisting that I'd never have pulled a stunt to keep the cash for myself.

Carol seemed completely sincere and I sighed with relief on hearing it. 'That's a big load off my mind,

160

Carol, it's been bothering me since it happened.'

She poured coffee. 'There was never a doubt in either of our minds, Eddie, Kenny was raging when he heard some of the stories about you.'

'That makes me feel better. When you said he'd hit the bottle again around that time I thought it was the coup failing that maybe caused it.'

'No, definitely not, he was delighted that you and Jeff and the lads thought so much of him that you'd even try something like that. Though I have to tell you we'd already decided we couldn't have taken the money.'

'Why not?'

'It just wouldn't have been right, Eddie, there are people in racing much worse off than us.'

Arguing was pointless. The money wasn't a factor now anyway. I thanked Carol and she made me promise to come back and see Kenny soon, said she'd call me and tell me when he was back to his best. I agreed and we said goodnight.

On the drive home my spirits were high and my mood positive. Next day I'd push McCarthy hard for a helping hand.

*   *   *

Dominated as usual by his appetite Mac wouldn't face serious discussion till he'd lovingly ordered lunch at a nice hotel on the edge of the village. I stuck with clear soup and chicken salad, sipping mineral water against Mac's red wine as we waited in the quiet restaurant.

He listened warily at first then with increasing despondency as I told him what I knew about Conway and that I had tapes and a witness though I

161

couldn't mention the fixed race or tell him what had happened to Tutty at Conway's house.

He said, 'We can't make anything stand up just on tapes, Eddie.'

'Maybe not but it's a good start. A bit of legwork by your guys should help build things up.'

'The first thing we need to do is interview Conway.'

'And what if you can't find him?'

'We'll have to wait till he turns up.'

I fought the frustration. 'For how long?'

He just shrugged. I said, 'Mac, he might never turn up. You have to assume that.'

'Why? Maybe he's gone on holiday.'

I wished I could tell him about the fixed race. I blustered on about Conway not reporting for work at the clinic, about him taking the chance of being exposed there if his past work was investigated while he was absent. I made out the case for him running away from or being abducted by some villains he'd maybe crossed but Mac's face stayed resolutely unconvinced.

Throughout the meal I kept chipping away at him. I said, 'Look, let's just assume for a minute that everything I say is true. If Conway never turns up you're going to have to start an investigation anyway so you might as well do it while the trail is still warm.'

'Don't see your logic, Eddie. What concern is it of ours if he never comes back?'

'Wouldn't you like to know how many jockeys with damaged brains are trying to get horses over fences?'

'That's supposition.'

'Mac, come on! We've been through all this! You know Conway did Bill Keating's scan, you should be trying to find out exactly who else he scanned and checking your records, interviewing people.'

'Making a rod for our own backs you mean?'

'No! I mean finding out how many lives that little bastard has buggered up!'

The waiter appeared at my shoulder and said calmingly, 'Some wine, sir?'

Mac smiled and sipped his.

I ended up threatening Mac that if he didn't take some action I'd break my theory to the Press and give them the tapes. That unnerved him and he made a vague offer to 'take a look at it' but I pinned him down to the promise of a full investigation and he ate his apple pie and cream with considerably less gusto than the first two courses.

For once in his life Mac decided to do things the easy way and by the end of the week he'd persuaded the police to search Conway's house. When they turned the place over they found no clues to the fat man's whereabouts but they did find three things which suddenly turned Bill Keating's case into a murder inquiry.

Among a set of files in a locked tin box was Bill's original brain scan showing the damage that would have cost him his riding licence. Attached to it by a paper clip was the faked scan which Conway must have stolen from the Jockey Club. McCarthy admitted that the little man had free access to the Records' Room.

They also found in his garage a chisel which, after forensic examination, proved to be the tool used to punch a hole in the exhaust of Bill's horsebox.

And they found blood on the floor of the basement. It was probably Tutty's but I couldn't reveal that.

A warrant was issued for Conway's arrest and

163

while the whole story couldn't be told until he was found we managed to get enough released to the Press to make it clear that Bill Keating had not taken his own life. Mac's department, as usual, got all the credit though that didn't bother me. I felt my own sense of achievement and satisfaction, albeit temporarily: I still badly wanted to track Conway down.

Jockey Club chiefs promised a security review and considered the option of ordering new brain scans on all jockeys. But because it was so close to the end of the season they decided to wait until June. I was confident they wouldn't have found anything but clear scans anyway. Trouble was which of them, if any, were fakes?

Among the renewed emotional turmoil for Cathy and the children there was a sense of relief. Profound shock at his murder, of course, but some personal consolation in knowing he hadn't killed himself nor the two horses that had shared his deathbed.

On the Sunday before Cheltenham I went to the little churchyard and stood by Bill's grave for five minutes. I spoke to him in my mind, told him I'd done what I could and said I'd keep on trying to find Conway.

I looked up, picturing that battered old smile of his filling the sky. From somewhere in my childhood memory I managed to string together the words of a prayer for him. I left that peaceful little place feeling pretty damn pleased with myself.

A dangerous conceit.

CHAPTER EIGHTEEN

The police interviewed me about Conway and on learning of Tutty's involvement in making the tapes they pushed to discover where he'd gone. I said he'd simply thought it was getting too dangerous and had opted out, told me he was going to Ireland to find work.

I couldn't tell them about the planned coup and Tutty's fate when he'd tried to get the money. Anything to do with the coup had to be edited out of what I told the authorities to protect Jeff Dunning and the lads.

I did give the police the details of the veiled threat I'd received during my meeting with Ernest Goodwin in the car park at Huntingdon, told them what he'd said about Conway going on a sea voyage and all that. It was dutifully noted and by the first day of the Cheltenham Festival I'd heard nothing more from them.

With both the police and Mac's department involved in the hunt for Conway I reckoned my conscience could stand me having a break from it all for a week or so to concentrate on Cheltenham.

It turned out to be a brilliant meeting for our stable with Allesandro winning the Supreme Novices' Hurdle by five lengths and Touch Line getting up to win the County Hurdle by a short head under one of the best rides I think I've ever given a horse.

The stable owner, Gary Rice, had particular reason to celebrate as the victories seemed to signify a change of luck for him. Recently it had all been bad.

On the Friday before Cheltenham the yard's brand

new horsebox had been stolen on its first racing trip. Someone had driven it away from the Market Rasen car park. Gary had paid forty-five grand for it just three days before.

Twenty-four hours later he lost his Porsche 911 as well. Somebody stole it from outside his house, not a peep was heard from the sophisticated alarm system. The police rated their chances of recovering the horsebox a lot higher than they did the Porsche.

Three weeks earlier Gary's house had been burgled while he was away on a business trip. The thieves had decided to start their own art collection with most of Gary's. He'd lost several very valuable antiques too.

At a big party to celebrate a successful Cheltenham Gary told me that he hoped this turnaround in his fortunes proved the old saying that bad luck comes in threes. I said I'd bet his insurance company shared his hopes. When Gary's losses in the last month were totted up they topped the million pound mark.

Gary had taken each blow as 'just one of those things'. But the more I thought about it the more I was inclined to think someone was targeting him for personal motives and the first person that came to mind was Neumman, the jock who rode for Gary before I got the job.

Our stable had been in excellent form approaching Cheltenham, something Neumman would have found particularly galling. Also, Neumman had some spare time on his hands having suffered suspensions totalling ten days for rough riding.

Two things stopped me mentioning my suspicions to Gary: one, I had to admit a personal bias and dislike of Neumman which coloured my judgement and two, I was wary that Gary would ask me to try and find some solid evidence against him. I was enjoying my self-granted leave from the Conway case and didn't want to get involved in anything else.

As it turned out it was a wrong decision. Subsequent events showed that if I'd taken an interest in Gary's misfortunes at that point I might have saved myself and others an awful lot of pain and trouble.

*   *   *

Gary Rice had business interests in Barbados, an island with a strong racing fraternity, many of them Brits.

He also had a marine transport business based in Barbados which sailed regularly between there and Britain with various cargoes including bloodstock, much of it his own. Gary would send British bought horses over to race on the island. The standard of competition was lower than the UK and his trainer there had been turning out a steady stream of winners.

He had a big estate on Barbados most of it covered by sugarcane which was processed in a factory he also owned. The five hundred acre plantation ran alongside a purpose built training complex housing twenty-three of his horses.

On April 14th the main house at the plantation was almost totally destroyed by fire which was blamed on a smouldering cigarette end. Okay, said Gary, just another unfortunate incident but fifteen days later, in the early hours of April 29th, an explosion at the sugar processing factory caused several hundred thousand pounds worth of damage. That was put down to a faulty fuel pump. The only good news was that no one had been badly injured in either incident.

But between England and the Caribbean that made five very costly blows to Gary in around ten weeks and he was already beginning to suspect a personal vendetta, when it was confirmed. On May 1st Gary's trainer in Barbados, a guy called Berman Carroway, received a telephone threat to the effect that he should leave Headlands, Gary's estate, by the end of that week.

That's when Gary called in a firm of private investigators.

During this period there'd been no movement on the Conway case. Despite the police alerting Interpol and McCarthy utilising all of his international racing contacts there hadn't been a whisper about Conway. The prospect of him having been genuinely abducted and maybe even killed was becoming more believable.

Gary Rice knew all the details of the Conway case, he'd insisted one evening that I entertain him with the full story which I did on the promise he'd keep it to himself until Conway turned up.

On May 20th with the jump season cantering lazily into its final few days Gary invited me to dinner at his house near Ludlow, said he had an interesting tale to tell me.

Although there were just two of us in his cavernous wood panelled dining room Gary had hired a catering firm to prepare dinner. He didn't employ a cook because half the time he wasn't at home.

He sat across from me at the big teak table as impeccably turned out as ever in an expensive dark blue suit and white shirt. His tie was pale blue with small yellow diamonds and a heavy Rolex hung on his wrist.

His teeth and the whites of his eyes threw a startlingly bright contrast against the handsome deeply tanned face and his thick dark brown glossy hair topped off six foot of athleticism.

What do you give the man who has everything?

With the season winding down I could afford some carelessness in my diet and I enjoyed four excellent courses, accepted a large brandy but declined a cigar. By the end of the meal I had plenty to think about.

Throughout it Gary had been pushing crockery aside to slide papers and photographs across to me. The first thing he showed me was a black and white ten by eight picture of a man whose face I knew but couldn't quite place.

Gary prompted me. 'Think back to around this time last year. We'd been out for a meal and came back here for a drink, you, me and Charles. This guy was with us.'

I looked again. A thin man in what looked like a safari suit: black curly hair receding at the front, olive skin, close set dark eyes, long chin, Arabic looking though as my memory scratched around I recalled he had an English name. 'Er, Clarence, no ... Clen ...'

'Clemence.'

'That's it, you'd taken him on that day as an agent for the transport work.'

'That's right, drumming up cargo business between here and Barbados.'

'That's where he's based.'

'That's right.' He gestured at the picture. 'That's him leaving the Harbour Master's office in Bridgetown last week.'

'Right.' I waited.

'I know it's a long time ago but do you remember when we came back here that night, did Clemence

169

come through the front door behind me?'

I smiled. 'Gary, it's all I can do to remember that night at all, we all had a skinful, didn't we?'

'We had a few but I know the very first thing I did that night when I opened the door because it's the first thing I always do, I punched in the code to disarm the alarm system.'

I looked at him, at the photos, the investigators' reports and I said, 'And you think Clemence remembered the code and passed it to the people who burgled you back in February.'

Gary smiled and tapped his nose with a beautifully manicured finger. 'I think he didn't bother passing it on, I think he did it himself.'

'You do or your private eyes do?'

'Let's say they pointed me in a certain direction. Look . . .'

He slid more papers across.

'. . . The records from Archangel.' That was Gary's cargo boat. '22nd February, the weekend of 11th and 12th March, on each of those dates Clemence was in England.'

The dates were highlighted in yellow on the pages as were three more.

Gary pointed at them. '14th April, the fire at the plantation. 29th, the explosion. 1st May, the threatening call to Carroway. Guess where Clemence was on those dates?'

'Barbados.'

'Correct.'

'Who else does he work for?'

'That's what my guys are now concentrating on but here's the interesting part from your point of view.' He passed me another piece of paper. 'That's an inventory of the Archangel's cargo when she left

170

Southampton for Barbados on 10th January last.'

The yellow highlighter picked out 'Horsefeed: samples: 100kg in large packing case'. The case had been uplifted from the offices of a company in Newbury, a company unfamiliar to me and the delivery note said it would be collected by an agent in Bridgetown.

Another sheet of A4 floated across to me. 'That's an inventory of the stock that was unloaded in Bridgetown.'

There was no highlighting bar. I scanned down the page. No packing case with horsefeed samples.

Another sheet, headed Loss Report which said that the packing case had been lost overboard during the night of 13th January in heavy seas and that a crewman had been disciplined for not securing it properly.

Gary said, 'Four months ago. We're still waiting for the insurance claim.'

'Which makes you think the case didn't contain horsefeed.'

He smiled indulgently and I knew there was something I hadn't cottoned onto. He said, 'When did your man Conway go missing?'

I thought back. 'The 8th January I think it was.'

'The case was collected from Newbury on the 9th. Also didn't you say your little secret squirrel guy at Huntingdon told you Conway had gone on a sea voyage and wouldn't be coming back?'

CHAPTER NINETEEN

We spent the next few days making plans. The Archangel was due to leave Portsmouth on 2nd June and part of the cargo would be three horses Gary had bought at Newmarket. He was sending them to be trained in Barbados. I was going to accompany them then spend a few weeks holidaying at Gary's estate with a ride in a jockey's invitation race at the Garrison Savannah racetrack thrown in.

At least that would be my story to Clemence who'd be one of my travelling companions. The plan was to play it open and friendly, see what signals Clemence gave out, maybe get him drunk, do some eavesdropping on his conversations with the crew and just generally nose around, hopefully without alerting suspicion.

Gary was confident that Clemence had no idea he was being watched. Even if he did come across as wary maybe I could pick something up from the crew. The guy who'd been disciplined for the loss of the packing case in January might just be sufficiently aggrieved to let something slip.

By leaving on the 2nd I'd be missing the last three days of the jump season but it wasn't as though I was vying for the jockeys championship or anything and I would be riding in Barbados, in the warm sunshine on a nice little flat course.

While Clemence was away from the island, Gary's firm of investigators would concentrate on his activities there. Within three days of our meeting they'd discovered that the Newbury company the packing case had been collected from had since ceased trading leaving no information on the whereabouts of its directors.

It had been a private company registered in the Isle of Man and as such Gary said it could prove impossible to find out who had set it up. He told me

172

the directors may simply have been two strangers picked off the street whose names were used to set up the company which they would then sign over to the real owner without his or her name having to be revealed anywhere. All legal in an offshore company.

The company had registered its business as 'Bloodstock Products' though the investigators could find no one among the other tenants of their building who could recall seeing regular deliveries or pickups. Their office had been small and staffed only by a receptionist.

In the week before departure I tried several times to set up meetings with McCarthy. I left messages on his machine saying I had important news on Conway but Mac proved very elusive. He had his secretary ring me to say he was extremely busy and would call me soon.

The twice I managed to get through on his mobile we were mysteriously cut off and I began to wonder if he was following leads of his own, ones he didn't want me to know about.

The more I reflected on how neatly and suddenly Bill Keating's case had been tied up the more I thought it stank. Conway had been very wily and it was unlikely he'd leave damning evidence lying around.

If he holed the exhaust in Bill's horsebox why not simply dispose of the chisel? Why keep it? Why keep Bill's fake brain scan at home? Surely it would have been much easier to hide at his place of work. And why only Bill's scan?

If it had been Conway's habit to retain the damaged scans then the chances were that more than one jockey was involved so where were those scans?

There had to be a strong possibility Conway was

set up. When it was just puny little Malloy who was after him all that came my way were threats and blind alleys. As soon as the Jockey Club and the police get involved evidence is suddenly plentiful and easy to find.

Supposing Conway didn't kill Bill Keating? Supposing whoever did kill him wanted the police to think Conway was the culprit? Simple, take Conway out of the picture and plant the evidence at his home. If Conway's body was in the packing case lying at the bottom of the Atlantic then the police would be searching for him for an awful long time.

But it still took me back to square one: who did kill Bill Keating and why?

Maybe a few days spent with Harold Clemence would offer some clues. We didn't want to make a big thing of the fact that I'd be supervising the horses on the voyage. Clemence only found out on the day before departure.

Whether the prospect of my company made him wary or simply bored I don't know but next morning, horses safely loaded and all cargo on board, Clemence still hadn't appeared. As the skipper went through the final preparations I asked him where Clemence was. He told me Clemence had informed him last night that he still had some business in England and would be flying back to Barbados in a couple of days.

I tried to reach Gary Rice but couldn't. I had no choice but to sail and hope I could pick something up from the crew. At 7.22 on the morning of 2nd June we left Southampton for the nine day trip to the Caribbean.

What I know about boats could be written on the back of a *Capstan* packet. All I can say about Archangel was that you could walk the length of her in sixty-two strides, her engine sounded like it was trying to burst upwards through the deck and the crew seemed competent and, for the most part, friendly.

There were six of them, all black Bajans. The ship had always been a working cargo vessel and on outward trips the big hold was filled almost exclusively with bananas, the smell of which still pervaded everything below decks.

I spent the first three days trying to get on good matey terms with everyone in the hope of picking up something on Clemence, making the best of his absence. But it turned out that only two of them had travelled with Clemence on previous trips, the skipper, a muscular little bloke who liked to be called Mr Dann rather than captain and a big guy known as George. George was six five tall, skinny with a booming voice that could be heard all over the boat.

George was more than happy to talk openly about Clemence though he didn't give away any secrets. Mr Dann was much more reserved and sometimes I'd catch him silently watching me.

The fine weather held and the horses, on deck in wooden stable-boxes, gazed out by day and night as though looking for the gulls which had fascinated them for hours as we left port.

Since getting back my licence a couple of years ago I'd almost forgotten what it was like to work so closely with horses. Whether riding races or schooling for trainers, jockeys arrive to find the horse waiting, fully tacked up and ready. When they dismount the groom takes the horse away and the jockey mounts the next one on the production line.

Each day now I'd feed, water and groom the three, finding myself surprised by the salt caking in their rapidly growing coats. One of them, aptly named Old Nick, proved a poor traveller whose temper worsened the further we went. Four days out I gave up grooming him and I opened his door only to carefully put food and water in.

The whipcord gelding had made his mark on the crate carrying him before it was even loaded.

Swinging high above the ship on the end of the crane jib at Southampton he'd kicked a hole in the side of his box and was still lashing out as the crate was bound hard against the starboard railings by a half inch thick steel hawser.

About halfway through the voyage Old Nick gave three of us a real fright when he got cast in his box at two in the morning. Big George had come running for me, shouting and banging on my cabin door. He had a gun and wanted to shoot Old Nick who was thrashing around on the floor trying to get up.

Sometimes horses lie down and roll in their stables. Occasionally they find themselves stuck against a wall unable to stretch their legs to get up. Some lie quietly till help comes. Some panic and lash out. Old Nick had smashed through the adjoining wall of the next box.

I managed to calm George down sufficiently for him and Carson another crewman to help me get Old Nick upright again. The operation involved me sitting on the horse's head, immobilising him long enough to let the others drag him by the tail till he was clear of the wall and able to rise. The horse's mad thrashing had cost him an eye. I patched the socket up as best I could and prayed it wouldn't get infected.

The remainder of the voyage passed without any enlightenment but not quite without further incident.

I'd spent some time during the trip reading up on

Barbados and as the lights of the island came into view around dusk on 11th June I stood at the rail and recalled what I'd learned.

Barbados measures twenty-one miles by fourteen. It is the most easterly of the West Indies. Top exports: sugar, rum and oil. Two hundred and sixty thousand people live there, most of them Christian. They spend Barbados dollars and their life expectancy is seventy-three years.

Reflecting on life at seventy-three I went below to start packing. When I next came on deck I was contemplating death at twenty-nine.

I was in my cabin when I heard the explosion and felt the boat lurch to the left then swing round throwing me against the upright of my bunk. My first thought was that somehow we'd hit the harbour wall or something before I remembered that we were still too far out for that.

The boat seemed to right itself then almost as quickly slip downwards again. Pushing away from the bed I grabbed the door handle. The long passage outside tilted badly leaving me a slope to negotiate as I tried to get back up on deck.

I could hear shouts and curses. I turned round and using the walls for support forced myself along the passageway towards the stairs.

I smelled smoke, fumes.

Away to my left ahead of me I could hear what sounded like a huge monster slurping and sucking in water.

Stepping out onto the deck I almost fell sideways down its forty degree angle. The crew were desperately trying to launch the lifeboat on the low side, shouting, almost screaming in panic.

The horses.

Almost hanging from the rail I hauled myself across to where the three boxes were and yanked the doors open. The horses inside were trying to turn their quarters towards me and the door thinking that was where the enemy was, that was where the defensive kicks should be aimed. But they kept overbalancing, crashing sideways against the back wall to make the planks creak and heave at the squealing nails.

If the boxes were still fixed to the deck when we went under they'd have very little chance of survival. If I could get the horses out they stood a strong chance of swimming ashore.

I needed help.

Making my way as best I could I reached the dipping rail and the panicking crew, three of whom were hacking with axes and knives at the tangled ropes which still held the lifeboat suspended swaying just feet above the water.

I grabbed the shoulder of the first man I reached. 'I need help! I need some help with the horses!'

Without even turning to look he cursed and lashed out backwards with his elbows trying to push me away. I said, 'Hey, come on! Don't panic. We'll all get off.'

He ignored me and kept struggling with the ropes. Behind me I heard two mighty whacks in quick succession and as I turned to look I saw a steelshod hoof bursting through the rear wall of the middle box. Three more kicks followed smashing a large hole in the wood. It gave me an idea.

Beside me one of the big guys was raising a long axe to strike again at the ropes. I knew he wouldn't surrender it easily and I needed it very quickly.

The sea was through the rails now.

178

When he was at full stretch I punched him hard just below the right armpit. He grunted and the shaft of the axe slipped through his loosening fingers. I grabbed it and hauled my way back up to the box.

As Old Nick continued kicking at the planks I worked on the edges higher up battering till the nails came out. As the planks began springing free the horse sensed escape and pushed his rump against the weakening wall. I stopped swinging the axe and stepped to the side as the big chestnut quarters came through, a jagged plank edge piercing the sweating skin.

Suddenly the boat bucked and lurched sickeningly and I fell backwards as the horse burst through the wall. Panic-stricken, he fought to keep his feet but the deck moved like a splintering treadwheel under his hooves and he slithered down towards the rail and the gathering sea.

The water was quite calm, bubbling and gurgling almost pleasantly as it gradually swallowed him and the boat. The other two still cowered in their boxes.

I looked to where a steel hawser anchored the boxes firmly although the deck angle was almost impossible.

I was lying flat now, my feet resting on the lower rails of the side of the boat. Without knowing for sure I sensed that the crew had gone. Just me and the two horses left. I knew I could make it. We were no more than five hundred yards from shore and the water would be warm. I was a strong swimmer.

I stretched full length to swing the axe one-handed at the cleats holding the hawser end. The axehead missed and bit deeply into the wood surrounding the cleat. Wrenching the blade clear I swung again aiming for the damaged part hoping to weaken it but the head hit the steel cleat this time, ringing the vibrating shock back along my arm to numb my shoulder.

Changing the axe to my left hand I tried again hitting the wood on the other side of the cleat. Beneath my feet the sea sucked again, clearing its throat as the boat turned slowly till the deck stood vertical, throwing the two horses heavily against the walls of their boxes.

I watched the bulging planks, willing the nails to break free. But they were holding and the poor beasts were going to go down with the boat. I tried a final swing of the axe but as I raised it with my left hand the boat finally gave up and turned slowly over.

As I pushed myself clear I heard the sound of metal tearing through wood then the pinging swish and crack that told me the cleat had finally given way, torn from the deck by the weight of the boxes.

As I tumbled into the water more sounds of rending wood and squealing nails came and I hoped and prayed that the boxes had smashed apart releasing the horses.

Horses are reasonable swimmers and there had to be a fighting chance we'd all get back safely.

If the boat didn't drag me under.

CHAPTER TWENTY

It was going straight down as though launched vertically towards the ocean bed. The speed it sank at caused a minor whirlpool which began sucking me back as I tried to swim free.

The water was warm, there'd be no problems

surviving the temperature if I could just get clear of the pull, the swirling bubbling arms trying to hold me back, drag me in and down.

For just a few seconds I felt I might not make it but I kicked and swam hard upwards, breath burning my lungs. Eyes open I saw the watery stars and let go the searing breath six inches below the surface, my lungs expelling it like a whale spout.

Burst the surface. Suck in air. Cool fresh sweet air.

Waves just gentle. Get my bearings. Shore lights through the dusk to my left. No lifeboat. No horses.

Then I heard splashing away to my right. I swam towards the sound. It was one of the horses. He was swimming out to sea. I went after him, caught up and managed to grab his headcollar. It was Old Nick. He'd never caused me anything but trouble.

Though thin-legged, horses' wide ribcages hold plenty of air and they swim fairly easily. If I could just guide him we'd both make it ashore. I couldn't see or hear the other two.

I dragged Old Nick's head around. I'd forgotten about his injury and recoiled in shock at the slimy seaweed hanging from his empty eye socket. Recovering quickly I dragged the stuff out only for a wave to wash black water into the cavity.

Turning him back towards shore I struck out as best I could, one hand gripping his headcollar. His legs caught mine as he paddled forward. The only safe swimming place was behind, clinging to his tail but that would have meant no direction up front. I resolved that if he fought, if he turned even once from the direction of the shore I'd let him go.

He kept going.

The darkness was almost total now and I wondered why they hadn't turned the lifeboat, tried

181

to find me. Where were the coastguard, the rescue services? Surely the crew had alerted them.

I checked the shore lights again. We were drifting off course. I hauled again at his head, 'Come on you bastard or I'll leave you!' And he came round.

I knew we were swimming straight, moving forward but the lights never seemed to get any nearer and I wondered if I'd completely misjudged the distance. I was growing tired, beginning to feel sick. I'd swallowed a few pints of water.

I pressed on but nausea surged and I vomited into the clean sea then opened my mouth to let the salt water wash out the foul taste.

Felt like we'd been swimming for hours. My mind was confused. Too much effort. Too much adrenaline swilling around.

I swam with closed eyes stopping myself from looking at the lights till I'd counted to a hundred.

Around nine hundred they started coming closer. At eleven hundred I knew we would make it. At twelve hundred Old Nick turned again trying to swim at right angles to the shore. I cursed him, hauled at him but he seemed determined and I was on the brink of letting him swim to his death when I had an idea.

Pulling off my T shirt I reached up and forced it down over his eyes or his one remaining eye effectively blinding him.

He stayed with me now but his strokes grew more laboured, he was finding it harder to keep his head above the surface and it was a long exhausting final hundred yards or so before our feet touched sand.

The lights I'd seen were way above us now on the cliffs. The moonlight was bright enough to show we'd landed in a small cove. I let the horse go and sank exhausted onto the white sand, lay on my back listening to the waves washing gently up the beach.

Suddenly I heard a soft thud and felt the ground vibrate as Old Nick went down on his side just yards from me. On hands and knees I moved towards him. His breathing was heavy and irregular. I eased my T shirt from his head and patted his neck, 'You're just tired, you'll be okay.'

Forcing myself to stand I walked towards the cliffs hoping the moon would pick out a path upwards but I could find nothing. The cliffs formed a crescent around the bite of sand and I could find no safe way of negotiating the climb in the dark.

But the night was warm, sleeping out would prove no hardship so I went back and lay down close to Old Nick whose breathing seemed to have settled a bit. I had plenty to occupy my thoughts but sleep must have come quickly. The next thing I remember was waking up in the blindingly bright sunshine lying beside a dead horse.

Old Nick lay on his side stiff-legged like a fairground horse fallen from a carousel. Small crabs scuttled around his body and black flies were feasting in his empty eye socket. At first I thought he'd simply died of exhaustion but I found a huge gash in his thigh which he must have got during the sinking. He'd performed miracles even to reach the shore. Poor bastard.

I looked out to sea: no sign of Old Nick's travelling companions. I hoped they'd made it ashore somewhere else but I doubted it.

The cliffs enclosing the cove were over a hundred feet high but I could now see a path leading up.

I scooped my yellow T shirt from the hot sand. The morning sun had dried it and I shook it clean, put it on and headed up the cliff path. At the top I turned

183

again to look out over the blue water: nothing but a few boats.

A walk of around a mile brought me to a main road where I hitched a lift to Bridgetown in an old truck carrying coconuts which drummed and rattled so loudly I could hardly hear the driver speak. I'd told him I'd pay if he'd take me straight to Gary's estate in Saint John's district but between my unkemptness and uncertainty about where the place actually lay he decided he'd just drop me in the capital.

I spent the journey trying to put my thoughts in order. What had caused the explosion? Had it been an accident? If it had then it was Gary Rice's sixth and costliest so far. Was Clemence's absence significant? Was the target simply the boat and cargo or was I meant to go down with it?

My thoughts went back to that dark car park at Huntingdon and Ernest Goodwin's warning about potential violence if I didn't give up on Conway. I quickly discarded the notion, any violence from that quarter was sure to be much more direct. Having said that, if Conway disappeared from the Archangel then they might have been happy to take their chances of me going down in an unfortunate 'accident' on the same boat.

That opened another theory. If Clemence had sussed we were on his trail and the boat somehow held evidence to prove Conway had been on it then the sinking would prove most convenient for him and his paymasters whoever they were.

The general surroundings gradually took my attention as we bumped and bounced along the potholed road leading down into Bridgetown. I became aware of the strange assortment of buildings, the colourful people.

Men of all ages, mostly black, clustered around the numerous rum shops drinking and playing dominoes in the shade. Kids threw a basketball at a ring nailed to a telegraph pole. People moved around slowly. From brilliantly coloured wooden shacks no bigger than a one car garage smiling women and children waved as we passed.

Approaching the capital the houses grew more opulent, the traffic increased, horns sounded incessantly, a cacophony of different tones. There were big blue buses and yellow minibuses. A huge Rastafarian drove a donkey cart loaded with fruit.

The whole atmosphere made me smile, temporarily took my mind off the fact that somebody might be trying to kill me. The coconut man dropped me at a taxi rank and I thanked him and told him I was a jockey and that he should look me up if he was at the next racemeeting.

He smiled, humouring me, 'Sho thing, Mistah!'

I was half tempted to make my first stop the local police station but decided it would be better to go straight to Gary's estate and call him first. A talkative taxi driver drove me on the twenty minute trip to Headlands.

After climbing for about two miles we swung into the estate through big buff coloured pillars bearing a brass plaque with Headlands on it in six inch lettering.

I recalled what Gary had told me about the place.

The eastern border of the huge plantation housed his racing interests in the shape of a training complex with twenty-five boxes, a big white house, several smaller cottages scattered around, a big swimming pool and terrific views.

185

Set on land well above sea level if you jumped on a horse and galloped east in a straight line for just over a mile you'd take off from cliffs eight hundred feet above the Atlantic and hear only huge waves crashing on the reefs below as you fell.

It was just past noon when we pulled up in front of the big white house. Insects buzzed and chirruped among the white, pink and yellow shrubs in the garden which stretched a couple of hundred yards on all sides to borders of colourful bushes.

Behind these in the corners loomed groves of coconut trees.

The area between the lawns and the front of the house was block paved in silver grey with a darker grey path leading to the high entrance door and hall.

As the taxi stopped the door of the house opened and Gary Rice came out, his face breaking into a wide smile when he saw me. He even applauded lightly.

'Small world,' I said.

He laughed, white teeth gleaming in the sunshine. He wore floral shorts and a baggy lemon T shirt. 'Any money in those shorts?' I asked, 'Mine is floating around off the coast.'

He hurried back inside and returned with twenty dollars which he insisted the delighted driver keep.

An arm around my shoulder he led me into the cool terracotta tiled hall, through the house out onto a long terrace overlooking the garden giving me brief hugs all the way and offering variations of, 'Thank God, I thought you were dead'.

We sat at a white table on the terrace and Gary introduced me to Letitia, the maid. She was a big lady though her roomy black and white uniform covered most of her body fat. But her shoes were too tight and

186

brown flesh spilled uncomfortably over the edges. She insisted on laying a blue and white check tablecloth before pouring drinks for us.

I settled for a cocktail of fruit juice and ice. Normal feelings like thirst and hunger were beginning to reassert themselves.

Gary was leaning across the table still staring at me like I was his long lost lover. 'What happened?'

I told him.

'Sorry about the horses. Did my best.'

'Don't worry. You're safe, that's the main thing. The police have been here this morning, they had no report of the sinking though it seems the Harbour Master did. They've gone to interview him.'

'When did you arrive?'

'Came in on the dawn flight.'

'You got some news on Clemence?'

'Not a lot. I heard he skipped the trip and I know he flew back here last Friday.'

'What day's this?'

'Tuesday.'

'The whatth?'

'The fourteenth.'

I nodded, rubbed my stubbly chin and drank some more, trying to adjust to the sunlight and the powerfully sweet smells from the garden below us. 'When did you hear about the sinking?'

'Not long after I got here. I knew the boat should have docked yesterday evening. I rang the port authorities.'

'So one of the crew did report it?'

'Looks like it.'

'But nobody sent out the rescue services.'

'Nope.'

'D'you think it was an accident?'

'I very much doubt it but whether we can convince the police is another matter.' Gary reached across to the drinks trolley and poured both of us more juice.

I said, 'I suppose it depends on the cause. If a boiler blew or an engine or something...'

'The boat was carrying explosives.'

I sat forward. 'Pardon?'

'Explosives. Part of the official cargo.'

'For who?'

'They were for underwater work on Martinique. A new harbour's being built there.'

'I'm not trying to be wise after the event here, Gary, but with your recent record wasn't that just a teeny bit dangerous?'

'I didn't know till this morning we were carrying it. Clemence handled all the orders.'

'Well that explains it, then.'

Gary told me the explosives should have been in a safe container, should have been bombproof. He also told me the reason for his sudden visit: Carroway, his trainer, had quit and moved out.

'When?'

'Saturday, the day after Clemence got back here.'

'Another phone threat?'

'Backed up this time by burning four of my horses to death.'

I stared at him. 'When?'

'Friday night. Come on, I'll show you.'

CHAPTER TWENTY-ONE

He led me into the L shaped yard of white slatted wooden boxes, with shiny blue doors. A dozen

188

curious equine heads looked out at us. At the top right stood the blackened remains of a short row of boxes, a burnt shell rising just a couple of feet off the ground.

Their close neighbours were charred but sound. 'How'd they save the others?'

'Lots of fire extinguishers and brave lads.'

'So why couldn't they rescue the horses?'

'Somebody had shoved padlocks through the bolts in each door.'

'Dirty bastards!'

We stood staring at it. Gary told me the police had interviewed everyone in the yard. 'Did you mention Clemence to the police?'

'No, not yet. There's nothing we can pin him down to just now and I was thinking he might be more useful if he was still in circulation.'

'How much longer can you afford to have him in circulation?'

'Not for long, the insurance people are already shitting themselves.'

'You insure all your stuff with the same company?'

'Uhuh. Well, all my racing stuff and everything over here.'

I pulled a painful face. Gary grimaced, 'I know, the old no claims bonus is long gone.'

We were about to go back inside when we heard faraway hoofbeats coming nearer. Gary said, 'Second lot coming back. Want to see them?'

'Sure.'

Within minutes they appeared by the burnt boxes and wound their way in to spread out in the yard, their lads dismounting, not a white face to be seen. The horses looked healthy enough but there was a generally depressed air among the staff.

'Who's running things just now?'

Gary pointed to a little bloke in khaki breeches and an orange sweatshirt. 'Amory, he's the head lad.'

'Will he cope?'

'I don't know, I'll watch him over the next few days.'

As Amory headed the others in leading the horses in a cooling walk round the yard he nodded to us, forcing a smile, not looking particularly confident.

Suddenly we heard a shout and a girl came running into the top end of the yard, black skinned, black dreadlocks bouncing as she tucked a pink T shirt into tight black breeches. She sounded angry, 'Hey, Endell yuh bastard! Yuh promise yuh wake me! Yuh said you mek sure I ride second lot! Yuh didn' knock mah do'!'

She reached the object of her abuse, a youngster a few inches taller than she was at around five six, walking a lanky chestnut round. 'Endell, yuh heah what I sayin?' He smiled looking impish and the other lads and girls smiled and chuckled.

Gary was smiling too. He said, 'The amazing Kari Parsons.'

The closer she got as they walked towards us the more clearly I saw her. Older than I'd first thought, early twenties, very attractive despite a large square scar on her cheek. Lithe and athletic and obviously quite wild.

Gary said, 'That's her brother she's yelling at, Endell.'

It was only when she raised her fists to try and punch her brother that I noticed her hands were bandaged. It obviously hurt her to use them so she tried elbowing him instead. He laughed and the others began shouting encouragement. Some of the

190

horses started getting a bit jumpy.

Gary gave Amory, the head lad, a minute or so to intervene but he just walked round sheepishly so Gary called her over. She marched across and stood in front of him as though she saw Gary every day.

Fine featured with soft looking skin she stood, big bright eyes burning indignantly, chin thrust upwards, the scar on her left cheek almost proudly displayed.

'What's wrong, Kari?'

'That bast ... that Endell he tol' me las' nigh' he call me this mo'nin tuh ride out. He nevuh call me, he lie, he knew muh pills mek I sleep.'

'Let me see your hands.'

She stuck them under her arms. 'They okay, Mistuh Rice.'

He held his own hands out insistently and slowly she offered hers. They were bandaged from wrist to just below her fingertips where it looked like they'd been deliberately peeled back. Tiny islands of blisters could be seen. Gary pointed them out and said maybe she should wait another day or so.

'I okay Mistuh Rice, tough skin!'

'Can we maybe talk about it later, Kari, I've got a few things to sort out.'

She considered it, obviously not pleased but simmering down gradually since it was the boss. She glanced at me. Her spirit alone put me on her side but I thought I'd better offer no more than a non-committal smile.

Gary said, 'This is Eddie Malloy, my jockey from England, you've heard me talk about him.'

'I'm gonna be a jockey,' she declared in almost a challenge to me.

'We could use some of your spirit,' I said.

The compliment took some of the fierceness out of her glare. Gary said, 'Can we see how you are in the morning, see if you can ride then?'

She nodded. 'I be okay.'

'We'll see.'

'I will,' she said turning away, determined to have the last word then marching past the rest of them with her nose in the air.

We walked back towards the house. Gary said, 'What do you think of Miss Kari Parsons?'

What I thought was that she was far and away the most attractive girl I had ever met. 'They should name a hurricane after her,' I said. 'What happened to her hands?'

'Got them burned trying to save those horses on Friday night. She had to be held back from climbing into the boxes, was sure she could persuade them to jump the locked doors.'

Jeez, a hurricane right enough.

*   *   *

Gary soon realized that Amory wasn't quite up to running the place and returned him to his head lad duties. Amory seemed very relieved. Gary said that with the exception of a couple of short trips to Europe he intended to remain on the island until the police sorted things out.

I agreed to stay and help out with the proviso that I had to be back in England for the start of the new season in six weeks time. Also I wasn't as confident as Gary in the abilities of the police to nail the saboteurs. I wanted to know a lot more about Gary's agent, Clemence, and what involvement he'd had, if any, with Conway's disappearance.

192

I also wanted to know who had reported the sinking of the Archangel and why he hadn't mentioned that one person and three horses were unaccounted for.

Gary offered me the choice of a room in the big house or a cottage to myself in the grounds. I chose the cottage which was roomy, with white clapboard walls and a broad porch running all the way round decorated with plants and hanging baskets.

Inside it was painted lime green with cool polished wooden floors, rush mats, air conditioning, brass ceiling fans, a wide pink jacuzzi bath and a four poster bed covered by an elaborate canopy hung with lace curtains.

Gary smiled as I looked around. 'It was meant as the honeymoon suite. I've got a dozen cottages dotted around the estate. My intention at the start was to run a holiday place here, just haven't got round to it yet.'

'So who's using them?'

'Stable staff mostly.'

'Beats the hell out of a hostel.'

He handed me a key. 'As soon as you're settled I'll drive you into town and get you some new clothes.'

'It won't take much settling, it's not as if I've anything to unpack.' I thought ruefully of my kit bag and the two bottles of fine malt which had probably helped depth charge it to the bottom of the sea.

'You want to go now, then?'

'Why not?'

In Bridgetown I got what clothes I needed on Gary's credit card. He hired me a blue Mazda which was the best car they had. Then we went to the police station where Gary introduced me to the guy in charge of the investigations into his recent accidents, a Detective Sergeant named Jerome Handler.

Handler said he hoped I had better luck than Berman Carroway. I explained I wasn't the replacement trainer, just there to help out for a few weeks. Handler said he hadn't yet got round to checking any details at the Harbour Master's office but he'd do so that afternoon and get back to us.

I suggested to Gary that we pre-empt him. Gary wanted to visit Clemence's office so we agreed to split and meet up in half an hour.

The harbour was just a couple of minutes walk from the Police Station. Squinting in the sunshine and trying to take in the mixture of smells carried in from the water I headed for the seafront.

At the Harbour Master's office I had to wait fifteen minutes before a fat white guy serious and uncomfortable looking in a shirt two neck-sizes too small appeared.

He told me he did have information about the Archangel but was reluctant to divulge it to a 'civilian'. I tried being charming but it didn't work so I told him about my friend in the Police Station across the road and suggested he may want to spend an hour or so giving a full official statement to him.

Sweating, he looked at me, cold-eyed, wanting to tell me exactly where to go but weighing it against falling an hour behind in his work.

I said, 'Give me five minutes and save yourself a lot of time and hassle.'

He stared then agreed, 'I have to get my papers.'

He came back with a blue folder and confirmed that the loss of the Archangel had been reported to him at nineteen twelve last evening.

'Who reported it?'

194

'The captain.'

'Mr Dann?'

'That's right.'

'Did he say if there were casualties?'

'No casualties, all crew and passengers taken off on lifeboats.'

I tried to see the form he was reading. He slid it further away from me.

'What time did the boat go down?'

He stared warily probably wondering how much more detailed the questions were going to get. He said, 'Why do you want to know?'

'I've got a personal interest.'

'It sank just after eighteen hundred hours yesterday.'

Right time. 'And the cause of the sinking?'

'Subject to an inquiry.'

'A big hole in the side perchance?'

He didn't answer.

'Caused by an explosion?'

He gathered his papers back into the folder and got up. 'A report is being prepared for the police, Mr Malloy, I suggest you direct further questions through the friend you have there.'

'I think he may want to come over right away. I think you might have to drop everything else and do that report for him.'

He shrugged. His eyes went cold again and he turned to leave. I said, 'Can you tell me where to find Mr Dann?'

He kept walking.

'Please! It's urgent.'

He turned and smiled, 'Ask your friend in the police force.'

I waited in the car park for Gary as arranged and

195

promised myself a pair of sunglasses as, narrow-eyed, I watched him come towards me.

'Any luck?' I asked.

'Nah. Clemence hasn't been seen since he came back on Friday and he's only telephoned once.'

'Or so his office tell you.'

'I don't think they've much to hide, Eddie. It's just a little place that hires out office and secretarial facilities to a number of different people, all they really do is take messages. What about you?'

'The skipper reported the sinking at just after seven so it must have been pretty much the first thing he did as soon as the lifeboat docked.'

'But he somehow forgot to mention you were missing?'

'Seems like it.'

'So not only was it not an accident, it looks like Mr Dann could have been in on it?'

'He'd sailed with Clemence before on almost every trip. He definitely did not want me to be rescued, he's got to be in the frame somewhere but why risk everybody else's life including his own?'

Gary slid his sunglasses up into his thick hair. 'No risk really, was there? You were what, maybe five hundred metres from shore, two lifeboats, calm sea, you only got into trouble because you tried to save the horses.'

'So if the boat was sunk the boat was the target?'

'Or the cargo, if you'd gone down with it maybe that would have been a bonus.'

'Thanks a bunch.'

He smiled. 'Not for me, for whoever's behind it.'

'What about the cargo then? What else were we carrying?'

He pulled a sheet of paper from his pocket and we

196

dissected the contents over lunch in a nearby bar. But there was nothing special on board, including the horses which were regular passengers for several of the carriers who worked the route. Nothing of immense value apart from the boat itself.

The next step seemed to be locating Mr Dann or Clemence but Gary was uneasy about bringing our suspicions into the open while his firm of investigators were still working on Clemence, still trying to get something solid.

I chewed some juicy mango flesh. 'But what if they don't? It could take months and if he is behind all this God knows what it will have cost by then.'

'True.'

'I mean even if we could link him to Conway, even if it was Conway's body in that packing case all Clemence has to say was he was doing his job, winning orders. He'll deny any knowledge of the contents of the case and deny responsibility for losing it over the side.'

Gary scowled, bit his knuckle absent-mindedly.

I said, 'Now what I would like to find out is if any other packing cases left England especially around the time of your break in, your car theft. Where did the paintings and the antiques end up? Where did the Porsche go? What happened to the two horses in your missing horsebox? What's the chances we'll see them soon under other names racing round the Garrison? If we can tie any of those down to Clemence then the hardest part's over, we've proved he's a criminal. That would make it much harder to deny involvement if Conway's body was in that packing case.'

Gary brushed back his hair with his fingers only for it all to slide luxuriantly forward again. He sipped

197

pineapple juice. '*I'm* convinced, Eddie, you're preaching to the converted but it still doesn't tell us where we go from here.'

'Well if Clemence is so hard to pin down let's try for Mr Dann, see what he has to say.'

'Fine, you're the boss.'

We went back to see DS Handler, asked him to find out where Mr Dann lived, told him Gary needed him to fill out a report form for his insurance company. Handler said he'd see what he could do.

Struggling to keep up at times as Gary teased me I followed his silver Merc in the Mazda tooting as I passed the coconut man who'd given me a lift this morning.

Late afternoon Handler rang. Mr Dann's address was care of Clemence's office who claimed they had no personal information on the skipper other than next of kin, a sister living in Virginia, USA.

He had to be somewhere on the island. He was a sailor and I reckoned if I spent enough time hanging around the bars in the harbour area there would be a fair chance of finding out more about him.

Endell Parsons, the stable jockey and brother of the fiery Kari, volunteered to take me on a pub crawl in Bridgetown that evening. He drove a little red sports car expertly avoiding potholes, even in the darkness that early sundown brought to Barbados.

He was fine featured like his sister though his eyes were set much wider apart. Short dreadlocks bobbed like tiny dark snakes as he talked animatedly. He had strong very white teeth and a general look of natural cheeriness. About five six he'd have weighed no more than eight stone.

He wore pink shorts and a multicoloured beach

shirt. Yellow flip-flops slapped against the driving pedals.

He told me about the racecourse where I was due to ride next week, about all the characters, the horses, his ambitions, his women, which brought me onto the subject I really wanted him to talk about, his sister.

He was a bit reluctant at first, protective, but as the night wore on and we moved from bar to bar alcohol loosened his tongue and I learned a fair bit about Kari Parsons.

The big scar she had was cut into her left cheekbone by her father when she was thirteen. He'd wanted Kari to work as a prostitute and she'd refused. It seemed the father had abused both of them throughout their lives and Kari, a year older than Endell, had been the strong one, the one who, finally sick of the treatment they were getting at home, led Endell away when he was fourteen.

They went on the run moving on each time their father caught up with them until finally finding peace when he was stabbed to death in a knife fight three years ago. That was when they both settled down at Gary's estate where they'd been ever since.

That was as productive as the night got. Endell talked to a few people and three or four mentioned a place called the Southern Parish Club where Mr Dann sometimes drank. We went there and stayed till 2 a.m. but he never showed.

Next day Gary asked me to represent him at the races. The stable had three runners, Endell was to ride. I travelled in with him. His sister Kari accompanied Amory the head lad in the horsetrailer.

Endell cheered me up on the drive to the races, bumping through potholes, tooting at every pretty girl we passed followed by suitably suggestive calls

199

and gestures. All the girls took it in good part.

Endell explained. 'See, what yuh gotta unnerstan' here, Eddie, is that sex is big fun. Big fun. It's out in the open. People talk about it an' do it an' enjoy it. Pregnan' woman she got status here, guy with loadsa kids is a big hero.'

'And that's the kind of hero you want to be?' I said.

He laughed. 'Workin' on it, man, workin' hard!'

The racetrack was laid out on the Garrison Savannah, a big parade ground where the British forces used to drill when stationed there in the early part of the century.

Its main business now was sport, mostly racing. We got there a couple of hours before the first race and, with great enthusiasm, Endell showed me around, taking pride in acknowledging all who spoke to him, showing off to me how many people he knew.

To each he introduced me as 'big time jock from Englan', gonna be champ nex' year'. Many said they'd heard of me, most out of politeness and some because they thought they should have. I had more invitations for drinks than I could handle and I was impressed by the genuine friendliness and lack of formality.

There was very little social segregation, no sour faced gatemen or strict dress codes. It made me realise again how much the English class system had to answer for.

Endell had a ride in the first and left me with instructions to go and join the horse's owners in the bar but I thought I'd wander around on my own for a while.

The course was filling up both in the stands and the free area in the middle. Punters themselves had the same outlook the world over. Happiness, hope and

200

anticipation—until the first race was run and the age old search for excuses started.

There was a real buzz about the place as people drank glasses of rum, and beer from bottles, laughed and planned and argued the case for their fancies.

The sun shone in a clear sky, glinting on the white rails, pushing the temperature to the mid-eighties.

The track itself was tight and constantly turning, six furlongs round and narrow, the turf well watered. A sand training strip ran alongside the track on the inside of the rails.

The horses came out for the first and I watched them canter to the start, the jockeys crouched and stylish like the best Americans. Many steered with blue, orange, yellow or red bridles adding to the bright colours all around. Anyone flying over this tight circle would be looking down on a moving kaleidoscope of brilliant intensity.

I wandered down past the stables area where horses were being walked, saddled, groomed. One tiny black lad held a hose spouting a powerful jet of water over the leg of a narrow bay horse. The sun's rays showed a rainbow in the bouncing spray.

Four men sat laughing and shouting at a round white table balanced unevenly on the grass. At least a dozen open beer bottles were spread around. They wrestled untidily with newspapers and flourished racecards in each other's faces arguing loudly the merits of their selection.

Smiling at the prospect of what this place would be like come the last race I turned away but some familiarity in one of the voices clicked the tumblers in my memory bank.

I turned to look at him. His big broad back was towards me. I walked closer, coming in from the side.

It was the same guy. Last time I saw him he had a gun in his hand, wanting to shoot Old Nick.

It was George, the big sailor from the Archangel, and there had to be a very good chance he would know where Mr Dann was.

CHAPTER TWENTY-TWO

The whole area was busy so the group didn't notice me as I circled the table at a distance of about twenty-five paces. I wanted to see if I recognised any of George's partners from the boat.

He was the only one.

Decision time. Should I approach him or just hang around and follow him after the races? The correct choice depended on another crucial question, one I didn't have the answer to: was George implicated in the sinking? He was the only one besides Mr Dann who'd sailed with Clemence previously.

The fact that no one called out the rescue services that night suggested that the whole crew were involved. Then again, if they were, Clemence or Mr Dann would have to have paid all of them off and risked somebody talking too much.

Then the key factor came to me, the one which told me the majority of them couldn't have been involved: there was blind panic that night after the explosion. If they'd known it was going to happen everyone would have been ready, the lifeboat would have been thoroughly prepared. Instead they'd jammed its ropes in their haste to lower it.

I watched George. The man next to him was engrossed in study, his racecard close to his face.

Seeing him distracted George slyly stole his beer and drank it.

So, I was assuming George wasn't involved in the sinking. Next questions were, did he know where Mr Dann was, and, would I be able to get the information from him if he did? I turned an idea over in my mind as the first race went off and when it was finished and George's group had thrown away losing tickets and settled down for the post mortem I wandered across to the table and stood at his shoulder.

Seeing the eyes of his friends look up he turned, took a moment to recognise me then gave me a welcome far heartier than our acquaintanceship deserved. His reaction told me that either he was trying to cover the fact that he'd never expected to see me again or that he was going to hit me for money before we parted.

He introduced me to his friends. One said, 'Hey English, you know Manchester? I gotta girl there. Goin' over one day.' His friends jeered and laughed. I asked George to come and have a drink so I could talk to him. He was out of his chair so fast he knocked it over.

George said he was glad to see me. His understanding of what had happened that night was that Mr Dann had told everyone on the lifeboat I was safe, that he'd seen me launch the other lifeboat and that he'd report everything to the coastguard. He hadn't seen Mr Dann since.

I could tell George was anxious to begin the process of milking me for cash, talking about a 'sure thing' in the next race, claiming he knew the jockey.

I promised to invest in it and have some on for him too and his big eyes sparkled and widened and he slopped some beer down his pale green shirt. I said, 'George, I've been talking to my boss and he says I've got to buy another boat here. He says I should get Mr Dann to help me pick it.'

He frowned and shook his head, 'No need, Mistah Malloy. I de man fuh boat buyin'. Mistah Dann spen' too much. Bad luck too askin' Mistah Dann. Yuh boss doan' wan' bad luck on new boat.'

It took me five minutes to persuade him it had to be Mr Dann. He finally agreed when I promised him a job as first mate on the new boat and said he could come along when we bought it.

After all that and two more rounds of drinks it turned out he didn't know where Mr Dann was or where he lived, said he moved around from woman to woman. But he did know where his favourite drinking hole was. He also knew that he played dominoes there at least three nights a week.

The Southern Parish Club, the place Endell and I had spent hours in last night.

I gave George twenty dollars to bet his 'sure thing' and told him there'd be another hundred if he could find Mr Dann for me though I stressed George wasn't to speak to him. 'Just call me at this number if you find out where he is.'

He took the piece of paper I'd torn from the racecard and I left him to finish his drink.

I hurried down the steps and stood against a pillar waiting for George to come out which he did about ten seconds after me and in a hell of a hurry. We were moving against the flow of the crowd wending its way back to the stand as the runners for the second cantered to the start but George's height made him easy to follow.

If he'd been bullshitting me back there he was a

204

superb actor but I couldn't take the chance of him going straight to a phone and calling Clemence. Within a minute his sole intention became obvious as he approached his buddies whooping and shouting and waving the money I'd given him, kissing the notes three or four times before sitting down again to no doubt kiss them goodbye.

I watched Endell ride a fine race to lead all the way in the second and hold on by half a length after his horse had tried to run out at the tight bend by the stables. It was customary for the winning owner and trainer to lead the winner back in past the stand.

With Endell smiling widely in the saddle Amory and I did the honours.

The stable's other runner was beaten in a photo finish. After racing Endell was keen for us to stay on and party. He told me he'd picked out a couple of girls. I told him I wasn't really interested as I was hoping to persuade his sister to have a drink with me that evening.

He looked puzzled. 'En' one fuh you, anyway,' he said, meaning the girls he'd spotted, 'both fuh me!' We laughed and I left him to it, intending to go to the stables and find his sister but she found me first, almost running straight into me as I left the paddock area.

In cream shirt, black breeches and tan boots she looked wide-eyed, excited, the scar on her cheek standing ridged as though engorged with blood.

'Mistuh Malloy, where's En'll?'

'He just left. Is something wrong?'

She looked up at me, unsure whether I was the first who should be told. She licked her beautiful full lips and said, 'De trailer gone! Somebody stole 'er!'

'When?'

205

'Now! I tek Capricorn aroun' to load 'er up, trailer gone!'

Capricorn was the last of our three to run. 'What about the other two horses?'

Opening her arms and shrugging helplessly she said, 'They gone, too.'

'Where's Amory?'

'Donno.'

* * *

Amory turned up safe. The horses didn't. They were found that evening at the bottom of the cliff near Headlands. The eight hundred foot drop onto the rocks had broken almost every bone in their heavy bodies; Sentimentalist, a beautiful grey filly, had a part of the twisted trailer axle through her neck. The trailer itself, a big American type, thirty grand's worth, was a wreck of matchwood and twisted metal.

The police were baffled. Gary was shattered. Kari was devastated. Sentimentalist had been hers and she'd also lost one in the fire last Friday. When DS Handler turned up to take her statement she shouted and cursed at him damning to hell Handler and all his colleagues for being unable to stop the mayhem.

Her brother Endell had to lead her away and calm her down. Handler said he'd return later. Endell stayed with Kari all evening. Gary Rice arranged to buy dinner for an influential politician in the hope he could chivvy police investigations along and I spent several uncomfortable and fruitless hours parked outside the Southern Parish Club hoping to catch Mr Dann.

It was a miserable weekend for the yard. We'd lost six horses, everyone knew why Carroway, the

206

trainer, had gone, they were aware of the fire at the plantation and the explosion at the sugar factory. Gary had to go to Stockholm for a couple of days but he got everyone together for a pep talk before leaving telling them they'd be rewarded well for their loyalty if they saw this through.

Gary's political contact had promised to do what he could to maximise police involvement but the firm investigating Clemence seemed to have hit a brick wall. The only people he'd worked for in the past as an agent appeared to be legitimate companies though the investigators were painstakingly checking those companies for any tie ups.

They were also trying to get inventories of cargo carried from England on other shipping lines around the time of the thefts of Gary's property.

I spent a total of fourteen hours over the next three nights in or around the Southern Parish Club. Not a sign of Mr Dann and I was beginning to wonder if he too had been consigned to a packing case awaiting an ocean burial.

On Monday 20th June, McCarthy finally found time to return the numerous calls I'd made before leaving England.

'I could have been dead by now, Mac.'

'What do you mean?'

'I must have tried to get you ten times before I came over here.'

'I was very busy, Eddie.'

'On what?'

'Several things.'

'You're never too busy to return my calls when you want something from me.'

'Well funny you should mention it ...'

Mac had heard about the sinking but wasn't

ringing just to sympathise, he wanted to pick my brain about Gary Rice asking how well I knew him, what his main business was, stuff like that.

'Why do you want to know, Mac?'

'Can't really say just now.'

'You can't say but you want me to tell you all I know.'

'I'm doing somebody a favour, Eddie, you know what it's like.'

'Come on Mac, I work for Gary, he pays my wages.'

He sighed heavily. 'You know Bruce Cronin?'

'The owner?'

'Uhuh. He's also the MD of Silverdale Insurance, they handle a lot of racing stuff.'

'Yeah, I know them, based in Newbury.'

'That's right. Did you also know that your boss insures all his stuff with them and that this claim he'll be making for boat and cargo will be his seventh loss in eleven weeks?'

There were more claims to come but I didn't mention them.

'Yeah, well he's got problems.'

'He's got problems! This will take Silverdale's payout to over two million on his stuff alone.'

'They're an international company, Mac, they can stand it.'

'Not for much longer, not on top of all the other stuff they've been hit with lately. Bruce says there have been more claims in the past four months for fire, theft and wholesale damage than they've had in the previous two years and Rice accounts for a fair slice of it.'

'So they think Gary Rice is ripping them off? A guy who's got more money than you've had calories?

They think he'd risk killing his stable jockey and his boat crew? Get real, Mac.'

'But how much money has he got? Everybody hears all these multimillionaire stories but nobody really knows what he does for a living.'

Convinced Gary was straight I was getting angry. 'I can tell you what he doesn't do, he doesn't rip off insurance companies. And he doesn't run moaning to his friends when his luck turns bad. You can bet your life Silverdale Insurance and Bruce Cronin don't do too much complaining when they're counting the profits in millions.'

'Bruce is—'

'And, by the way, you'd be better dropping the old pals act and helping Gary Rice find out who's targeting him. Solve two problems then.'

McCarthy, as usual, persevered but got nothing from me but more hassle. I said, 'You must have better things to do. What about Conway, that's who I rang you about two weeks ago.'

He went quiet, sounded like he'd forgotten. I said, 'Conway, the little con man with the brain scan, remember? The guy who's supposed to have killed Bill Keating?'

He seemed suddenly on edge. 'That's a case for the police.'

'I know but haven't you been keeping tabs on it?'

'Not our job.'

He was beginning to sound uptight giving the impression he wanted to end the conversation.

'Why not?' I asked.

'It's not our problem any more.'

'But—'

'Look, I'll have to go. Speak to you soon.'

I hung up wondering why Conway's name made McCarthy so nervous.

CHAPTER TWENTY-THREE

Next day, Tuesday, I was due to ride in the invitation race in the afternoon so I got up early to ride out with the first lot. I entered the yard to the sound of gunfire.

All the box doors, top and bottom, were fully closed. Forming a semi-circle, sealing in the feed room door in the corner, stood four of the black grooms talking excitedly, crouched and ready to spring. Two carried spades, the other two had machetes. As I got closer I saw that Kari and Endell were the ones with machetes.

Around them lay the slashed bodies of maybe a dozen big grey rats, flies buzzing at the drying blood.

The window of the feed room had two smashed panes and standing on a beer crate aiming through the gap with a rifle was Amory, the head lad. He fired three in rapid succession shouting, 'Bastards! Bastards!'

Behind locked doors horses neighed in fright, their hooves clicking and scraping as they moved nervously around.

I hurried across and asked Endell what was happening. Poised staring towards the feed room he answered without looking at me.

'Somebody t'row rats in de feed room! Hun'reds!'

Amory's rifle jammed and he cursed and stepped off the crate trying to fix it. A few seconds later a big rat leapt through the broken window and lay dazed for a moment as it hit the cobblestones. The four beaters rushed at it screeching and swinging their weapons.

The rat recovered and bolted clear as metal struck sparks from the ground and curses filled the air.

Amory looked up at the window, wary now of stepping back onto the crate in case another rat jumped straight at his face. I hurried over to him. He was sweating, hands shaking as he reloaded the rifle.

'How many left?' I asked.

'Bullets?'

'Rats.'

'Plenty, plenty, plenty!'

'How'd they get in there?'

'Doan' know, jus' wan' 'em out!'

'You're not going to do it this way if there's a lot of them—'

Another one came flying past, brushing against my shoulder as it dropped. Amory yelped and aimed wildly as it landed and rolled over. The four beaters slashed at it as Amory tried to get a shot. I grabbed the rifle barrel, pushing it straight down. He looked at me in surprise. I said, 'You've as much chance of killing one of us or shooting your own foot.'

Kari's machete hit the rat's ribcage spraying blood onto clothes, some onto Amory's face. He screamed and backed away wiping the red smear madly with his pink T shirt. Kari whooped. Blood stained the white ragged bandages on her hands.

Grabbing the crate I rammed it against the broken window catching glimpses of a stream of grey bodies rushing around the feed sacks inside, their scurrying, scratching and squeaking making me feel sick.

The door looked secure though it had hurriedly been slammed shut pinning a broken grey body against the jamb. I called on Endell to get something to make a more permanent repair to the window. A

211

couple of minutes later he came back with small gauge chicken wire and a box of nails. We got three layers of wire up without any more escapees.

Amory and the grooms were angry I'd stopped them but I persuaded them that the rats must have been brought here and put in the feed room. If so it was unlikely anyone would have driven right into the yard, even in darkness, and unloaded them. I suggested we look round the rear of the building.

Still armed and bloodthirsty they filed grimly after me like some small band of rebels.

The feed room backed onto a rose garden. On the soft broad path beside it we found the tracks of a big car or small van. Among the flowers a plastic pipe led down to the ventilation hole. The mouth of the pipe had a bright red football forced into it. The ball was fixed to the sides of the pipe with broad silver tape.

Amory bent to rip it off. I stopped him. Rats would be bottlenecked in there ready to stream out. The lads volunteered to shoot and hack at them as they escaped but they'd miss far too many and the whole property would be infested.

We agreed the best bet was to dig a big hole right at the mouth of the pipe. More spades were sent for and we set about digging. An hour later we had a hole big enough to hold six men standing up.

Shortly afterwards we stood around the hole with a five gallon can of petrol, a sharp knife, two fire extinguishers and two old doors. One of the grooms was sent back into the yard with his spade to hammer on the feed room door and scare the rats again.

When we heard the banging Endell cut the tape, knifed the ball and pulled it free as the air rushed out. We all stepped back from the edges waiting for the exodus.

It didn't come.

Amory, at the far side of the hole, hunkered down to look into the pipe, 'De mouf jam wid dead 'uns.'

We all looked around at each other with the same thought in mind: any volunteers to clear it? Kari smiled wide and took the rifle, straddled the pipe mouth and rammed the gun barrel into it from above grunting as she worked it like a plunger, her loose denim shirt showing swinging breasts.

The dead bodies were pushed out first then a surging scratching squeaking river of rats became a mewling grey waterfall as they cascaded into the hole, biting, clawing, fighting to stay alive as others piled in.

It must have continued for three minutes and the dark sides of the oblong hole filled steadily like some hellish bath with bubbling grey hair, snapping teeth, long squirming tails and tiny desperate eyes.

Finally it stopped about two feet from the top and we quickly dragged the old doors across to cover the crawling mass. Through a narrow gap in the doors we emptied the full petrol can, made a bigger gap then stepped well away.

Two grooms stood at the house side, extinguishers ready and I lit a tightly screwed up ball of paper. Endell threw it through the gap.

There was a whoosh and a mild explosion as the fumes ignited blowing the doors six inches upwards then sending flames around their edges as they settled back. The thing I'll always remember about it was the terrible concert of squealing.

Kari seemed elated by it, seeing it as some revenge over whoever had caused her so much misery. I resolved to try and get to know her better while trying to convince myself the motive wasn't simply lust.

Endell and I left Amory and the others to clean up. Letitia, the maid, had already called the police.

We got changed and headed for our afternoon dates with two horses at the Garrison. Apart from riding in the race itself I was looking forward to seeing some of my weighing room buddies from England again.

Barbados was a popular holiday spot for the jump boys who could afford it though without Gary Rice this year that would not have included me. Six of us were due to compete in a special invitation race with the weights, normally at flat levels, framed accordingly.

Blakey was going to be there as was Jeff Dunning who'd organised the coup race. Jeff was quite a way below the top flight at home and I wondered how he'd managed to get an invite to ride here. Not that I was the most famous jock around; Gary had fixed the ride for me on one of his own horses.

This would be the first time I'd have seen Jeff since the Conway story broke and I was hoping to start repairing our friendship. Jeff and the others wouldn't know I was riding till they saw the racecard so there'd be plenty of ribbing when I walked into the weighing room.

And there was. They'd heard about the boat sinking and they teased me with predictable quotes about sea horses, water polo and midnight swims as well as the usual ribaldry.

One guy I hadn't expected to see was Neumman. He wasn't down to ride but he'd managed to get into the weighing room where he hung around stony faced and sulky each time our eyes met. I wondered how long he'd been on the island and who he'd come over with.

We cantered to the start and circled slowly enjoying the sunshine, recalling the discomforts of Plumpton in December, swearing we'd all lose a couple of stone and come and ride here permanently.

Back on a horse, among friends again, I felt great. Forgot about explosions, abductions and rats and shot out of the stalls determined to beat these guys so I could crow about it all through the winter.

And I'm sure I would have won if someone hadn't cut halfway through my right stirrup leather. I was leading the pack off the final bend when it snapped and I went down among the flashing hooves.

It was a nine furlong race, around half the distance any of us was used to riding so I was just guessing at the pace as I made the running. The course was barely six furlongs round, almost constantly turning. I was on a chestnut filly called Desert Girl. She seemed well balanced and keen, happy on the tight track.

The six behind were shouting but we were going too fast for me to hear what they said. I was laughing, loving this, the speed in the sunshine, the breeze cooling my face, the huge noisy crowd on the inside in streaks of multicoloured skin and clothes, the blare of the commentary so close.

As we went towards the final bend I was elated, I felt I'd kept just enough up my sleeve to ask the filly to quicken once more up the straight.

They were trying to get to me. I stayed tight to the rails. Sensed a nose snorting at my quarters. Heard whips on flesh. Adjusted my reins. Hit the last turn smiling, then the slenderest of warnings, a millisecond as I heard leather tear . . .

I was riding much shorter than usual, all my weight in the stirrup irons. If I'd been lolloping along in a three mile chase half sitting I'd have had a reasonable

215

chance of staying aboard but there was never a hope. The leather broke, my right leg snapped straight and I was on the grass, tumbling and rolling.

One horse seemed to jump over me then the kicks came, my back, my thigh, as though they were intent on keeping me rolling over. But in seconds they were past.

Heard the hoofbeats recede. Lay still.

Conscious. Eyes open. At ground level. Many feet close to my face, some booted, some sandalled, some trainered, some bare, their black toes fidgeting showing almost white underneath.

The body never adjusts to the potential shock of a fall at speed. Full internal emergency procedures usually start before you hit the ground and the gushing adrenaline can sometimes mask an injury. I went through my usual routine easing slowly onto my back and gently stretching and moving joints and limbs hoping for all the normal sensations, even pain which would carry the welcome news that I was not paralysed.

Everything seemed to be working. I looked up through a ring of mostly black inquiring faces at the blue sky and thanked God.

People were bending over me arguing whether I should be helped up or left alone till the medics arrived. By the time they did I was getting groggily to my feet. All around started applauding and I felt strangely embarrassed but I smiled and thanked them as two guys in white coats led me towards the ambulance.

The crowd, attached to me now for some reason, sauntered along behind. Even when the ambulance pulled slowly away swaying down the track they snaked after it singing and laughing in a fat dazzling conga.

Some place.

The Stewards held an inquiry then decided to call in the police. The stirrup leather had been deliberately damaged, cut partway through possibly by someone with a hacksaw.

After the doctor had poked and prodded and passed me fit a relieved looking Blakey and Endell walked me back to the weighing room to change. I was still dazed, bruised and a bit sore. The lads crowded round asking questions: was I sure I was okay? How did it happen? Who would want to cut the leather?

Jeff Dunning, suddenly friendly again, seemed particularly interested in why anyone would want to harm me. He asked questions aimed at finding out exactly what I was doing on the island. Was I still looking for Conway? Was I making any progress? Any suspects so far? He was very apologetic about doubting me over the lost coup money and suggested we meet later for a drink.

I said I'd call him.

Before leaving to pick Gary up from the airport I looked for Neumman. He was nowhere to be seen which was unusual. I'd have thought he'd want to be around to take maximum enjoyment from my discomfort.

I wondered if he'd been anywhere near my saddle peg before the race.

CHAPTER TWENTY-FOUR

Gary got off the Stockholm flight right on time impeccable as ever in a light suit, pale blue shirt and

217

speckled tie. Unlike the bedraggled sweaty tourists wandering dazedly through the Arrivals gate he looked like he'd just come from a refreshing half hour at his club.

He carried about four crocodiles' worth of overnight bag and gave me his usual sparkling smile as we shook hands.

The smile faded during the drive back as I brought him up to date on the latest 'accidents', the rats and the damaged stirrup leather.

He said, 'The way things are going the cops'll be moving in permanently at Headlands.'

'What about your man, the politician?'

'Seeing him again tonight for dinner.'

We spent a while discussing the invasion of rats. It marked a significant change in direction for whoever was targeting Gary. It was the first incident that wouldn't necessarily have cost him anything financially. Nothing substantial anyway. I said I thought we might have to start looking at why someone wanted him off the island or even off the estate.

He could think of no one who'd have anything to gain by forcing him to give up his interests in Barbados.

Mac's call about Silverdale Insurance was nagging at me. Just to help ease my mind I asked Gary straight out exactly what business he was in.

I could see he was thinking of ducking it. 'How badly do you want to know?' he asked me.

I shrugged, 'I suppose I could live without it.'

But he smiled and told me. He had numerous companies operating internationally concentrating mostly on the money markets. They traded in different currencies, precious metals. They borrowed cash, lent it out, brokered equities and bonds, raised loans on behalf of businesses and estates, managed credit card operations, and even literally made money with a banknote printing company in Germany.

His racing interests had started as a hobby but he tried to run things very much on a commercial basis. More big losses would make that impossible, make his assets, including employees, uninsurable.

'And it's just the racing side that's been affected so far?' I asked. 'No stolen gold, no fires at your moneymaking plant?'

He shook his head. 'Nothing, not a single problem among the other companies.'

When we reached the house Gary called all the staff together again, personally poured drinks for everyone and thanked them for standing by him. He repeated his promise to reward them well if they stayed on. Kari called out, 'Yuh heah what we done wit' dem rats, Mistuh Rice?'

'I did. Nice work.'

'You bet!' Kari said, smiling wide and holding up her drink to toast everyone. That brought a few smiles and I began to detect a more positive feeling among them, a determination not to be beaten. And the more I saw of Kari's personal qualities the more I admired her.

Chattering loudly they all went back to work, a few passing happy glances at me. I heard the words King Rat a couple of times. Funny what you have to do sometimes to earn respect.

Gary went up to the plantation next to give the same spiel to the workers there and by the time he got back the cops had arrived wanting statements from everything that moved. Handler was there and we spoke to him for some time though Gary didn't ask any favours. He preferred to organise those through his contact.

That night I took Kari to dinner and completely fell for her. Her exuberance and general love of life were evident in almost everything she talked about. She volunteered the information about the scar and told some horrific stories about life with her father.

She obviously cared deeply for her brother, Endell, and didn't resent his position as stable jockey in the least. She had her own ambitions and a zealot's belief that they'd be achieved. I wished I was a big owner or trainer who could help make her dreams of being a jockey come true and resolved silently to get a commitment from Gary to put her up whenever possible.

Over a final drink back at my cottage she let me unpeel the bandages and look at her injured hands. Most of the blistering had subsided leaving just red patchy skin though there must still have been some pain there. I thought of her this morning grasping that rifle and thrusting hard to break the bottleneck of rats in the pipe. That must have hurt her hands.

Then again the pain she'd been through in her first fifteen years made something like that laughable.

In the early hours of the morning I moved to kiss her. She smiled and led me outside onto the porch to where the moon hung large over the sea. Looking up at it she said, 'I wan' it to be romantic, like I read in books when I was li'l.'

I wasn't sure if this wild tomboyish woman was winding me up but I took the chance and kissed her very gently, very softly but long and deep and the memory of her swinging breasts, of her swaggering athletic entrance into the yard the first time I saw her made me want her very badly.

'Come back inside,' I said.

The moon lit her face. She looked at me, tempted I could see but her romantic ideals held up. 'Not tonigh', Eddie, not firs' nigh'. Mek yuh t'ink I a slut.'

As she tried to pull away I held her trying not to seem too desperate. 'I won't, honestly, Kari, I won't!'

I sounded extremely desperate.

She eased herself out of my arms. 'Tuhmorrow nigh',' she promised smiling and slipped away to her own cottage. I went to bed feeling deliciously frustrated.

*　　　*　　　*

Next morning over breakfast on the terrace Gary told me he'd arranged for the Archangel to be salvaged in the hope of finding some evidence.

'When's that happening?'

'Probably take about a week.' He picked up an orange, bit into the skin and peeled slowly sending the scent across on the mild morning breeze.

'Waste of time and money, Gary.'

He shrugged, kept peeling.

I said, 'All they'll find is a big hole in the side and a chance to make jokes about something fishy going on.'

He said, 'You never know. Experts can tell if an explosion's been set off deliberately.'

'After the evidence has lain at the bottom of the sea for two weeks? Good luck to them.'

'It's all we've got at the moment, we'll have to run with it.' He bit into an orange segment sending a narrow squirt of juice onto the tablecloth.

Frustrating. I went back to the lines I'd been thinking on yesterday. 'Are you certain there's no one who'd want to scare you away from Barbados?'

He frowned, chewing his orange in slow motion, shaking his head without much conviction.

I said, 'Fine it down. Is there anyone who wouldn't want you here, on this estate?'

He thought again then smiled and said, 'Only on a friendly basis.'

'What do you mean?'

'Phil Campbell, a good friend of mine, he spent half of last year trying to buy me out.'

I sat forward. 'Of here?'

'The lot, stables and all.'

'What did he want it for?'

'It wasn't him exactly, his company. He's the MD of a company with the second biggest sugar business on the island, plantations, refineries, transport, the works. Just looking to acquire a few more acres.'

'How hard did he pitch for it?'

'Very hard. But I know exactly why.'

I waited.

'There's been speculation for the past eighteen months that the Government want to take over all the sugar production. They already control around half of it and word was that they'd be willing to pay premium prices to buy people out.'

'And did your man know you knew that?'

'Course he did. He put his cards on the table, offered me a good price, one that he'd end up losing on if the Government thing didn't come off.'

'Which it hasn't?'

'Not yet but there's still every chance.'

'So Mr Campbell would still be interested if the place came back on the market?'

222

'Eddie, forget it. Phil's company already have over five thousand acres including the two estates adjoining mine so it wasn't as if this was exactly do or die for them. Anyway, I've been good friends with Phil for years. He's been on the phone commiserating over my problems here.'

'When?'

'Just before I left for Stockholm.'

Letitia brought tea on a trolley and poured two cups. Gary sat down opposite me in a cushioned chair and drew the saucer slowly towards him across the yellow tablecloth.

I said, 'It's worth looking into, Gary.'

His look hardened, 'Eddie, I'm his *daughter's godfather.*'

I stood firm. 'So you can't judge it objectively.'

His eyes rolled skywards. I pressed on, 'Let me have a look at it, Gary. No harm done if it's all above board.'

'I'll tell you what to do first, come and have dinner at his house tomorrow night.'

'What are you trying to do, make me like him?'

'Just come and meet him. You're your own man. Do what you like afterwards.'

'And you'll back me?'

He nodded solemnly and finished his tea. '*Carte blanche.*'

I agreed then we discussed security, decided what was needed. Gary asked me to ring around and take care of it.

I organised high powered security lights around the yard and the plantation buildings. The main houses were already alarmed. I ordered a review of all the systems, an electronic sweep for bugging devices and booked twenty-four-hour guards with

223

rottweilers to patrol the whole estate.

As dusk fell that afternoon I decided to soak in the jacuzzi before taking Kari out to dinner again. Just as I stepped into the bubbling water the phone rang. It was George, the big sailor from the Archangel. He told me Mr Dann had just walked into the Southern Parish Club.

'Are you there now?'

'Yes, suh. Waitin' fuh ma money!'

'I'll be there in fifteen minutes. Meet me outside.'

I drove at speed, parked and crossed to where George stood by the entrance to the club. He smiled wide, nodding as I crossed the road towards him. I said, 'He still in there?'

'Sure is!'

'Where's he sitting?'

'By de window. Playin' dominoes.'

Knowing how sly he could be I told him to wait while I peeped carefully through the doors. Mr Dann was there with three others.

George told me which car was his, a sleek red Toyota. I paid the big man off but he wouldn't leave till I assured him it wasn't yet boat buying time and that my business with Mr Dann tonight was nothing to do with him.

Tackling Mr Dann in the bar would have been silly so I settled down to wait in the car, knowing I might be there all night but reasoning that I might get lucky on the basis that he'd brought the car. Maybe it was just a flying visit.

An hour and a half later he came out and got in his car, put his lights on and pulled away at a leisurely pace. I followed. He set off northwards up the west coast for about ten miles then turned off to the right.

Approaching the turn I cut my engine and lights

and rolled the last hundred metres or so in what light there was from the moon. I got out, softly closed the door and walked towards the opening.

It was a long driveway, fifty paces maybe. The red Toyota sat in darkness. Then a light came on in the house. Cautiously, keeping to the edges, I crept forward.

Small cottage, once white now shabby, patchy. The window of the room where the light had just been switched on was on the left side, just low enough for me to look through if I stood on tiptoe.

I did, clutching the ledge, peering in. A small room. Mr Dann was alone inside, bent over, lifting stuff out of a box. I smiled. He was a wiry little guy but I was confident I could handle him. Suddenly from behind a single hand clasped my throat and a voice from a foot above me boomed, 'Come join we, Mistah Malloy, have a beer.'

Then he laughed and carried me inside.

CHAPTER TWENTY-FIVE

The giant had to duck to get through the doorway into a room at the back of the building. He put me down and shut the door behind him. He'd been sort of cackling under his breath as he'd carried me in but went completely silent now and stepped back against the door standing half to attention, a huge black guardsman.

Clemence sat at an old table set diagonally in the corner staring cold-eyed and thoughtfully rubbing his long chin. A bare light bulb reflected dully in his receding hairline and made his yellow short sleeve

225

shirt look dirty and his olive skin look even darker.

To his right, slouched in a wooden chair against the wall, was another big black guy shiningly bald, stern faced and silent, his wide jaws chewing lazily as he stared at me. He wore a pink vest with Sun of The Beach printed on the front. I wished he was on the beach now.

Mr Dann did not come in, leaving just the three of us.

The room, the whole house, smelt of stale piss and marijuana. Heavy dirty curtains covered the window. The floor was bare boards. Rubbish choked an old fireplace. Thoroughly depressing. Gloomy. Dangerous.

There was an air of menace you could have cut with the big knife Clemence produced from a drawer in the table. He laid it alongside a stainless steel corkscrew. Reached in the drawer again: stainless steel nutcrackers. Carefully placed beside the other instruments.

Half a dozen open beer bottles stood on the table. Clemence moved them so I could see his array of metal. Nobody had spoken yet. I'd expected jeering and mockery for being such a sucker, I'd have been more comfortable with that. Instead it was just cold professional ominous silence.

Clemence slowly opened the other drawer in the table. My eyes fixed on his hand like a rabbit on a snake as he pulled something out. It was a small melon. My mind searched crazily trying to make sense of this new ingredient. It drew a blank.

Clemence reached in again: a small sealed string bag of walnuts this time. He put them beside the melon. At least they went with one of the other items, gave me a shred of hope. He bent then to a crate at his feet and came up with a bottle of beer, put it down beside the walnuts.

Then he picked up the knife. He looked at me. I tried not to swallow, to let that bobbing Adam's apple convey the fear I felt. All three were looking at me though my eyes were fixed on Clemence's.

He lifted the melon, cut it in half, put the knife down, ripped the loose seeds out with his hands flinging the soggy mess on the floor, bit deep into a piece and, juice streaming down his chin, smiled a big white toothed smile. I almost smiled back in relief.

He took the corkscrew then and levered the top off the beer, cut the walnut sack open and started cracking nuts; all potential instruments of torture accounted for. Some tension-easing breath came out of my nostrils.

He drank and popped a nut in his mouth, I could see shards of it on his big glistening teeth as he said his first words, 'You don't learn very quickly, Malloy.'

No smile now just patient chewing.

I didn't reply.

'Mr Tuttle warned you, Mr Goodwin warned you. The boss did not want to harm you. He insisted you be given every chance. Now, regrettably, he has asked me to try and persuade you more forcefully to keep your nose out of things, to go home and resume riding horses.'

The big guy hit me from behind just below the ribs. Blinding pain. Sickening. I went down. Lay grunting, trying not to vomit.

Clemence said, 'Is that sufficient, Malloy? Will that make you go home?'

Couldn't answer. Gasping for breath. Angry that he'd always had the upper hand, this boss guy, whoever he was.

I pushed myself to a sitting position. The giant moved in again, his head hitting the light bulb. Clemence glared at him and put up his hand. The big guy backed off.

The creaking bulb swung in a circle glowing on each of us in a crazy pass-the-parcel of light. I tried to work out what to do. Couldn't. If the big guy hit me again I'd be out. A couple more after that and I'd be dead.

I sat there in pathetic bewilderment angry with myself now for being so stupid, so arrogant as to think I'd just catch up with Mr Dann and beat some information out of him.

Clemence looked past me at the giant and said, 'Take his pants off.'

I turned quickly, lashing out as he came at me. He was almost seven feet tall, laughing. His huge left hand gripped my shoulder lifted me and squeezed, virtually paralysing my right side. He pushed, bending me backwards over the table and grabbed the waistband of my flimsy khaki trousers. He ripped them open and down, boxer shorts tearing at the seams.

'On the floor,' Clemence said. He threw me down on my back. I grunted grasping my genitals in useless hope of retaining some dignity, providing some protection.

I looked up and Clemence stood over me.

In his right hand were the steel nutcrackers.

My stomach lurched. I felt my face blanch. Suddenly all the old jokes didn't seem funny any more.

The bald guy was there now too, still chewing slowly. Clemence said to him, 'Open his legs.'

He knelt at my feet, pushed my ankles apart.

Clemence looked down. 'Are you going home?'

My anger boiled over. 'I'm staying here so you can tell your boss to go fuck himself. And fuck you too!' I said.

'You won't be fucking anybody for a long time Malloy.'

I glared at him with a mixture of defiance and hate. No fear showing I hoped. He nodded and the giant bent over me and pulled my protecting hands clear as easily as a kid would move a doll's limbs.

Clemence smiled. 'Maybe I am not scaring you enough.'

He turned to the bald one. 'Give me that gum.' The guy stopped chewing and looked as puzzled as I felt. Clemence pushed his hand towards him, 'Give!'

The guy spat it into his hand and gave it to Clemence who put the nutcrackers between his teeth and pulled the sticky gum in two. He then fixed a piece inside each of the jaws of the instrument.

I almost forgot my terror as I stared trying to figure out what the crazy bastard was doing. He turned then to the table and took a beer bottle cap and stuck it to the gum. Carefully he did the same on the other side then held it up to the light showing the caps' jagged edges pointed inwards.

I almost passed out before he touched me.

He grinned. 'An expensive lesson, Malloy.'

I said nothing, wondering only how long the pain would take to push me into unconsciousness. All my previous agonies came back to mind: the breaks and fractures; a leg, both wrists, collarbones, ribs, all the result of falls. Falls in the mud and cold of a British winter. A beautiful safe British winter.

How would the pain compare with those limb breaks? With the incident last year when I was whipped till I bled?

Clemence got to his knees beside me his sweaty hands easing my penis aside.

I shut my eyes.

'Delicate,' he said softly.

A touch of the cool steel on my thigh.

The giant's acrid breath on my face.

Then my right testicle pushed gently, ridiculously gently, between the ragged jaws.

No snapping closed.

Slow, steady pressure increase. But the first ounce, the first gram sent a starburst, a constellation of agony upwards through every organ, every strand of intestine, every electrified nerve along its full searing length till merciful, heavenly overload blew the fuse box in my brain.

*   *   *

It must have taken me a full minute when I woke to recall what had happened. I lay on my side in the gloom, on the stinking floor where they'd left me.

Badly dazed. Trying to figure things out, where the ballooning ache in my groin had come from.

There was heat on my bare thigh, uncomfortable, just a spot the size of a coin. I reached to rub it. The heat hit my hand then. Groggily I looked round. Through a small hole in the curtains came a single circular shaft of light like a laser beam. I eased myself out of its path.

At least it was morning. At least I was alive.

I turned to lie on my back staring up at the dead bulb, the grimy flaking ceiling. Where were they? In another room? When would they come back?

The pain wasn't terrible now. Just a big spherical

230

ache in my groin and lower gut. I was scared to try and get up in case I couldn't, in case all the pain would come back.

I thought about Kari and almost smiled. She'd be proud of me. I was proud of myself. The way I felt I'd probably never sit down again let alone bump along on a horse but I was bloody proud that I'd held out, hadn't begged for mercy.

Then I remembered how I was supposed to be spending last night. And I remembered I'd dashed out without telling Kari I couldn't make our date.

My mind returned to the present. Where were Clemence and the gorillas?

I eased myself up a bit, leant on my elbow. Bottles and scattered walnuts still littered the room but if there was anyone else in the house they were keeping perfectly still. All I could hear was some birdsong and the distant sound of big waves breaking.

Gradually I worked myself into a sitting position, sweat beading on my scalp and brow. I forced myself to look down, to check the damage.

My penis lay bruised and limp against my thigh as though in mourning for its broken grotesquely swollen supplier.

I had to close my eyes again.

At least I was alive and everything was still there. How well it would work again was another matter but nothing had been separated from my body.

Castration had been my biggest fear. I resolved to be much more sympathetic to geldings in future. If I ever rode again.

God, what a story for the lads.

I almost laughed.

Still not a sound from the other rooms. Maybe they'd gone. It took two or three painful minutes to get to my feet. Couldn't put any weight on my right leg or it sent an explosion of pain upwards. I hobbled very slowly across to the window. Pushed a small gap in the curtains ... Nothing. Just trees, heavy undergrowth.

I leant on the desk staring at my torn trousers. Picked them up. Enough left to cover me though I'd have to hold them together. The grey boxer shorts were in tatters. I set about trying to get the trousers on. It took almost ten minutes.

Made it to the door. Turned the handle and hoped. It opened.

Nobody in the hall. No noise. Along the grubby hallway undisturbed, praying the front door would be unlocked. It was. I got out.

The sun shone on me. The scent of flowers and the sea cleaned the house stink out of my nostrils. I rested a moment against the wall, looked along the drive towards the road.

Wondered if my car was still there. Took hundreds of tiny steps to cover the fifty paces. Made the last few, through the opening, with eyes closed. Another short prayer. Opened them. The car was there.

The keys were in it. Only one problem left— driving. I managed to engage first gear and stayed in it all the way back to Bridgetown. I stopped by a callbox. Got a coin from the glove compartment and called Gary saying a silent please with each ring that he'd be there.

CHAPTER TWENTY-SIX

Gary picked me up and took me straight to a private hospital where a young doctor winced (though not half so violently as I did) as he inspected the damage. I told him a horse kicked me. 'Bloody good aim,' he said.

He told me they'd have to wait till the swelling subsided before they'd be able to give an accurate assessment of the 'long term effects'. There was little the hospital could offer but bed rest which I argued could be taken just as well back at the yard.

But Gary insisted I stay in overnight at the very least just in case. I was too sore and worn out to argue and they checked me into a big bright room with flowers, TV, telephone and views out over the gardens.

Cream pyjamas and a dressing gown were thrown in and Gary promised to bring some clothes for me. Blinds closed and air conditioning humming hypnotically I fell asleep and woke a couple of hours later to find Gary back at my bedside. He'd brought clothes and bad news.

'I'm selling up, Eddie. It's not worth it.'

Groin still anaesthetized by the injection I pulled myself into a sitting position. 'You're kidding!'

He shook his head, swept a swathe of his dark hair away with his fingers. 'Nah, this has brought it home to me. They could just as easily have killed you. The longer it goes on the more danger everybody's in. The more chance somebody will get killed.'

I was mad. 'Gary, come on, you're over-reacting! I've had the equivalent of a punch in the ribs and a very solid kick in the bollocks, they hardly held a gun to my head! You're not going to let them beat you just for that!'

He was staring at the floor, shaking his head. 'It's my responsibility, Eddie.'

'Well it's my balls, Gary, and if you think I ain't going after Clemence again once I can walk straight you're dreaming.'

He looked at me. 'I'm sorry, Eddie. This was never meant to be much more than a hobby for me and it's turning into a fucking nightmare.'

'What about your man in parliament? Get him moving. Tell him to get the cops off their arses and catch these bastards!'

'I'm afraid he's backing off a bit, has been from the start. A little bit too sordid for him.'

'Speak to DS Handler, then, he's okay, he'll do what he can.'

He shook his head again. 'No, Eddie, I'm moving out.'

'So they've won . . .?'

He wouldn't look at me.

'They've sunk your boat, killed, what, six maybe eight of your horses now? They've burned your boxes, filled your feed room with rats, tried to do me in at the races, had a go at using my right bollock in an amazing new Bajan recipe and now you're giving in! No reprisals? No revenge? Come on, Gary!'

He got up. 'Sorry, Eddie, I can understand how you feel. It's for the best. You'll see that when the fizz goes out of you.'

'Listen, Gary—'

He put his hand up, that steely business air suddenly about him. 'You listen, Eddie, it's over. I already spoke to Phil about the estate.'

I said, 'He's still very interested, right?'

He nodded. 'We're meeting tomorrow to put it on a more formal basis.'

I pushed myself forward. A stab of pain made me grimace. I said, 'Gary, listen, he's probably the guy

234

behind all this in the first place.'

'That's nonsense, I've already told you.'

'Try this then, do me a favour and try this. Meet him and say you're happy to sell up. Tell him what's happened to me and make it clear I'm scared and I'm heading back to England as soon as I'm well enough. Tell him you've already set things in motion. Then give it a couple of days by which time I'll be up and about again, then arrange another meeting.'

'Uhuh.' He was beginning to look thoughtful.

'Then, at that meeting, tell him you're having second thoughts. Tell him Malloy doesn't want you to sell up, that he's rebelling now and wants to stay here. Say that you feel indebted to me for what I've been through and that you need some time to think.'

'And what will that achieve?'

'I'll bet that within twenty-four hours the heavies are back gunning for me. They'll be concentrating even harder on persuading me to go back home. Very quickly.'

'That won't prove that Phil's put them up to it.'

'It'll keep him in the frame.'

He shook his head. 'No, Eddie, I've always had a good relationship with Phil, I'm not going to backtrack on a business deal.'

'Okay. Fine. You say you're seeing him tomorrow, you haven't formally offered him the chance to buy yet. Just try that line, tell him I was angry that you were thinking of selling and you just want a few days' breathing space till I come out of hospital. That's nothing more than the truth.'

He stood up, went to the bottom of my bed, gripped the metal rail then nodded reluctantly. 'All right, but I'm giving it a week maximum.'

Just after Gary left DS Handler arrived to take my

statement. I told him we couldn't keep meeting like this but he wasn't amused. He knew that even if they found Clemence and his gang they'd simply offer unbreakable alibis.

The doctor wanted me to stay at least three days but I couldn't afford the time. With Gary ready to admit defeat I had to turn something up very soon.

Next afternoon Endell, in luminous orange vest and yellow shorts, came to pick me up.

He fussed over me, carried my bag and took great care to settle me on a big blue rubber swimming ring which lay on the passenger seat. When I saw it I thought it was a wind up and looked across at him expecting a fit of giggling but he seemed quite subdued and didn't cheer up much during the careful drive back, though it might have been concentration: I'd warned I'd kill him if he hit even one pothole.

Towards the end of the journey it was obvious he was worried about something. I asked, 'What's up, Endell?'

He went on, 'We los' some guys up at de plantation.'

I looked at him.

'Las' night,' he said.

'Lost? Dead?'

'Naah! Jus' ran away.'

'Why?'

'Obeah.'

'What?'

'Obeah. Black magic. Trouble.'

'What happened?'

'Two guys gets dead lizard in matchbox. Two gets Duppy dust. They all gone.'

'What does that mean? What's Duppy Dust?'

'Powduh bones, maybe grave dirt. Duppy out to

236

get 'em. Bad signs fuh dem dat's scare' of Obeah.'

'People still believe in all that black magic stuff?'

'Some do.'

He was looking pretty apprehensive himself. I said, 'Do you?'

He laughed nervously as we pulled into the yard. 'Me? Naah!'

'Does it leave enough workers to keep the place going?'

'Fuh now but lots of 'em scare' dey gonna be nex'. Duppy real bad news.'

We stopped by the house and he helped me out. 'What's the Duppy?'

'Evil spirit. Some gets terrors over 'em, go jump off cliffs 'n stuff.'

Endell took my bag inside. I limped in after him wondering what these people would try next. They certainly had a hell of a repertoire.

Gary had arranged to meet Phil Campbell for lunch at Campbell's golf club. I waited anxiously for him to come back and tell me that Campbell had completely blown his top when Gary told him my determination was making him think again about selling.

But when Gary returned he told me Campbell hadn't seemed particularly perturbed. Campbell had said he'd be disappointed if things fell through but he hoped they wouldn't.

I thought he'd be confident they wouldn't because he'd be doing everything possible to persuade me to go. By this time Gary didn't know whose side to take though I got the impression he still believed in Campbell's honesty.

'Let's see what happens,' I said and hobbled painfully off to lie down.

We didn't have long to wait.

Just after eight o'clock that night my phone rang. Before answering I clicked on the tape recorder I'd had installed by the alarm people.

I picked up the handset. 'Hello.'

'Malloy.'

'Uhuh.'

'Can you spare a couple of minutes?'

English voice. Couldn't place it. I said, 'Who is this?'

'Don't talk, just listen.'

'I like to know who I'm listening to.'

'You're listening to the guy who's just about to save your life.'

He said, 'Are you listening?'

'Keep talking.'

'There's a flight to London tomorrow afternoon at five thirty. I want you to make sure you're on it. Find yourself a nice little place in England and stay there permanently. Don't come back to Barbados. Clear?'

'Can I say one thing?'

'What?'

'Whichever travel agent you work for you want to tell your boss you're badly in need of a refresher course in customer courtesy.'

The breath hissed through his teeth. 'Malloy ... What did I say to you? I told you you should listen. You didn't listen. YOU DID NOT LISTEN! I'm going to go through it one more time. I am going to try and make it very clear to you. Up till now we have been very patient. Your quota is completely used up. You are not fucking around with amateurs here, you're way out of your depth.'

Something in the voice, the tone, the menace was familiar to me.

238

He went on, 'Now we want you to be a good boy, a good little boy and run off back home. Amuse yourself there. Play with your toys. Do not go back to Barbados.'

'What if—'

'Listen, bastard! No what ifs. No more warnings. Be on that flight.'

The line went dead. I remembered where I'd heard the voice before. I played the tape back just to double check. I was sure, then.

I managed a smile and poured a drink, eased myself delicately into the big soft maroon armchair. This was the key to let me through the main door. It wouldn't give me all the answers but it was a start.

I called Gary, asked him to come to the cottage. I played the tape back. I didn't smile, tried not to show any satisfaction in being proved right.

Gary said, 'It still doesn't implicate Phil.'

On evidence, he was right. 'I accept that but it still gives us six days to find out more.'

He looked puzzled.

'You gave me a week, Gary. Hear me out, I've got a plan.' I explained it.

CHAPTER TWENTY-SEVEN

Next day Gary drove me to the airport and accompanied me through the terminal almost as though he was forcefully putting me on the plane. I was confident someone would be watching my departure. I left on the five thirty flight and Gary went back to arrange secret investigations into Phil Campbell's private and business life.

239

Gary hadn't been keen on the snooping but I persuaded him that what Campbell didn't know wouldn't hurt him. If he came up clean there'd be no damage to their relationship.

I landed at Gatwick just before 9 a.m. British time on the last Monday in June, got myself a hire car and set off north on wet roads under overcast skies, fat clouds. The radio broadcast solemn warnings of probable interruptions to play at Lord's and Wimbledon.

Welcome to a good old-fashioned British summer.

The rain resumed as I joined the A5 heading west and conjured up a storm of almost tropical intensity. By the time I reached the yard the dark clouds had wrung themselves white and the sun shone.

Padge, the head lad, was sitting on an old sack on the wall, the sunshine making his red hair blaze like gold. Steam rose all around him from the drying ground.

As I pulled in he looked up and smiled. I got out and limped towards him, happy to see a friendly unstrained face. He had a saddle in his lap, lovingly rubbing saddle soap into it in small circles. He watched me make my way clumsily towards him and smiled. 'You look like you shit yourself.'

'And welcome home to you, too.'

'Christ's sake, what happened?'

I couldn't put up with the ribbing till I felt better so I tried the one I'd used on the doctor, 'Got kicked by a big chestnut bugger at Gary's place.'

He looked incredulous. 'Really? And here was me thinking somebody'd been at your bollocks with the nutcrackers.' And he almost fell off the wall laughing.

I should have known Gary Rice would never have

240

been able to keep it quiet.

The new season was still five weeks away and things were comparatively quiet. Some of the early types were doing roadwork. Charles had gone to Scotland for two weeks' hillwalking.

Padge, subdued chuckles still occasionally bursting into fresh guffaws, helped me up to the flat with my gear. All was quiet, tidy, as I'd left it. The sun shone through the twelve square window panes. I sat at the little pine table and realised this was the first time that this had seemed like home to me. Padge, silhouetted against the bright window, said, 'You okay?'

I nodded.

'You sure? Anything I can get you? A cuppa? Some sandwiches? Large whisky? A truss?' At which he fell into another fit of laughter. I looked for something to throw at him and he went haring gleefully down the stairs.

The door banged behind him.

I sat in the silence for a minute.

Looked at the light on my answerphone. Still. Unblinking. No racing, no contact from the outside world. I ceased to exist until the tapes went up again at Bangor. Sometimes that steady little light made me feel terribly lonely. Not today.

That telephone held the link I'd been waiting for. The guy that called me in Barbados on Wednesday had called me before. On the phone I was looking at now. Last October. At two in the morning. To tell me to forget about the death of Bill Keating.

Turning everything over in my head during the past twenty-four hours I'd wished a number of times that I'd taped that call back in October. I was almost certain it was the same guy but that would have

241

confirmed it and maybe given the cops something to work on.

Gary and I had spent ages kicking it around looking for connections. Somewhere between the tiny village of Lambourn on an autumn day and a large estate in Barbados in midsummer was the link to Bill Keating's death and Gary Rice's troubles.

Somewhere in between came Conway.

We were assuming for the moment that Phil Campbell or his company were behind things but Gary could think of no link whatsoever between Campbell and England.

One of the first things Gary's investigators were trying to find out was if Clemence had ever been on Campbell's payroll.

My suspicion on listening a few times to the threatening call was that it had been made from England. Twice he had warned me not to return to Barbados: the first time he'd said don't *come* back but the second time he said don't *go* back.

I couldn't be sure but it was a fair enough bet to merit the trip across. Even if the whole scam, whatever it was, was now concentrated in the Caribbean there had to be some trail left over here.

My coming home served more than one end: it gave the impression they'd beaten me. Now that they thought I was running scared it should make it easier to root around quietly in England where it had all begun.

I called Peter McCarthy.

He wasn't in. I left a message.

I stood at the window. The clouds had all gone leaving a bright blue sky. Tempted to go and sit in the sunshine I decided my painful bits couldn't stand the stairs again and settled for a seat at the table where I

242

must have dozed off.

The phone woke me. It was McCarthy.

He said, 'Should have known you were back. Felt it in my water this morning.'

'Since when did intuition become your strong point?'

We small talked for a minute or so then I asked if anything had been heard of Conway.

'Not a thing. To be honest nobody's killing themselves to find the man. Why are you still interested?'

'Just natural curiosity.'

'That's not how I'd describe it, Eddie. Innate, pathological maybe but *natural*? I don't think so. Have you got something new on it?'

'Pushing in that direction.'

There was a longer than normal pause. When he spoke again the lightness had gone from his voice. 'What do you know?'

'Is there something *to* know?'

'What's that supposed to mean?'

'Just that I seemed to throw you there for a minute when I said I was pushing towards something new.'

'Why should that throw me?'

'You tell me.'

'You must have had something in mind!'

'Mac, what's the problem here? Why so defensive?'

He half laughed, trying to lighten things again. 'I'm not being defensive! Not in the least.'

'You don't know anything new about Conway's disappearance?'

'Not a thing.'

I tried to catch him flat. 'I think he's dead.'

That pause again then, 'Why do you think that?'

'Various reasons.'

'Like?'

'No single thing, a combination.'

He sighed. 'Eddie, if you know anything you're obliged to tell me.'

'As soon as I do know something I will tell you, it's all theory at the moment. Why don't we meet?'

'I'm tied up for the next few days.'

'Where are you going to be? I'll come to you.'

'It's difficult. Can I call you?'

'When?'

'Soon.'

'Tomorrow?'

'I'll try.'

He got off the phone in a hurry and I hung up under the distinct impression that he knew more than he was saying though that was nothing new for Mac.

That evening Padge and a couple of the other lads invited me to The Corner House, our local pub, promised they'd pay for all the drinks to celebrate my homecoming. Touched by their kindness I thanked them both warmly and, the soul of naivety and innocence, laughed and joked with them on the short sunny walk.

As we went through the door into the bar there was a loud cheer and about a dozen of the regulars held loaded nutcrackers in the air. They squeezed them off in a barrage like a military salute. Shell shards scattered everywhere. I flinched involuntarily at the sight and sound and everyone pissed themselves laughing.

By the time I got into bed hindsight and whisky had dulled things enough to bring a smile. I lay in the dark thinking the world wasn't that bad at all and that it would be a hell of a lot better if Kari Parsons was beside me.

Not that I'd be able to do anything.

Despite the alcohol I didn't sleep for a while. I was convinced there had to be a thread running through all this, a common denominator. Within minutes of waking next morning it came to me.

CHAPTER TWENTY-EIGHT

Sitting at the small table by the window with pen, pad and a mug of coffee I put Bill Keating's name at the top of a page and Gary Rice's at the bottom, wrote England by Bill's and Barbados by Gary's. I stuck Conway right in the middle of the page then started jotting down words: brain scan, heroin, murder?, boats, burglary, threats, horses, dead horses...

That's where I stopped. No blinding flash, just a connection, tenuous maybe but something worth looking at.

Bill and Gary were both linked to dead horses. Gary's had been killed deliberately.

So why not Bill's?

I sat back, chewed my pen, vaguely aware of the clip clop of hooves below in the sunlit yard. Following my earlier theory that Conway had not killed Bill Keating, that he'd been set up neatly with the planted chisel and brain scans, I decided to make the definite assumption that Conway was not the killer.

No matter how long or how obliquely I thought I could not come up with another suspect or another motive that led to the next natural assumption: Bill Keating had not been the target.

Simple.

But we knew the exhaust had been deliberately damaged, the tailgate closed, the engine switched on so there was only one answer left—the intended victims must have been the two horses. Whoever killed them almost certainly hadn't known Bill was lying unconscious in that stall.

It made sense. Bill would never have killed the horses. Anyone out to kill Bill and make it look like suicide would almost certainly have known that and could have made a much more convincing case if they'd set the horses free.

I now had two links: dead horses and phone threats from the same man.

So who was behind it?

Someone who's involved in trying to screw Gary Rice. Someone who didn't mind killing a few more horses in the process. Made a point of it in fact as part of the campaign.

Problem was the first two horses didn't belong to Rice.

Who did own them, then? Whoever it was may have been the first target.

That had to be the next step. I got up, rang McCarthy, left a message on his answerphone then tried his mobile number. No response.

I showered, moving a bit more freely though the bruising, showing in the full length mirror, was in technicolour now. I shaved, dried myself off, dressed, made more coffee, all on automatic pilot my mind working at top pace.

I couldn't hang around waiting for Mac. I rang Cathy Keating. We got the pleasantries over with and I told her I was following up on a reported sighting of Conway. I didn't like lying to her but if

Bill's death was to be raked over once more I wasn't sure how she'd take it.

Last time we'd met I felt she just wanted to put it all behind her and try to forget. I had little doubt she'd welcome the news that Bill's death had been nothing more than a grim coincidence, an accident, but until I could prove it I wasn't going to raise her hopes.

Still, she sounded uneasy. I said, 'Cathy, all I need to know is who owned the horses that were in the box that evening.'

'What's that got to do with it?'

'Maybe nothing, it's just a hunch that might lead us to Conway.'

'I can't remember. Bill picked them up, did all the paperwork. I think he planned to drive them north overnight, to a new trainer in Yorkshire.'

'What was his name?'

'Can't remember. Sorry.'

'What about the trainer they came from?'

'Somebody here, in Lambourn ... Ohhh ... now what was his name? I think it might have been Pete Curland. It was a couple of two year olds if I remember. Curland ... Curland ... I think it was Pete. Why don't you ring him?'

'Good idea. I'll do it now.'

'Will you stay in touch?'

'Sure. Can you keep this under your hat until I come back to you?'

'Of course.'

'Okay, I'll call soon.'

Now the problem with contacting Curland was that he might be involved somewhere. I wouldn't call him unless I had to. I was sure I could get the info I wanted from Mac if only I could get in touch.

By 2 p.m. he still hadn't phoned. I tried his number

247

again. He answered. I said, 'Why didn't you call me? I left a message on your machine.'

'I've just got back, been shopping with Jean. I am supposed to be on holiday you know. Where's the fire anyway?'

'I need to see you, need some information.'

'So what's new?'

'Come on Mac, you can spare me an hour. I'll drive down.'

'When?'

'Now.'

'Forget it! I'm going fishing.'

'I'll come with you.'

'You'll scare the fish.'

'Okay, get me some information and I'll leave you in peace for the day.'

'What do you want to know?'

I told him.

He moaned in frustration. 'Eddie, tell me you're not back on this Conway thing again?'

I was getting frustrated with his stonewalling each time Conway came up. 'Mac, what is your problem with Conway? Don't you want this whole business sorted out?'

'I told you, leave it to the police, it's a murder inquiry.'

I was very tempted to tell him it wasn't any more. 'So what? If we can help them out we—'

'Eddie! Listen, Conway is bad news for the Jockey Club. When the papers got wind of those tapes of yours last time the coverage wasn't exactly relished in Portman Square. It all seems to be dying down now. We'd like to leave it that way.'

'I'm sure you would so you'll appreciate hearing that I don't think Conway killed Bill Keating and if you can just help me out with some information I might be able to prove it.'

'Eddie . . . oh, it's pointless talking to you, when do you need this for?'

'As quickly as you can get it, three at the latest.'

'Give me half an hour.'

He was back within the deadline. 'The horses were called Killian and Cartographer, unraced two year olds. They were bought as yearlings in America by a bloodstock agent who must have sold them on to the only registered owners, a private company, though he could have been acting on a direct commission from them.'

The horses were well bred and each had cost a substantial sum, a total of five hundred and twenty-five thousand guineas. Why would anyone want to kill two such valuable animals before they'd even set foot on a racecourse?

'Did the owners have any other horses in training?' I asked.

'I'm having that looked at, as I said they were owned by a small private company. We need to do some digging.'

'Mac, can you think of any other horses who've died in say the past year in something that could look like an accident?'

He thought for a while. 'I wouldn't say I can but there'd be no real reason for my department to know, especially if it's accidents we're talking about.'

'It was just a thought. Would you mind asking around, quietly?'

'You're giving me bad vibrations on this, Eddie.'

'That's not what The Beach Boys told me when I met them.'

'Very funny. I'm going fishing. Goodbye.'

I had to find out more about the company that owned Killian and Cartographer.

The obvious way was to speak to the trainers who'd had their horses. The trouble was that last time I'd made a few calls asking discreet questions about Bill Keating these bastards got to know about it within hours so they had some very close connections in the game.

They thought I was out of the picture and I wanted to keep it that way as long as possible so I had to be very careful who I spoke to.

Pete Curland, their last trainer, was no more than an acquaintance of mine and I couldn't be sure how he'd react to a direct approach. I wished Charles was here, he could have called Curland and asked questions on my behalf. I went downstairs to find Padge. He was holding a horse while the farrier shod him. As I appeared in the doorway of the stable he smiled long and hard, silently milking the nutcracking moment from last night.

I said, 'What did you do for amusement while I was away, Padge?'

He laughed and I could tell by the way the big farrier smiled that he too had been let in on the joke. I said, 'When you're finished I could do with a favour.'

With a mock groan he said, 'I told you I'm not rubbing that cream on it again.'

'Very funny. I'll be up in the flat.'

Ten minutes later Padge was dialling Curland's number. He told Curland that Charles had asked him to get a reference for a prospective new owner and gave the name of the company which owned the dead horses.

Curland remembered the company but said he'd never met anyone personally. The horses had been

250

sent to him direct from the bloodstock agent and the only contact he'd had was with a secretary from the company. They'd paid bills promptly and asked simply for a monthly report on the horses' progress.

Curland didn't think the horses were likely to match up to their price tags though he said he was confident of winning a couple of small races with them. He told the owners this in his third monthly report and a day later the horses were removed.

As far as he could remember they were supposed to go to Claude Kenton in Yorkshire. Padge called Kenton and tried the same line.

Kenton could only confirm that the horses never reached him and that he too had only dealt with a secretary for the company that owned them.

We carried mugs of tea out into the late afternoon sunshine. I was moving reasonably well now, almost managed to share the sack that covered Padge's perch on the wall but settled for leaning against it.

The words on my pad upstairs ran through my mind, the two links, phone threats, dead horses . . . a third link began to form. Apart from the trauma of the incidents in Gary Rice's case the real sufferer had been his insurance company.

Insurance.

Padge rolled a cigarette. He said, 'Where is the pleasure in owning horses, especially ones you've paid a nice few quid for, if you don't even speak to the trainer?'

'Maybe they weren't in it for pleasure. Business.'

'Not a very successful one then when your assets get gassed.'

I smiled at him. 'Unless you're heavily insured.'

'Couldn't insure them for much more than their purchase price.'

'Maybe not but let's suppose you are in it strictly for business. You buy an expensive yearling— Cartographer cost them three hundred and fifty thousand guineas—insure him for say four hundred thousand allowing for some improvement by the time he gets on a racecourse, then send him to a good trainer, someone who can give you a fair assessment of his potential.'

Padge was listening hard. A magpie rushed down, landed in the tree above us and cocked his head almost as if he wanted to hear the rest of it too. Padge glanced up, saluting the bird out of superstition and said, 'Go on.'

I said, 'Now supposing the trainer says he's bloody good, you've got a bargain or even, he's well up to standard you'll easily get your money back, great. You race him, hopefully win a few quid then send your investment off to stud.'

Padge grinned. 'A bit over simplified, Eddie.'

'I know but the trainer, if he's honest, will be right more often than not. On the other hand supposing he says, you've bought a bit of a pup here, we'll win one or two small races with him but there's no way you'll get your cash back.'

I saw by Padge's face he was coming round my way.

I said, 'Now just to be sure, if your first trainer tells you that, you move the horse on for a second opinion. As soon as you're sure you've made a mistake how do you get your money back?'

The smile spread slowly and the sun glinted in Padge's blue eyes. 'Off the insurance company.'

'Correct.' I felt almost elated.

'But you couldn't do that more than once.'

'Why not? Why the hell not? You just use a

different company each time.'

'Nah, they'd soon spot it.'

'How? Horses are dying every week, limb injuries, twisted guts, they'd just be chalked up as another statistic.'

'Be in the papers, surely?'

'Why? They're unraced, nobody knows of them, they're just mid-range expensive. Stay well below the million mark and you'd hardly raise a flicker of interest.'

'You might be right.'

'Worth working on, isn't it?' I was excited.

Padge smiled again. 'Wouldn't like to try to stop you.'

I was on a run now.

CHAPTER TWENTY-NINE

I called Cathy. She said, 'Twice in one day, to what do I owe the pleasure?'

'Sorry Cathy, I'm sort of thinking on the hoof here, still following up this Conway thing.'

'Did you find out what you wanted to know about the dead horses?'

'I'm a bit wiser than the last time we spoke, that's why I'm ringing you again. Did you have any hassle from the insurers of those horses?'

'I didn't claim on my insurance, the horses' owners had insurance, and the company paid out.'

'Yes but didn't they try to counter claim you for damages?'

'They'd have to have proved negligence which it obviously wasn't. It was—' She faltered.

253

I said, 'It's okay, I know what you mean.'

'No, I'm all right.' She composed herself and continued. 'As the verdict at the time was suicide, it was deemed a deliberate act. They accepted there was nothing I could have done to prevent it.'

'Right. You don't happen to remember who they were?'

'The insurance company?'

'Yeah.'

'I think I've got a letter somewhere. Want to hold or will I call you back?'

'No. Fine. I'll hold.'

A couple of minutes later she was back. 'Beckett and Kelly.'

'Sound more like flyweight contenders at Belfast Town Hall. Got their number?'

She gave me it.

'And who signed the letter?'

'K. Castle. Think it was Keith from memory. A very nice man. Oh, hold on, I'm sure he gave me a card at the time. I think his home number was on it.'

I held again and got the number.

'Thanks Cathy.'

'Can I expect another call tomorrow?'

'Every chance.'

'Eddie, you sound excited about this.'

'Well, I suppose I am a bit. Another good friend of mine is in trouble and links with Bill's case have started to pop up. It's early days.'

'Should I be preparing myself for anything?'

I silently chided myself for not being able to mask my exuberance. Bill's widow could hardly be expected to share it. 'I don't think so, Cath, not for any bad news anyway.'

'As soon as you know something for sure will you

come and tell me?'

'Of course I will.'

She hesitated then said quietly, 'Ring me if you need anything else.'

I called Keith Castle. He wasn't in. His wife asked if I'd like to leave a message. I said, 'I need to speak to him urgently. Can you tell him it's about Killian and Cartographer?'

I left my number.

Next I rang Gary in Barbados and explained my theory so far. I could tell he was unsure as to how impressed he should be. 'Sounds brilliant but where does all the shit that's been happening here tie in?'

'Don't know yet but at least we're sort of up the first three rungs of the ladder.'

'The way my luck's been we'll fall off near the top but keep on kicking.'

'Your investigators turned anything up on Phil Campbell yet?'

'Not a thing so far. Phil looks as clean as the proverbial whistle at the moment.'

That wasn't what I'd been hoping for. 'Your guys got much more to do on it?'

'They reckon they'll finish for Tuesday morning.'

'Any chance of putting some of your people on the trail of this private company that owned Killian and Cartographer, try and find who owns the company?'

'I'll see what I can do but if they're set up in the same way as that Horsefeeds mob in Newbury, the packing case lot, then it'll be a waste of time.'

'It won't, Gary, it might be another very solid link.'

He agreed and I gave him the company details as Mac had passed them to me. 'How long will it take?' I asked.

'Christ knows.'

'Put your best guys on it, Gary.'

'You wanted my best guys doing Phil Campbell, how many best guys do you think I've got?'

I laughed. 'Hire some more.'

There was nothing else I could do till this guy Castle called me back from the company who'd insured Killian and Cartographer.

It was the next morning before he did though he apologised saying he'd got home late and didn't want to risk disturbing me. He couldn't meet me today but was happy to discuss things on the phone.

I explained about my friendship with Bill Keating and told him something of my involvement since. 'Now various things have happened which make me think that the deaths of those two horses were not an accident.'

'What sort of things?'

I explained my theory. 'Do you think any of that holds water?'

'Substantially. Have you spoken to the police?'

'Not yet. The case is closed as far as they're concerned and I think they'd want some pretty solid evidence before they'd look at it again.'

'Is that evidence likely to be forthcoming?'

'That depends. I'm trying to find out exactly who owns this company that owned the horses. What have you got on them?'

'Give me five minutes, I'll call you back.'

He came back with a head office phone number and the address of the private company along with the names of two directors neither of which I recognised. They were based in Stafford. They'd been customers of Castle's company for just eight months and had paid the premiums for the two horses in advance.

256

'Their deaths must have put a hole in the profits.'

'We have a very sound business, Mr Malloy, though no one likes to sign a cheque for almost six hundred thousand pounds.'

'You must have done some pretty thorough investigations yourselves last autumn.'

He shrugged, 'We had little choice but to agree with the Coroner's verdict.'

'How much contact do you have with other equine insurers?'

'Very little other than from a competitive point of view, keeping an eye on the market.'

'How do you think they'd feel about an approach from you on the basis that others may have been ripped off? It would be interesting to know if this company has claimed on any other horse deaths.'

'I'll get started right away.'

He gave me his mobile number.

I rang the Stafford number Castle had given me for the private company and asked to speak to Mr Grafton, one of the names listed as a director.

The girl who answered didn't know what I was talking about and a few more questions brought the information that the company in question had closed down three months ago. The place was now a pet shop. The girl hadn't a clue what the business of the company had been.

I asked if there were any other shops in the building she was in: newsagent and a hairdresser on either side. I got both their names then their numbers from Directory Inquiries. The newsagent told me he'd only ever known there to be a secretary in the office when the company was there. They'd traded for less than a year and he thought they had something to do with horseracing.

'Horsefeeds?' I asked.

'Mmmm ... Might have been. Can't remember.'

My frustration was now tempered with growing confidence. I had to be on the right track. I called McCarthy again and told him I was driving down to see him.

After much moaning about how precious holidays were he agreed to meet me for tea in Newbury. Ninety per cent of Mac's destinations had the consolation of waiting calories.

When I reached the Camden Hotel Mac was perched on the edge of a dangerously sumptuous sofa. If he sat back he'd need assistance to get his bulk upright again. I seldom saw him casually dressed but his belly bulged out of a beige polo shirt over brown cords and loafers.

He didn't look that happy to see me though he cheered up considerably when the cream tea arrived. I settled for black coffee and tried to time my questions to finish them as his mouth emptied.

At first I thought I detected some of the nervousness he'd displayed on the phone when I'd mentioned Conway. But when he realised I was on a different tack altogether he seemed to relax more.

He listened to my theories with just the occasional grunt and at the end didn't show much enthusiasm for helping. He said, 'You seem to have set everything in motion, Eddie. Just a matter of waiting to see what comes out in the wash.'

'Fine but a helping hand from your boys wouldn't do any harm.'

'We're very busy at the moment.'

'What with?'

'A number of things. Confidential.'

'Come on, Mac, you can spare at least one man to

start nosing around.'

Dabbing at his mouth with a napkin he said, 'How can I justify it? Who do I say has made the formal complaint?'

'Since when did everything have to be official?'

He shrugged. 'It makes life difficult for me when it's not.'

He was ducking and diving, knowing he'd wind me up. I tried a softer approach, sat forward across the table, smiled. 'Mac, you know that was why I was put on this earth, to make your life difficult. Now do me a favour and put someone on this.'

He looked exasperated. 'To do what? I told you, you've already done all the right things. Why don't you wait and see what comes of that?'

'Mac, you're missing the chance to get some brownie points here. If you're in this from the start you'll be able to take the credit.'

Which he did anyway, usually without having earned it.

That tempted him a bit and he hesitated before making a face. 'I don't know, let me think about it.'

'Till when?'

'A couple of days.'

'I haven't got a couple of days! These guys could be setting up another horse killing right now. What's the point of your people coming in on Friday if they kill another couple of horses on Thursday? Start looking now! Give me some help and maybe you'll get them before the next one.'

We had a long argument then. He accused me of being fixated with finding Conway 'dead or alive'.

I stared at him. 'You would rather it was all just brushed under the carpet, wouldn't you? What about Cathy Keating? What about Bill's children? Don't

259

you think they'd quite like to hear that not only did Bill not commit suicide but that nobody hated him enough to kill him either? If Bill's death was an accident don't you think they'd sleep a little bit easier for the rest of their lives?'

He had sufficient grace left to blush slightly. I asked, 'Why do you want Conway to stay missing?'

He glanced around again. The only others in the big lounge were a couple with three quite noisy children. Nobody was going to overhear us but Mac lowered his voice anyway. 'We don't need this whole brain scan thing blowing up again, that's why.'

I sat back watching him almost squirm and I knew he was hiding something.

The brain scans.

It clicked.

I said, 'How many more false scans were there besides Bill's?'

He looked at me, morose, defeated. 'Two,' he said quietly.

'Who?'

'I can't tell you.'

'How did you find out about them?'

'Had all the scans in the files compared against the false one in Bill Keating's files.'

'In case Conway was using copies of the same scan?'

He nodded.

'And he was?'

Nodded again.

'Now the Jockey Club are covering it up.'

He rallied slightly as he donned his official cap. 'It's not a cover up. We simply chose, in the best interests of racing's image, not to release the news.'

'A cover up by any other name would smell as

260

lousy, Mac.'

'Very poetic, Eddie, but I told you, no cover up and no lasting harm. The two jockeys concerned will never race again.'

'And that makes it all right, does it?'

'The world is not a perfect place. You should know that as well as anybody.'

I sighed, 'You know the worst part? You'll probably manage to keep it under wraps. Conway's probably lying at the bottom of the Atlantic.'

He tried not to look too cheered by that but it was hard to hide. I gave up on him. 'Well, Mac, I hope you enjoyed the tea. I'll pay on the way out. Call me when you get your conscience back.'

I felt angry and annoyed all the way home. I'd known Mac for quite a while and although he'd almost always take advantage where he could, he usually stuck up for the underdog. I wondered just how much pressure his bosses were putting him under on this one.

The long drive had brought back much of the discomfort in my groin and I had to take the stairs up to the flat one at a time. I felt even more frustrated to find nothing on my answerphone. I'd been hoping Gary would have turned something up by now.

I poured a large whisky and spent the rest of the evening jotting and doodling trying to figure out who the other two jocks were, racked my brain for people who'd shown the same symptoms as Bill Keating. I came up with nothing.

CHAPTER THIRTY

Next morning Keith Castle rang to say he'd set things in motion with the other insurance companies and would get back to me as soon as he heard something.

'When's that likely to be, Keith?'

'Very difficult to predict. One or two of them are large organisations where the wheels grind slowly.'

'What do you think, a day, two?'

'Not for the big ones, Mr Malloy, we may be talking a week or more.'

'Shit.'

I moped around the flat. All I could do now was wait and see what others came up with. Just after four Gary called to tell me that the company who'd owned Killian and Cartographer had, like the Newbury one, been registered in the Isle of Man making it impossible to trace the owner.

But that confirmed the likelihood that the owner of both companies could well be the same person which, again, if we accepted Conway's corpse had been in that packing case meant the links were strengthening all the time.

The business of this company was apparently horse grooming equipment. Gary said the investigations into Phil Campbell were almost complete and he should have a report tomorrow.

I called McCarthy and could almost sense him flinch at the sound of my voice. 'Mac, any news on that company who owned Killian and Cartographer? Did they own any other horses?'

'I haven't spoken to my office, Eddie, give me ten minutes.'

He rang back. 'None. That was their only venture into ownership.'

'Shit. Listen, what I need is a list of all private companies in say the last five years who've owned horses.'

He groaned, 'Eddie, come on! We've got other things to do!'

'Not as important as this, Mac, and you know it. You might not like it but you know I'm right.'

'It'll take ages.'

'No it won't. Surely Weatherby's will have it all on computer?' Weatherby's are the Jockey Club's administrators.

Another groan then a resigned, 'Leave it with me.'

'Mac! What I need especially are private companies who have owned winners.'

'I thought you were sure they were just having them killed all over the place.'

'If they're working the scam I think they are then at some point, if they've been going long enough, they'll have bought a decent horse, one which would have earned more than its insurance value.'

'And then what are you going to do?'

'I'm going to try and find out who accepted the winner's trophy on behalf of the company.'

He didn't say so but Mac was impressed. Two hours later he called back to tell me he had a list of 259 companies thirty-one of which had owned at least one winner. He also had the names of the winning horses and the races won.

I gave him Charles's fax number. I then refaxed the list to Keith Castle's company with a message that it should help speed things considerably. All he had to do now was check with other insurers to see which of the companies had claimed on dead thoroughbreds, especially unraced ones.

Then I sat down to concentrate on the winners. There were eighteen different horses who'd won the thirty-one races between them. All were owned by different private companies. Ideally I'd like to have known which of those had been registered in the Isle of Man but finding that out might take days.

The horses' victories were spread over four years at flat tracks mostly in the midlands and the north. I broke them into areas covered by certain racecourse photographers ending up with just five lists, then I rang round the photographers all of whom I knew quite well.

I raised two personally and told them what I wanted and left messages for the other three. I could have got the results more quickly by visiting the *Racing Post* offices or *The Sporting Life* but I didn't want to alert newsmen.

All the photographers called back before the day was out promising pictures by Saturday morning. This was Thursday evening.

* * *

Just after one on Friday afternoon Gary rang. When I heard his voice I almost dreaded what he was going to say. For although things were going well here I badly needed confirmation that Phil Campbell was behind the campaign to get Gary off the estate.

If we couldn't establish a strong link in Barbados then all we'd be left to work with would be this insurance caper, I'd be tunnelling from one end only.

'Eddie, we can find absolutely nothing wrong with Phil Campbell's business, his personal life, his wife or kids, his cook, his maid or his cat. The most outrageous thing he's done was get himself a speeding fine.'

I felt myself steadily deflate as he talked.

Gary went on, 'Unless you're asking me to believe that Phil has gone from that to organising total mayhem then I think we're going to have to exonerate him.'

I sighed and conceded, 'Gary, I'm sorry for doubting your word on Phil Campbell but I'll tell you this, unless we turn up more than I'd hoped for over here it's going to be a bloody long haul.'

He let me wallow in despondency for a while then said, 'What I just gave you was the bad news, Eddie, I've got some good news as well.'

I almost held my breath.

'Ever heard of a man called Joe Hawkins?'

'Kenny's brother.'

'That's right. Do you know him?'

'Not exactly. Spoke to him once in hospital when he was visiting Kenny with their mother. Not the most pleasant guy in the world.'

'Who were you visiting?'

'Kenny, remember he was paralysed in that car smash?' My mind went back to that day at Newcastle when Jeff Dunning suggested rigging that race on Kenny's behalf and Neumman had poked his nose in saying we should let his bigshot brother take care of him.

'Right. Did you know Joe Hawkins has business interests in Barbados among other countries?'

'I know he's got a few quid.'

'Got fingers in a number of pies from what I hear.'

'What's his business?'

'Anything that makes money and from what my guys have found out it doesn't give him sleepless

265

nights if he inadvertently breaks the law. Within the last six months he's bought two plantations over here and he's in the market for more.'

I perked up.

He paused then went on. 'About eighteen months ago Phil Campbell took on a new finance director called David Bernstein. Six months ago, around the time Hawkins moved into the plantation business, Bernstein started socialising with him, dinners, golf, racing, it seems they're pretty close.'

He was building up to something, I could feel it. 'And?'

'We've had a look at Bernstein. He used to be a highflier on Wall Street till they jailed him for thirty-two months for insider trading.'

I smiled, 'So we've got two crooks, and one works for a company that's been trying to buy your land. And they met six months ago?'

'Uhuh.'

'When did your troubles start?'

'In England, late February. Didn't get going here till mid April.'

'Doesn't quite tie in. Do you think Phil Campbell knows who his financial director is running around with?'

'I very much doubt it but I'll find out tonight.'

'Is it wise to ask him outright?'

'Eddie . . .' It was an admonishment, a reminder I'd already had my bite at that particular cherry.

'I'm sorry, Gary, you're right. What do we do next?'

'I'm not finished yet. Back in February one of Joe Hawkins's many companies bought half a million pounds worth of stock in Saint Simon Insurance.'

I waited.

266

Gary said, 'They're Silverdale's main rivals in the UK.'

'Silverdale, your insurers?'

'That's right.'

'When in February did Hawkins buy the stock, before or after your house was burgled?'

'Three days before.'

Another link in the chain.

Gary promised he'd try to get more info from Phil Campbell that night.

'Okay. In the meantime I'll try and tie Joe Hawkins into this insurance scam over here.'

'With the horses?'

'Yeah.'

'I thought Silverdale hadn't insured those?'

'They didn't, it was a smaller company but if it was Hawkins's man who threatened me on the phone back in October there must be every chance he was running that racket. That's probably what gave him the idea for trying to bust Silverdale if he's behind these attacks.'

'Maybe but I'd have thought a couple of horses were small beer for him.'

'I wouldn't be so sure. If you can afford to keep buying well bred horses without the chance of losing money you've got a very reasonable chance of getting a classic winner sooner or later. Then you are talking big bucks.'

'True.'

'I'll nose around a bit, maybe pay Kenny a visit.'

'He's hardly going to drop his own brother in it.'

'I don't think they got on. Kenny's straight. I never even heard him mention Joe.'

'Okay, whatever you think.'

'Good luck tonight.'

267

'Thanks.'

With renewed hope I flicked through my diary for Kenny Hawkins's number.

*   *   *

Kenny's wife Carol said she was sure he'd love to see me this evening. Said it would be a chance to make up for last time when Kenny had got so drunk he'd passed out before I got there. She seemed strained. The relief at the prospect of my visit was almost tangible.

'How's Kenny been?'

She sighed, 'Terrible if you want to know.'

'Still boozing?'

'He's drinking too much, Eddie, but even when he's sober he's impossible, he's ... I, I shouldn't really be telling you this ... I'm sorry.'

'Carol, I'm always willing to listen if it helps.'

'No, it's not right. I don't feel so bad moaning to my mum about it but I, well I sort of feel like I'm betraying him.'

I understood exactly what she meant.

'Look, I'm sure a visit from you would pull him out of the dumps for a little while at least. He hasn't seen anybody for months.'

'What time suits then?'

'Half seven?'

'Fine.'

'I won't tell him you're coming. It'll be a nice surprise then.'

By the look on Kenny's face when I walked in that evening it was the worst surprise he'd ever had in his life. From his wheelchair in the silent room he stared at me like I'd come back from the dead to haunt him.

He'd put on at least two stone making his naturally chubby face even fatter looking. His dark hair was short but uncombed around his prominent ears and there was a generally unkempt look about him. He wore a light grey open necked shirt and dark green cords.

'How are you, Kenny?'

He still stared, transfixed. 'What are you doing here?' He seemed almost horrified. Carol stepped in. 'Kenny! I invited Eddie for dinner. For Christ's sake what's wrong with you?'

He ignored her, wheeled his chair urgently towards me, dark ringed eyes staring up into mine, pleading even before he spoke. 'Eddie, please get out of here.' His tone was quiet, rational.

Carol seemed incensed. 'Kenny! Don't you dare talk like that to a guest!'

He turned venomously on her. 'Shut up! Shut the fuck up!'

The high colour in her face started draining as she stared at him. He looked back up at me, veins standing out on his throat, pulse beating in his neck. He fought for control of his voice, gained it and spoke in a steely monotone. 'Eddie ... Go away. Don't come back here again.'

I tried to talk to him but he cut me off immediately. He looked sane, rational but totally serious about not wanting me there. I nodded to Carol and left.

When I got back to the flat there were two messages from Carol on the answerphone almost hysterically apologetic. She asked me not to call but to meet her next day for lunch at a country house hotel we both knew.

I spent the rest of the evening trying to figure Kenny out. No success.

CHAPTER THIRTY-ONE

Next morning's mail brought fifty-two different photographs of trophy presentations to winning racehorse owners many of whom I recognised. I found the one I was looking for in under a minute. He featured twice, two different horses. I'd met him only once, in a dark car park at Huntingdon: the mature, pleasant, educated, handsome Mr Ernest Goodwin, the acceptable face of Mayhem Incorporated.

It was too early to ring Gary, the middle of the night in Barbados. I called Mac, told him I now had solid evidence and asked him to find out what he could about Ernest Goodwin. The courses where he received the trophies may have had some personal information on him though I warned Mac that Goodwin was probably an alias.

'You don't say?'

Mac seldom stooped to sarcasm but he knew I wouldn't give this thing up, knew that he was too far into it to pull back now, he'd have to keep helping me even though he didn't care at all for what was being uncovered. If he thought the publicity surrounding Conway had upset digestions at Jockey Club dinners he was heading for revelations that would make the Conway PR just an aperitif.

He grudgingly promised to see what he could do on Goodwin. At eleven I drove south for lunch with Carol Hawkins.

We met at a small country house hotel about an hour's drive from Carol's house. She looked only slightly less strained than she had last night but her blonde hair shone and smelt of fresh shampoo. She wore a black two piece suit over a beige top of very fine wool. Her make-up was neat and understated; soft grey eye shadow and very pale pink lipstick.

I kissed her lightly. She smiled and asked if I'd mind not eating after all, she'd lost her appetite.

So we sat drinking coffee on fine Regency chairs at the window of a wood panelled room and looked out over acres of parkland. Carol was obviously acutely embarrassed, almost ashamed of Kenny's behaviour last night. I reassured her as best I could, told her not to worry.

'He's been terrible for weeks now, Eddie, I hardly recognise him as a human being any more never mind the man I married. He sits in the bedroom for hours just staring out of the window, hardly talks, ignores the kids completely. I was hoping seeing you would pull him out of it, he always liked you.'

'It wasn't this bad last time I saw you, was it?'

'Nowhere near it. He'd been drinking a lot after that bad patch in February but he seemed to be coming out of it.'

February.

That month kept coming up. Joe Hawkins bought his half million pounds worth of shares in February. Gary Rice suffered his first big insurance loss in February. I asked Carol if she knew what Kenny and Joe had argued about that day.

'He wouldn't tell me. They'd been fighting for ages over the insurance claim for the accident.'

Insurance.

'How is the claim going?' I asked.

Carol's strained look was suddenly dulled further by an obvious depression. 'Kenny dropped it,' she said quietly.

'Completely?'

271

She nodded.

'Why?' I was incredulous. As I remembered it they'd been talking of over a million, sounding confident of success.

Carol's shoulders rose in a sad, heavy shrug. 'I don't know, Eddie, I'll never know. Kenny just told me the subject was closed.'

My mind was starting to sort things out, make adjustments, pin down the elusive link that was now just hovering there.

'When did Kenny last see his brother?'

'Eddie, if you think it's just some family tiff that's making Kenny behave like this you're wrong . . . I'm sorry, I didn't mean to be rude it's just that—'

'Carol, it's okay, don't apologise.' She looked miserable and I wanted so much to tell her exactly why her husband was behaving the way he was. Everything had slotted into place. I just needed one point confirmed. 'Carol, Kenny's claim was against the local council, wasn't it?'

'Well, yes but it was their insurers, really.'

'Their insurers wouldn't happen to be a company called Silverdale?'

'That's them, I think. Why?'

'Just wondering.'

I was very wary of hurting Carol. If Kenny wanted to hide his secrets from her then it wasn't for me to break what now felt like a trust even though Kenny had confided nothing to me. But it would all come out very soon, that was inevitable.

She was still trying to explain, 'He won't even see Joe now, won't take his calls, doesn't reply to his letters. Joe comes on screaming at me then accusing me of turning Kenny against him . . .' Tears welled up. '. . . calling me, calling me all the bitches

272

of the day.'

She pulled a handkerchief from her small black bag. Feeling desperately sorry for her I reached across the table and took her hand. 'I'm sorry, Carol, I didn't mean to upset you.'

She squeezed my hand then pulled away. 'I know, I know ... it's not your fault, Eddie, does me good to get it out.'

She wiped the tears, composed herself, got a small mirror from her bag and tidied her make-up.

'Carol, I think I might be able to help Kenny.'

'How?'

'Well I think he's maybe just taken a bit too much on since the accident, got involved in one or two things that haven't worked out.'

Sadness turned to worry now on her face. 'Something bad?'

I wasn't sure how to answer. 'Put it this way, not bad enough that we can't make it right.'

'What is it?'

'I'm not sure just yet. Did Kenny see anyone else around the time of the big fallout with Joe in February?'

'He never goes out just gets the occasional visitor. He had two or three of the lads in around that time.'

'Jockeys?'

'Yes, old friends. Like you.'

I smiled. 'Nobody else?'

'Just a man from the Jockey Club but that was just an informal visit too, to see how Kenny was recovering.'

'What was the man's name?'

'I can't remember. He seemed very pleasant, said it was just a social call. He stayed about half an hour.'

'Would that be about a week after I came

273

to dinner?'

She thought back. 'Around then, I'd say.'

'What did he look like?'

'Big. Over six feet. Well built. Well, a bit pudgy round the middle really, dark hair.'

'Quite curly? Bit of a double chin?'

'That's right. Do you know him?'

'Peter McCarthy.'

The line of questioning started dawning on her. 'Is Kenny in trouble with the Jockey Club?'

'Not any more, he's not.'

But McCarthy's in big fucking trouble with Eddie Malloy.

I asked Carol to say nothing to Kenny and promised I'd call her within a few days.

By the time I got back to the car I was raging. I tried to call McCarthy, he was at Sandown races. I drove there at dangerously high speed and found him by the weighing room comfortably back in dark suit, white shirt and tie, and hobnobbing with two Stewards and a tall lady in a wide straw hat.

I resisted the strong urge to march straight up and confront him. When he finally caught sight of me he didn't look pleased and drew his conversation out as long as possible before admitting defeat and striding towards me very businesslike and official.

'Eddie, I'm busy today.'

I glared at him. My eyes felt like they were burning. He couldn't have failed to spot the anger and the almost vicious intent. I said, 'You want to have it out here?'

He glanced nervously around at the big crowd. 'We'll go over to the stables.'

I marched towards them sensing his reluctance. 'Just five minutes, Eddie, I've got a meeting.'

274

'Fuck the meeting!' I growled without even looking at him.

Neither of us spoke again till he'd signed me in past his security man at the gate of the racecourse stables and we had walked to the far end of a row of boxes. He checked the ones nearest us making sure they were empty then stood stiffly, staring at me. He said, 'What is it?'

'You visited Kenny Hawkins in February. Why?'

I could tell immediately that was the last thing he'd wanted to hear. He tried a weak bluff. 'Confidential matter between Kenny and the Jockey Club.'

'Bollocks! Blackmail is what you call it, Mac!' I jabbed a finger at him, knew I was sneering in anger. 'I never *ever* thought you'd stoop to that, Mac! Never!'

His shoulders drooped and he looked away, head down. I paced in front of him, trying to calm myself but I was almost tearful with rage and frustration and a strong feeling of betrayal. Mac had helped me get my licence back, I'd always trusted him. I must have called him every name I could think of before the steam started going out of me.

He stood looking suitably ashamed, genuinely sorry. 'Eddie, it wasn't my idea, I hated doing it, detested it but Lord Greenboro insisted, he gave me no choice.'

Greenboro was the Senior Steward of the Jockey Club, effectively McCarthy's boss. 'Obeying orders, Mac, eh? Like they did at Auschwitz?'

He looked away again.

'So Greenboro was big buddies with Bruce Cronin, the chairman of Silverdale Insurance? Kenny had his million pound claim in against Silverdale then Greenboro gives Cronin the news that Kenny

Hawkins was one of the jocks who'd had a false brain scan from Conway?'

He nodded.

'So! The good old school tie network strikes again! Senior Steward or not Greenboro had no right to give Cronin that information! No fucking right whatsoever! That was confidential. Kenny would never have ridden again anyway, you knew that, Greenboro must have known it. There was no need for disciplinary measures! Kenny Hawkins's life, the lives of his family were in fucking tatters and the Jockey Club can't even act human? For once in their history they can't even act human!'

'He would never have got away with it anyway, Eddie, it would have come out in court.'

'How do you know?'

'Silverdale would have demanded another brain scan, they'd read enough in the papers about Bill Keating's case. Their doctors would have claimed Kenny could have suffered a blackout when driving over that bridge. The man had brain damage.'

I stopped pacing and turned on him. 'Any damage shown by Silverdale's brain scan could have been put down to the car crash!'

'It couldn't, Eddie, believe me! We checked on that. Any competent surgeon could have proved Kenny's injury was historical.'

'That doesn't mean to say the crash barrier wasn't faulty.'

'He'd been having frequent blackouts, for God's sake! They'd have torn him apart in court. Kenny knew that, he could never have won that claim.'

'So why didn't you just let it go to court then?'

He didn't answer.

'You don't have to answer, Mac, I know the

276

reason. It was to save the shining pristine Jockey Club any more bad publicity. That's what it was at the end of the day, a PR exercise. Fuck Kenny Hawkins and his family, let's just keep our name out of the papers. Now I know why you've been acting so nervous when Conway was mentioned.'

I started pacing again. Mac glanced at his watch. I said, 'It kind of backfired a bit on Cronin, didn't it? Silverdale would have been better off by far settling Kenny's claim. How much have they paid out since to people like Gary Rice? Remember Gary? That was another little chore for you from Greenboro and Cronin, wasn't it? The night you rang me to try and pick my brain about Gary because Cronin thought he was into insurance fraud.'

I picked up a pitch fork that was leaning against a stable wall and stabbed carelessly in the dirt with the points.

I said, 'What would Cronin pay to catch the guy responsible for all these claims recently?'

'You think it has been deliberate?'

'I know it's been deliberate.'

'Do you know who's responsible?'

'What would Cronin pay, do you think?'

'For a conviction?'

'Uhuh.'

Mac screwed his face up, 'I don't really know. A lot I suppose.'

'A million?'

'Doubt it.'

'Why? Bet he's paid out five so far.'

'I don't know, Eddie, it sounds a lot.'

'Find out. Ask Cronin if he'll put up a million pound reward. Tell him you have very good reason to believe it will bring results.'

'I'll try.'

'Call me as soon as you've spoken to him.' I walked away without saying goodbye.

CHAPTER THIRTY-TWO

It was a beautifully warm still evening when I drove into the yard. I was much calmer, had been doing a lot of thinking, taking satisfaction in a perverse way for the damage Joe Hawkins had inflicted on Silverdale Insurance. I just wished it had been done without all the heartache it had caused.

Still, everything was now in place. I wasn't quite sure of the exact details. There were one or two options but it had obviously started properly with the death of Conway in January.

Kenny had been finalising his claim then. He probably knew that the brain scan thing could prove problematical if it got out but he'd have thought that unlikely. At that time Kenny couldn't have known I was setting Conway up for a fall.

It was more likely that Conway found out about Kenny's potential payout from the insurance claim and wanted a share of it. Conway's lifestyle had been way beyond the income two or three false scans would bring, there was every chance he was blackmailing the jocks concerned, threatening exposure. What an earner he must have seen in Kenny's claim.

But Conway made the mistake of not knowing who Kenny's brother was and Kenny made the mistake, I think, of telling Joe about Conway. The most Kenny would have been hoping for was that Joe

278

could do something to scare Conway.

Instead Joe had had him killed which must have horrified Kenny, made him want nothing further to do with his brother, made him refuse Joe's offer of big lawyers to help win his claim. That's when the arguments must have begun, the fights Carol had told me about.

On 10th February I passed the Conway tapes to Mac. A week later he visits Kenny and confronts him with the brain scan evidence. Kenny agrees to drop his claim. Mac says the Jockey Club will take no action. Kenny then finally tells his brother it's all over but Joe Hawkins can't stand seeing Silverdale winning so he sets out to ruin the company.

And he planned it so he'd take maximum benefit. He must have got the idea from the insurance scam he'd been running for years killing unraced horses, the one that started to unravel when Bill Keating died along with two of Hawkins's horses.

As soon as he knew I was asking questions about that his man had rung with the threat. I suspected then that whoever was behind it was getting info direct from a jockey. By virtually telling me when we met in hospital at Christmas that he knew we were planning the coup for Kenny, Joe revealed that he had access to the most secret weighing room plans.

My first suspect had been Neumman but thinking back to Newcastle the day the coup idea came up he'd slagged Joe Hawkins off whereas Jeff Dunning had been anxious to do everything for Kenny.

And curry favour with his brother at the same time?

Also after my fall in that Barbados race Jeff had been trying to pump me, find out what my plans were. And how had Jeff got the invite to ride in that race?

279

Had Hawkins pulled strings for him?

After that phone threat in October and the sabotaged jeep next day Joe Hawkins must have realised I was on the wrong trail anyway and when I latched onto Conway as the chief suspect in Bill's murder Hawkins had happily let me get on with it.

When Kenny told Joe that Conway was blackmailing him it gave him a double incentive to kill. He frees Kenny and sets Conway up as Bill Keating's killer, hopefully ending any further inquiries on that front. He must have scared Conway into producing Bill's scans then planted them along with the chisel for the police to find.

Aside from that Joe buys the shares in the rival insurance group, somehow gets hold of Silverdale's client list and starts working through it targeting the costliest risks first, hence Gary Rice's early losses in England.

Hawkins must have been cheering his good luck when David Bernstein approached him on Barbados and told him of the big potential profit in buying plantations and selling them on to the Government. One of the biggest private plantation owners happens to be Gary Rice so Joe can kill two birds with one stone: damage Silverdale and scare Gary off the estate.

The phone rang, interrupting my mental jigsaw compilation. It was Gary Rice. 'Eddie, good news! We've just found out that Clemence has worked in the past for this Joe Hawkins guy.'

'I know. Or rather I'd guessed.'

'What?'

I told Gary everything. He was elated, kept congratulating me, saying, well done.

'I wouldn't get too carried away yet, Gary.'

The reality was that Joe Hawkins hadn't made the semblance of a mistake. There was nothing to connect him directly with any crime. Sure, with Kenny's problems he had the motive for defrauding Silverdale but with claims coming in from a wide variety of clients, none of them with personal fraudulent intent, there was no way the insurance company could establish any overall connection.

The murder of Conway and all the general mayhem would have been carried out by lackeys like Clemence and Mr Dann. I was certain I'd find nothing to connect Joe Hawkins directly to any of the crimes.

Gary said, 'It's got to be worth going to the cops.'

'What with? All we have is a very tidy theory. No witnesses. No evidence. The only chance we've got is if Kenny will testify against him.'

'His brother? What are the chances?'

'About the same as a one-legged man would have in an arse-kicking contest. According to his wife, Kenny won't talk to anybody never mind the police. He barely talks to her.'

'Yeah, because his brother's fucked his head up completely. This could be the ideal time for Kenny to get clear of him. What do you think?'

'I think I'd better speak to Carol first, his wife.'

'What about her? Does she know enough to convict Joe?'

'No. Told me she didn't even stay in the house when he visited.'

'When can you go and see her?'

'I'm trying to draw a very fine line timewise. I've asked Mac to get Silverdale to put up a big reward to help catch the guy who's been doing the damage.'

'You didn't tell McCarthy about Joe Hawkins?'

281

'I'm not quite as daft as I look most times.'

'Sorry, Eddie. What did McCarthy say?'

'He's going to ask the Chairman. I'd like to hold off long enough for Silverdale to commit themselves then approach Carol and Kenny. That way they come out with at least some of the money they could have got from the claim. Problem is the longer I wait the more chance Joe Hawkins has of finding out I'm onto him at which point it's goodnight Vienna.'

'You'd better go for it now then, don't wait for Silverdale, go and see Carol and Kenny.'

'And then Silverdale get Joe Hawkins for nothing and Carol and Kenny get zilch? I think I'll risk things for a day or two.'

He tried to talk me out of it but I'd made my mind up. Bruce Cronin's use of his Jockey Club contacts had sickened me, they deserved to pay. Joe Hawkins was still in Barbados and as long as he stayed there I thought I'd be relatively safe. Gary promised to try and get a twenty-four hour watch on him saying he'd call if Joe made any suspicious moves.

'You'll be hard pressed. All his moves are suspicious.'

Gary chuckled and told me to be careful. I'd have to be. I'd already sussed that the only thing that had kept Joe Hawkins from killing or maiming me so far was the knowledge that it would have driven the final wedge between him and his brother. When Joe realised he was looking at life imprisonment I had the queasy feeling that all privileges would be withdrawn.

Sitting alone in the flat dwelling on the prospect of Joe Hawkins finding me out made me increasingly nervous. Just after eight thirty I rang McCarthy at home.

'You contacted Bruce Cronin yet?'

'I can't ring him direct, Eddie, he's the Chairman.'

'So?'

'He deals with Lord Greenboro.'

'Call Greenboro then.'

'It's the weekend, Eddie, for God's sake! I'll speak to him on Monday.'

It seemed Mac had quickly forgotten how ashamed he'd felt that afternoon. I fought to stop myself cursing at him again, tried to speak in a level voice.

'I haven't got until Monday, Mac. Neither have you.'

'What's that supposed to mean?'

'I'll explain when we meet tomorrow for lunch.'

'I'm busy tomorrow.'

'Be busy after lunch. I'll meet you at the Camden and I want an answer from Silverdale.'

'You're being ridiculous!'

'Get hold of Cronin. Ring Greenboro.'

'On Monday—'

'Now, Mac! Or I'll ring him and tell him exactly what I know and exactly what I think of him. I'll quote him a few of the potential Press headlines.'

'Leave it! I'll call you back.'

Within half an hour he did. Greenboro was trying to track Cronin down and hoped to have an answer for tomorrow.

'See you at noon in the Camden.'

*　　　*　　　*

McCarthy was waiting in the spacious lounge of the Camden Hotel when I arrived. Cavalry twill trousers and old roomy sports jacket were his choice for this

283

Sunday lunchtime though I intended to leave him, for once in his life, without much of an appetite.

He rarely touched alcohol and I was surprised to see him sipping a pint of beer. I nodded towards it. 'Pushing the boat out?'

He licked foam from his lips. 'Just shandy. What will you have?'

I took an orange juice and we went to sit by the window. 'You get Cronin?'

'Not yet. He's in France for the weekend.'

'What about Greenboro?'

'He's furious.'

'I'll bet he is. Probably already composing his letter of resignation. Is Cronin expected back tomorrow?'

'I think so.'

'I need a decision on the reward by Tuesday at the latest.'

'Impossible.' He sipped his shandy.

'You'd better make it possible, Mac. The guy behind this is a twenty-four carat bad man. He's got the word villain running all the way through him like a stick of Alcatraz rock.'

Mac half smiled. I said, 'I'm being completely serious, Mac, this guy killed Conway.'

He stared at me. 'How do you know?'

'I know. And pretty soon this guy is going to find out I know. He's got the best network of contacts you've ever seen. Once he's twigged about me he'll want to know who I've been talking to, who else might know about him.'

He laid a finger on his own chest. 'Meaning me?'

I nodded.

'But I don't even know his name!'

'I—'

He put a hand up. 'And I don't want to know!'

'Mac, it doesn't matter if you know or not, he's going to assume you do. He'll come after you for that alone.'

He looked disappointed in me. 'I don't like your tactics here, Eddie.'

'That's rich, Mac. That is very rich.'

Shaking his head slowly he said, 'Eddie, no offence, but I wish I'd never met you.'

I smiled taking some satisfaction from his gloom. 'And who's fault is that? You came to see me, remember? One stormy night three years ago in that old caravan? Came to con me into doing your dirty work.'

Hangdog, he glanced up at me.

I said, 'This is another little course to add to your experience as a gourmet, Mac. It's called Just Desserts.'

McCarthy left the Camden with a considerably increased sense of urgency. He went home to ring Greenboro again to try and get a contact number for Cronin in France.

I was taking another gamble with pushing Cronin. I knew he'd have to convene an emergency board meeting to approve a big reward and I had a strong suspicion that Joe Hawkins had a paid contact working at Silverdale. Somebody must have got him the company's full client list back in February.

I doubted that contact would be at boardroom level but there was a faint chance. If the contact was alerted Joe Hawkins would be the very next man to know I was on to him.

In my head I now deliberately drew a deadline of midnight Tuesday for tying everything up, getting Silverdale's commitment to posting a reward and

Kenny's co-operation including full statements to the police.

I knew when setting it that it might prove to be a deadline in the most literal sense of the word.

Back at the flat I called Carol and told her I was still trying to fix something up for Kenny and that it would help if I could come and see him on Tuesday afternoon. She was hesitant.

I said, 'You don't have to tell him I'm coming. I just want to be sure he'll be there.'

She sighed, depressed, very weary. 'He'll be here all right, Eddie. He hasn't moved out of his room for the last two days. Won't even eat now. Won't see the doctor or anybody else ... I'm at the end of my tether.'

'It'll get better, Carol, honestly. Are the children okay?'

'They're at my mum's. They're living there just now.'

She sounded awful, drained, defeated, condemned.

'Carol just hang on, things *will* improve.' I wanted desperately to make lots of promises, tell her all the good things that would happen if everything went to plan over the next forty-eight hours but I couldn't build her hopes up.

'What is it you're planning, Eddie?'

'Can you hold till Tuesday? I'll tell you then. It's just that I've got a few ends to tie up.'

'See you Tuesday then.' No hope in her voice, total resignation.

I slammed the phone down angry again at Mac and Greenboro and all the selfish bastards who'd done this to her.

I spent a long day waiting by the phone. Padge

286

called by in the evening, red hair frizzy from a recent shampoo. 'Coming down the pub?'

'Sorry. Busy.'

'You look it.'

I smiled. 'Waiting for a call.'

'Still dabbling around with those dead horses?'

'Sort of.'

'Did you find out who owned them?'

'Not exactly but I appreciate you making those calls for me.'

He waved away the thanks. 'Forget it. I'll be in The Corner House till ten if you want one.'

'Thanks.'

A few minutes later Mac rang. He'd got hold of Cronin.

'What did he say?'

'Every chance of a very substantial reward but he'll have to call a board meeting. His secretary's making arrangements now, trying to contact directors.'

'So when do we get an answer?'

'Maybe tomorrow. Tuesday at the latest I should think.'

'Ring me as soon as you know.'

That was it for the evening. No more calls to wait for. I decided I'd earned a large whisky and thought I may as well have it in the company of normal people for a change. I walked down to The Corner House to join Padge and his gang.

Forty proof alcohol and overuse of my brain dropped me gently into the deepest sleep I'd had since returning from Barbados and it took my mind a while to realise the ringing of the telephone at 3 a.m. was real.

I was still groggy when I picked it up. Gary Rice. 'Eddie!'

'Uhuh.'

'Joe Hawkins just left Grantley Adams airport.'

'Eh?' My mind, forgetting the five hour time difference, was trying to work out how you could fly at three in the morning.

'Joe Hawkins! He could be heading for England!'

Could be? 'What flight?'

'There are no flights to London till tomorrow. He chartered a jet.'

He chartered a jet.

The sentence bounced around in my head throwing out its full implications. He's in so much of a hurry to kill me he's chartered a jet.

'What are you going to do?'

I didn't know. My brain was still too heavy with sleep.

'I need to think.'

'You'd better get out of the flat, Eddie, he knows where to come.'

'Yeah. Ten hour flight, isn't it?'

'That's right.'

'Good. I'll go back to bed for half of it. Ring you in the morning.'

'Eddie—'

I hung up and shuffled back to bed. Half asleep nothing seemed so frightening. Anyway he wouldn't reach London till around one. I'd be long gone. Didn't know where to but long gone. I was sure. Set the alarm for eight.

And slept.

CHAPTER THIRTY-THREE

By 10 a.m. I had a bag packed and a destination planned. Two hours of driving north would take me into the wildness of Snowdonia among the mountains and rivers and remote little inns. If Hawkins found me there at least I'd die in a beautiful place.

I'd been trying Kenny's number since 8.30 with no success. I wondered if Carol had had enough last night and gone to her mother's. By the time I was ready to leave there was still no answer. It was essential I got Kenny away from there. If Joe was heading here first he'd be going to Kenny's next.

I decided to pass the responsibility for moving Kenny to McCarthy. I called his office. He was at an important meeting with Lord Greenboro, his secretary claimed she didn't know where the meeting was being held or when she would hear from him.

I watched my hand slowly ease the phone back into its cradle. There was no one else I could call.

Decision time.

It was after ten. Joe Hawkins would still be far out over the Atlantic. Three hours away. Pushing it I could be at Kenny's place in just over an hour. But what if Carol wasn't there? What if Kenny wouldn't let me in?

At least I could warn him. Shout through the door. Push a note under. I could be away from there and down on the Devon moors by the time Joe's plane landed.

Or I could head north as planned, take the chance that Joe would never harm his brother. But Joe would know Kenny was the only one who could get him convicted. Joe would have to silence him somehow.

Decision made. I'd go to Kenny's, call from my mobile every ten minutes on the way down, try to alert them as soon as possible.

I hurried downstairs and told Padge I'd be away for a few days and if anybody called he should say I'd gone abroad somewhere. I threw my bag in the back of the car and headed out.

About five miles down the road the engine spluttered a few times making the car buck then slow then stop. I cursed and turned the key. It wouldn't start. Then I saw the red warning light on the petrol gauge.

Empty. In the middle of nowhere.

Fuck it! I was sure I'd had enough petrol, positive I hadn't driven that far since my last fill up.

I didn't even carry a spare can and the nearest garage was about two miles down the road. I locked up and set out for it jogging on the grass verge, ducking under branches.

Maybe half a mile along a big blue Volvo pulled up twenty yards in front of me and as I reached it I heard the window whisper down. I looked in. A friendly looking guy, middle aged, smiled across. 'Is that your car back there?'

'Yeah, out of juice.'

'Want a lift?'

'Great, thanks.'

'Jump in.'

I did.

'Bad area for breaking down,' he said.

'It is. Just my luck.'

'Never many people about.'

'No.'

'It must be your lucky day with me coming along just at the right time.'

'Yeah, I appreciate it.'

He waited at the garage while I filled the plastic can I bought and drove me all the way back to the car.

'I'm very grateful. You've saved me an awful lot of hassle.'

'Well you know the old saying, if I can help someone as I pass along my way etcetera.'

He dropped me and waved cheerily as he turned and drove off. Almost restored my faith in human nature. A swarm of flies from the woods must have smelt me and as I stooped under the branches holding the spout into the tank mouth they buzzed around my head.

I cursed them, swatting with my free hand then someone said, 'They know shit when they see it, Malloy.' I'd heard it only twice before but I immediately recognised the man whose telephone voice held such menace.

I didn't turn towards it. My mind whizzed searching for options.

'There's nothing I'd like to do more than spread your brains all over the roof of your car. Just give me one little reason. Just once don't do what I tell you. Please.'

The petrol can gurgled the last few drops into the tank.

'Put the can inside the car, slowly and carefully.'

I did.

'Walk round to the driver's side. Slowly.'

I did and I saw him for the first time as he came out of the trees. Cropped dirty fair hair, almost yellow, blue eyes, thirtyish, surprisingly cherubic face. He

291

was around six foot wearing a black polo neck. He was aiming a pistol at my head as he moved along the passenger side parallel with me.

'Get in.'

He opened the back door and slid in behind me.

'Half a mile along there's a dirt road off to the right, take it.'

I did, my mind still trying to figure something out, still not accepting I was trapped. He made me drive deep into the woods to a clearing and park beside a big black BMW. We got out. He threw the keys to me.

'Open the boot.'

It was empty but for four loops of white plastic and a thin green tube which was what he must have used to siphon off my petrol.

'Lie down on your stomach and put your hands behind your back.'

I did it.

'Hands together, back to back.'

I didn't get it right.

'Palms outwards!' He kicked me in the ribs.

Palms outwards. He slipped a loop over and tightened it hard round my wrists, the plastic ridges rasping as the catch sped along.

'Get into the boot.'

I got in.

'Lie on your side facing the engine.'

I turned. Felt the rough carpet on my face, smelt petrol and upholstery cleaner. Whose blood had they scrubbed out?

He tied my feet too then locked me in the darkness and drove me bumping for what seemed like hours. I listened for outside noises, trying to work out where I was. We seemed always to stay in the country. There were no sounds of buses or honking taxis, no street vendors.

We stopped. I heard him get out. And I lay there helpless, hope fading. Waiting for Joe Hawkins.

It seemed ages. I struggled, wrestled with the plastic handcuffs but the thin hard band bit into my wrists. I lay still, losing track of time, fantasising that Mac would have come looking for me, spotted my car abandoned in the woods, followed the tyre tracks of the BMW magically along miles of tarmac. I pictured a ring of armed police outside just waiting for Hawkins, waiting to get him before they came and released me.

I worked on that image adding a little extra each time, a police helicopter hovering nearby, nightsights on the marksmen's guns in case he didn't turn up till dark ... I painted it, embellished it, almost made myself believe it.

A car drew up, squealing brakes, doors slamming, house door opening then closing then within a minute opening again. Footsteps grinding small stones beneath the heels, hurrying towards where I lay. A harsh voice cursing, growing louder, I heard my name then blinding daylight as the boot opened.

I closed my eyes, felt myself being hauled onto my back painfully twisting my arms and hands under me, forcing my pelvis up. I heard a terrible growling, the growling of vicious intent, the sound of pent up anger about to be released.

Then the blows to my face and head, my chest, ribs, groin, face again as he cursed me, slapped me, punched me, frustrated that he did not have more limbs to swing with, more bone to hurt with, the rage building in his throat till he was almost screaming, slapping and punching my face with both hands in a

293

frenzy that finally drove him to bend slavering across my face and bite viciously into my cheek.

Blinding pain.

His mouth stayed there, panting like a beast. I felt cool liquid run slowly down across my ear. His saliva or my blood. And wondered how many more beatings I'd face before he killed me. And I wondered how long I could keep the screams silent.

The boot lid slammed shut again then two car doors and we moved off. He braked hard throwing me back to my original position on my side. I listened to my own panting now as the shock of the attack started gripping. The panting of fear.

For myself. For Kenny. For Carol. That surely was where we were heading. I prayed they wouldn't be home.

But they were. The car was in the driveway as I walked up. No plastic cuffs now just a gun in my back. They'd killed the engine and coasted the last hundred yards. Parked a bit away from the cottage, cut my bonds, told me to be quiet as we approached. Hawkins, calmer now, had given me instructions which I had no intention of following.

Dusk was down. Carol would have locked up. The last person she'd open the door to would be Joe Hawkins and he knew that. He told me to knock and tell her in a calm voice that I'd just come to visit.

But I was going to die anyway so I decided I may as well die out here and let Carol stay locked inside where she'd have a chance of calling the police.

I stopped outside the door. Hawkins and his man with the gun stayed close to the wall.

'Do it!' Hawkins said.

I knocked. Waited. A minute. No noise from within.

'Again! Harder!' Hawkins rasped.

I obeyed and thirty seconds later heard the awful sound of Carol's small footsteps come through the kitchen. Her voice. 'Who is it?'

I called out, 'Carol! Don't open the door! Call the police! Don't open the door!'

Hawkins's man moved and clamped an arm around my throat choking the sounds. He put the pistol to my temple. I closed my eyes.

Carol, scared, said. 'Eddie? Eddie, is that you?'

Hawkins shouted, 'Open the door, Carol, or Malloy's brains will be all over your driveway.'

I tried to call out again but the hard bar of forearm crushed my windpipe.

It must have been a full minute. Hawkins stood calmly. He knew he wouldn't have to repeat himself. The key turned and slowly the door opened. Carol looked at all of us in puzzlement, trying to figure out the connection. Her face paled as she saw mine: I could see out of just one eye, my jaw was swollen and the bite wound in my cheek was open, smarting in the cooling air. There'd be blood too, I wasn't sure how much.

Hawkins smiled at her. 'Good evening. Nice of you to see us. I do hope my dear brother is home.' He pushed past her and his man prodded me forward.

Kenny wasn't in the living room. It was dark, felt unlived in, lit only by what was left of the daylight through the front windows. Hawkins turned in the gloom. 'Where is he?'

I watched her. She glanced at me, fear in her round blue eyes but not the terror I'd expected.

'He's in his room.' Her voice seemed strong.

Hawkins said, 'Tell him I'm here.'

'He won't come out.'

'Tell him I'm here. He'll come out.'

She walked through into the hall. Footfalls on the wooden floor. She called to Kenny. Twice. No response. She came back. 'He won't come out.'

Joe went to Kenny's room leaving me alone with the gunman.

'Kenny, come out, I've brought your mate along, your great pal . . . Come on Kenny, don't you want to see Malloy before he dies, pay your last respects?'

The gunman smiled, watching for fear in my eyes. I tried to hide it.

'Kenny, Kenny, Kenny . . .' falling tones. '. . . I told you Malloy would be trouble. I knew he'd be trouble but you didn't want a hair on his stupid fucking head touched, did you? And I did it for you. For the first time in my life I sacrificed my principles.'

That would have raised a chuckle under other circumstances.

Joe's voice came again, a steelier note now. 'Now I want the agreement cancelled, Kenny. The deal's off. I want you to know all the things he's done to me . . . Kenny, come fucking out here! I want you to know what this bastard has done! It gives me the right to cancel our deal! I want you to say we can cancel it! Kenny! . . . Kenny!'

His voice was getting out of control now.

'I want your permission! I have to kill him! I want you to say it's okay! Kennnnyyy!'

He was almost screaming. I heard him kick the door. Three times. I offered a silent thanks that the children weren't here.

'Barton!' Hawkins screamed the name and the gunman hustled me through the doorway along the hall. Hawkins had his hand out, impatient. 'The gun. Gimme the gun.'

296

Barton pushed me against the wall, gave Joe the pistol.

'Kick the door in.'

Barton grabbed my shirtfront and swung me out of his way, slammed me against the wall next to the door. Hawkins took a few steps sideways, pointing the gun but not looking at me, his eyes red with rage and impatience, his prominent ears crimson at the edges. Dried blood, mine, stained his chin.

Carol stood five paces down the hall watching the doorhandle of all things.

Barton could only get in one stride in the narrow hallway before crashing his boot against the door. It held.

'Again!' Hawkins cried.

It held again.

Hawkins moved closer to him, urging him on. 'Hit it closer to the lock!' The gun was pointing downwards now, not quite at my thigh, just off linc. As soon as Barton broke through I'd go for it.

Barton's pale face reddened as he concentrated then smashed against the door, his straight leg carrying all his force. The lock burst, the door swung in, Barton stumbled into the room. I made to go for the gun as Hawkins stepped towards the open door.

It must have been before Barton could even catch his balance. There was an air-bursting roar of sound, a thumping explosion and Barton came hurtling backwards through the doorway, his head slamming into Hawkins's groin as he went down.

Lunging forward as Joe Hawkins bent double, and lashed out kicking him in the face. He squealed and toppled onto Barton who had a gaping bloody hole in his shoulder. The pistol was still in Joe's hand. He groaned, tried to turn, to get up. I stood on the gun

297

hand leaning forward, pushing all my weight onto the heel that ground and cracked his bones. He cried out in pain as he let the gun go.

I grabbed it and jumped back instinctively, fearful that he would somehow reassemble himself perfectly and spring up again. I looked at Carol aware then that my eyes were staring almost out of my head. From down the hall she looked at me like I was a stranger.

I got the idea she was going to panic, become hysterical. I raised my left hand slowly, open-palmed. 'It's okay. It's all right, Carol.'

I moved back towards a semi-conscious Hawkins who still lay half across Barton who was losing blood in pools. It coursed darkly out along the floorboards seeping through cracks.

Very quietly, almost as though it would stop her panicking, I said, 'Can you call an ambulance? Tell them it's very urgent. And the police.'

Still staring as though seeing me for the first time Carol nodded slowly and went through to the living room. Then it dawned on me that these two men on the floor had filled my mind so horrifyingly, so completely for the past few hours that they still caused everything else to be blanked out. Kenny had been totally forgotten.

They both blocked the doorway. I had to bend forward and look in. Kenny was in his wheelchair by the bed. The room was almost dark. The rectangle of light from the hallway lit him, framed him. Thin wraiths of gun smoke drifted slowly around him. The smell of cordite was strong. Kenny was leaning forward, the stock of a shotgun resting between his useless feet. His thumb was on the trigger. Both barrels were under his chin.

His only body movement was a blink as his eyes turned from his brother to my face. He was haggard. A week's beard growth beneath dark ringed eyes, hopeless eyes that registered nothing when he looked at me, nothing when they swivelled back to his brother's prone body.

I glanced again at the thumb on the double trigger, hoped Carol would not come back just now. I didn't know what to do or say, couldn't be sure that even the mention of his name might tip him over, make him pull the trigger.

I heard Carol's footsteps. She came into the hall. I looked up, stopped her with my eyes. She stood still. I looked back at Kenny poised to blow his own head off. I was going to have to say something.

He spoke first though not directly to me. 'Been dying to do that for weeks. Dying to pull that trigger.' At the sound of his voice Joe moaned and turned onto his back, tried to raise his head to look at his brother.

Kenny's voice strengthened. 'Dying to pull the trigger! Do you hear me, Joe? Dying to pull the fucking trigger!'

His face was working now, coming manically alive, his jutting lower jaw making strange adjustments to let him speak, to accommodate the twin barrels still firmly jammed underneath.

I said, 'Kenny, it's going to be okay.'

He ignored me, stared at Joe who was groggily regaining full consciousness. Slowly, Kenny raised his chin, pushed the barrels forward, brought them horizontal, aimed them at his brother.

'Look at me, Joe,' he said. Joe tried to raise his head but it lolled back, eyes closed, bloodied nose pointing at the ceiling. Kenny put the gun between his legs again and eased the squeaking wheelchair forward till it reached the doorway.

Calmly levelling the shotgun again he stretched and pushed the barrels under Joe's exposed jaw. 'How does that feel, Joe?' Kenny smiled. I wanted to look at Carol but couldn't take my eyes off Kenny.

'I know how it feels and I wanted you to know. Before I pulled the trigger. I just wanted you to think about it.'

I considered grabbing the barrels. I had no love for Joe Hawkins but if Kenny killed him it was going to be awful hard to keep Kenny out of prison. If the ambulance got here soon it might be in time to save Barton whose breath was shortening.

'Can you feel it, Joe?'

Joe's eyes opened.

'I'm going to pull the trigger now. Goodbye, Joe.'

I reached down but was too late. Kenny pulled the trigger.

And the hammers clicked on empty chambers.

Kenny smiled and let the gun fall from his grip. Joe raised his head, narrowed his eyes at his brother. I doubted Joe even realised what had been happening. Kenny said to him, 'Gave both barrels to your friend. Funny how everybody else but you always ends up suffering.'

Carol came towards him as he started crying.

EPILOGUE

Six pints of blood saved Barton's life though he lost his right arm. He's on remand along with his boss. Both deny killing Conway but I traced Tutty and he testified that Barton had been one of the men who'd abducted Conway from his house. The police are hoping Clemence will crack and admit that Conway's body was in the packing case that went overboard from Archangel.

They're also plea bargaining with Clemence to build a solid case against Joe's attacks on Silverdale Insurance. At the moment the prosecution is relying on Kenny's word that Joe boasted of crippling Silverdale. One of the director's secretaries at Silverdale admitted passing information to Joe in exchange for money. That should help too in securing a long sentence for him.

While everything was happening at Kenny's that night the Silverdale Board were holding an emergency meeting and they approved a reward of £250,000 for the conviction of the perpetrator who'd cost them so much.

If they'd waited till the Tuesday morning they could, and probably would have saved themselves that quarter of a million. Carol wants to give me half of it but I've told her that if it comes through they should give fifty grand to Tutty and use the rest to try and get their lives back together.

Kenny has started psychiatric treatment and it looks like he's going to be okay. He's had a lot of encouragement from three successful trainers, all wheelchair-bound.

As of now I haven't found out if Jeff Dunning was Joe Hawkins's weighing room informant. Not that it matters any more. Everybody knows now that Bill Keating was no heroin addict and no quitter either and that means a lot to me.

Silverdale made me a good offer to go and work for them as an investigator. But I was never really tempted. I've just come back from two weeks' proper holiday in Barbados, tanned and fit and with memories that still make me smile when I think of the nights spent with Kari Parsons, the demon groom.

She had a lot of fun comparing the healing bite scar on my cheek to the old one on hers.

I nagged Gary into giving her her first ride for the stable while I was there and we cheered her into a close third at the Garrison.

Charles is back from Scotland raring to start his third season training. I just saw him bustling around the new horsebox helping to load today's runners with his usual enthusiasm.

I need to lose three or four pounds so it's just black coffee for breakfast. Then it's out into the sunshine with my kitbag and best light saddle for the drive up to Bangor.

It's the first day of the new season.

I've got four rides there.

And I can't bloody wait.